SEMBLANCE

The Midnight Society Book One

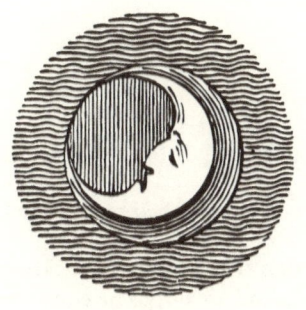

LOGAN PATRICKS

Archives Canada Cataloging-In-Publication Data

ISBN: 978-0-9917728-1-0

DEDICATION

To my lovely wife, who cheers me on every day, and to my beautiful daughter, who I hope never reads this book, but enjoys the fruits of its labor.

Strangecrow Books

First Edition

ACKNOWLEDGMENTS

There are many individuals as well who helped shape this book as well as spread the word of its existence. To my lovely beta readers Ms. Gabi Daniels and Ms. Kristin Zika, thank you for all your efforts in shaping this book, pointing out that "checkered shirts" on men aren't in fashion (ugh there goes my wardrobe), and reassuring me that the direction I went with this book was perfect. You two ladies eased a lot of my fears and gave me the confidence to keep on going.

To Danielle Young over at Consuming Worlds for being the first to share the cover of Semblance to the world.

To Tracie, who still loved my book despite using her razor-sharp spell-check eyes to catch all the "other" mistakes.

To my lovely wife who sat on the kitchen table performing manual labor formatting my book. I love you.

And finally to my daughter, who just crapped herself. I love you more than you can ever imagine and I will write you that young adult fantasy book very soon, just so you can read something of mine that's rated PG. I better change your diaper right now before the poop spreads up your back....

PROLOGUE

Now.

"You've got some fight in you girl," he laughed, his vulture eyes narrowing on me as if I were a heap of bloody meat. "I'll tell you what, because I enjoy a woman with brass, I'll let you choose your own poison. What will it be sweetheart? A hollow-point bullet exploding through your little, broken heart or a thirty-two story plunge onto cold, hard cement below?"

I was standing at the edge of the world, my back against the abyss that threatened to swallow me whole. The chill of the early spring wind bit into my heels, sending shivers up my spine. I stared into the barrel of the rifle and resolved to myself that I was going to die. Despite being terrified, I still had enough spite coursing through my veins to curse at the bastard holding the gun, the same bastard that murdered a man I cared deeply for.

"You motherfucker," I cried.

He smiled as he allowed my profanity to bounce off him like old rubber bands.

I closed my eyes and drew a deep breath. I felt like cussing out the universe for having it end this way, but let's be honest; every single decision I had made over the past month paved the yellow brick road that eventually led me to this not-so-wonderful land of loss and pain.

Aria Valencia, you naïve girl, you've made too many mistakes. If I could change the past, I would have done a dozen things differently. The only question was where to start my story?

CHAPTER ONE

Three months ago.

There were some days I seriously considered stripping at the Skin Bar a couple of blocks away from the university, just so I could make enough money for a nice hot meal and to save myself from another month of eviction threats from my red-faced Serbian landlord. However, the thought of my dad's spirit, God rest his soul, scowling at me while I shoved my breasts into some pervert's face was enough of a deterrent for me to think anymore into it. This was the life of a struggling music student, constantly fantasizing of ways to make ends meet.

Whoever said, "Money can't buy happiness" clearly never starved a day in their lives.

I picked up the local campus paper and flipped through the classifieds. They were littered with jobs for servers, which I had tried my hand at before, and loathed with a passion. Consider it a character flaw, but I was far too blunt and headstrong to put up with anyone's bullshit. Blame my dad for instilling in me a strong sense of pride and confidence from the day I was born up until the day he left this world.

Though people considered me a cheerful person, there were three sure-fire things that transformed this sweet, happy-go-lucky girl into a snarling beast that was best left imprisoned inside seven-foot thick steel walls.

The first was having my body inappropriately touched by drooling perverts. Unless you were my boyfriend, which no one was at the moment, then your hands were not allowed anywhere near my rear. Any attempts were met with an unholy wave of verbal profanities in addition to having all five of my fingers rake your eyes like they were dead leaves on a lawn.

The second was being judged unfairly, which was a constant occurrence for a classical performance music student. Every time I went on stage and performed one of Chopin's preludes on the campus's Steinway pianos—the most beautiful sounding instrument in existence—I was at the mercy of all the critics and their biased opinions. Granted, most of them left me with constructive criticism, there were the handful of critiques that infuriated me with their snooty perfectionism that made me want to give up this dream of mine altogether. But dad taught me never to quit and I always ended up picturing his Jedi spirit (yes I was a fan girl) and the look of joy on his face as I played. This carried me through the worst criticisms and those difficult times when I believed myself to be a failure.

Finally, the last item on my list of not-so-awesome things was hunger, which I endured a lot of lately. It was turning me into a Frankenstein-like-bitch.

I contemplated the serving job once again, almost giving into the temptation of having some pocket money, but decided that I wasn't in the correct mindset to deal with people. Also the threat of having my ass grabbed by drunken frat boys was not worth it for minimum wage.

I felt my stomach rumble and cursed at it.

"Stop complaining," I said to my belly. "I fed you a chocolate bar four hours ago."

Great, I was standing in the middle of the street talking to my stomach like only psychos or pregnant women did.

Hunger had struck at my sanity once again.

"Oh Aria," I wondered out loud to myself, "How are you going to survive another semester?"

I plopped down on my bed, exhausted and utterly defeated. My pride had given way to my hunger and for the first time in a long while, I had succumbed to the charity of others.

Justin had bought me lunch at the pub, which I refused at first. However, watching him eat his delectable burger while working on our musical counterpoint theory assignment was excruciating.

I lied to him at first and told him I wasn't hungry at all, but my stomach betrayed me and moaned like the chained ghost of Christmas Past.

"Oooooh, Cheeseburger," it howled. "French fries with gravy, oooooh."

It became such a distraction that finally Justin smiled and said. "Hey Aria, remember when you finished my music history assignment a couple of weeks ago? I still owe you for that one. Let me buy you a burger platter."

I had to hand it to my study buddy; Justin knew how to word things in a way that didn't make me look as pathetic as I actually was.

I gave in and nodded.

It turned out to be the most delicious burger in the world and I devoured it in a matter of minutes. I must have looked like a Neanderthal to Justin, but I couldn't have cared less at that point. I was lost in the finger-licking land of greasy beef and salty fries.

It was only after I had finished eating that I felt ashamed of accepting the meal. I hoped the look of guilt on my face wasn't too noticeable.

"You have ketchup on your nose," Justin laughed.

Damn it—guilt and ketchup. What an embarrassing combination.

The second I had some spare change I was going to return the favor and buy him a burger. I didn't want him to get any wrong ideas from me.

Justin was cute in a hipster sort of way—tall and lanky, baby-faced with sun-kissed hair and a fashion guru—but he wasn't my cup of tea. I didn't even like tea.

I always fell for guys that were more hard vodka than earl grey.

I suspected Justin had a thing for me but I ignored it, hoping that he would eventually direct his smitten eyes in another direction.

Justin's friendship was valuable to me, but that's all I saw it being—a friendship. Being broke didn't allow me the luxury of going out and meeting new people and so he became the centre of my social universe. I couldn't lose the current relationship I had with Justin.

Not now, and probably not ever.

I stared at the water-stained ceiling of my cramped studio apartment, sleepy from the grease oozing through my bloodstream. I longed to pass out for the rest of the evening but sleep had to wait. I had too much work to do.

I needed to figure out a way to survive another semester.

I logged onto my computer and checked my email, hoping that today my inbox provided me with some sort of salvation.

There were two types of emails that I usually received. The first was daily group coupon deals, which I checked religiously, hoping for some miraculous discovery that kept me fed for another week. There was one this one time that I discovered a deal for four microwavable pizzas for four dollars at the local grocery store and I practically came at the thought of having a steady supply of food for a week. Before stumbling across the holy grail of pizza deals, I had honestly considered crafting myself a makeshift bow and arrows and entering into the wilderness to hunt for some dinner.

The second type of email I got was rejection letters. Each week I sent emails to fifteen local entertainment establishments that housed pianos, inquiring about potential gigs along with a link to my webpage with samples of my music. And every week I received either some form of rejection or no response. It was hard to decide which was worse.

I desperately needed someone to cut me a break.

However on this magical night in March while scanning through my emails, I discovered that the China White club had emailed me saying they had an opening for a pianist this Saturday night.

I read the email over and over again in a state of euphoria.

"Dear Ms. Aria Valencia,

The China White Supper Club is interested in having you perform for us this Saturday on the Thirteenth of March. Please arrive promptly at 5:00 pm so we can discuss the set list as well as fit you into wardrobe. We are looking forward to your performance as you've come highly recommended.

Management"

For a moment I feared it was a joke. The China White was one of the more exclusive supper clubs in the city, one that only the elite dined at: movie stars, fortune five hundred business moguls, and people of social influence. If the wealthy needed to stuff their faces with succulent Chinese meals, they went to the China White.

It was unexpected and astonishing for them to contact me, especially since I never sent an email to them in the first place, but I was so giddy from the prospect of working the crowd at the China White—and getting paid for it—that I didn't bother thinking about the logistics of it.

I replied within two minutes.

"Dear Management @ the China White,

I would be delighted to play for your fine establishment this Saturday. You will not be disappointed.

Aria Valencia"

My destiny was waiting for me, whether I was ready or not.

By the time Saturday rolled around, I was high off of adrenaline. I felt like a fired-up athlete about to play game seven of a championship series. I was ready to go out there beating my chest and putting on the performance of a lifetime.

I burst through the doors of the China White, ready to tear the house down with my dexterous fingers and dazzle the eardrums of all that entered into the restaurant that night.

All I needed was someone to show me to the piano.

After a brief introduction and some pleasant conversation, Abraham Constantine, the owner of the China White, showed me to the dressing room instead.

He offered me a shimmering white gown that was more suited for an actress on the red carpet than a broke-ass music student in a Chinese restaurant.

I was nervous as I tried it on. I couldn't help but feel like a peasant deflowering an outfit fit for a princess.

Thankfully Abraham's kindness eased my nerves, his words as warm and soothing as chamomile tea.

"Lovely," he smiled. "You're like a princess wearing a glass slipper, but in this case replace the slipper with an elegant Vera Wang exclusive."

"Are you sure it's okay for me to wear this?" I asked.

"Absolutely," Abraham replied, rubbing his grey stubble chin. "This dress on another's skin would be an absolute sin. If I were twenty years younger, I would have made you my queen in a heartbeat."

"Your tongue is all sugar and spice," I smiled. I always had a misconception of the wealthy, picturing them as eclipse-sized assholes that shat all over the simpler ways of life, while wiping their rears on the sleeves of the lower class.

Abraham certainly proved me wrong. He reminded me of my dearly loved and missed uncle, both in physical features and characteristics. He was in his late sixties, aged by his light grey hair and the crow's feet around his eyes. However he walked and talked with vibrant energy that convinced me he was possessed by a twenty year old.

I also admired how he interacted with his employees, treating every one of them like his equal. I was surprised to see him consult with a baby-faced junior cook about the evening's menu selection.

He treated me, a poor girl dressed in hand-me-downs, with respect at first sight, shaking my hand graciously and asking me what music I thought was best to set the mood for tonight's dinner.

I had suggested some Chopin right off the bat, eager to show off my ability to perform his hauntingly beautiful and technically challenging pieces. I wanted the audience to witness my bravura on the ivory keys, hopefully garnering enough positive attention to get invited back for a second gig in the near future.

Abraham agreed to my choice, being a huge Chopin fan himself.

"The patrons should be arriving in about an hour or so," Abraham said. "Do you need to warm up? Our grand piano is a modest Borgato, probably not one as spectacular as the Steinways you're used to playing at the University."

"Are you kidding me?" I was surprised. To call a Borgato modest was like saying a Mercedes was as nice as a bus pass. "The Borgato's a stunning piano. You have excellent taste," I said.

"As much as I'd like to take credit for making the selection, I can't," Abraham replied. "It was donated by a benefactor, the same person that requested for you to perform for us this evening."

I was shocked and ecstatic to hear that someone with musical influence had heard of me, or even listened to me play, let alone recommend me for such an amazing gig.

"I don't need a warm up," I said. "I'm always ready to play."

"How about we feed you then?" Abraham asked. "How does Peking roast duck sound?"

I had starved enough over the past few years to appreciate a free hot meal. "You sure know how to sweet talk a girl," I replied.

I had performed countless times before in front of other music students and classical music aficionados. The people here tonight were different. They weren't classical music gurus or music critics. They were just a bunch of rich people here to taste the incredibly delicious duck while listening to a few songs.

Would they appreciate Chopin and the beautiful complexity of his music?

I felt the smooth ivory keys underneath my fingertips. There was only one way to find out.

I hit the first note, creating an instant bond between my mind and my art. I closed my eyes and allowed the spirit of the music to possess me, my hands no longer my own but an extension of the piano itself. I was its vessel—its mistress—and the intimacy we shared was one filled with beautiful and majestic music.

I began to play and was marveled by the brilliant acoustics of the room. The sounds of the piano filled every nook and cranny of the restaurant with its vibrant melody, and the building responded with a lively echo that flooded the space between the walls with the genius imagination of Chopin.

When I finished the piece, I quickly transitioned to another piece, and then another. Eventually I lost track of time, finishing song after song, pausing only to allow the final resonating note of each piece to fade into the air and seep into the hearts of my audience.

When I had finally finished my entire set and glanced up from the keys, I noticed that most of the tables were now empty.

I was disappointed. Did my music scare everyone off?

I looked up at the clock and realized it was almost midnight and the restaurant was just about to close. I had played for five solid hours without taking a single break.

Music had a tendency of speeding up time, making me lose track of the world around me. I lifted my hands off the keys and stretched them out, catching a glimpse of Abraham chatting with someone.

The woman sitting at the table was a real classic beauty. Raven-colored hair flowed down to her waist like water; counterpoint to her smooth milk-white skin and red lips the color of apples. She wore a ravishing designer ink black dress that made my Vera Wang gown look 'casual' and the diamonds around her neck and fingers reflected the lights from the chandeliers above, transforming her into a glittering dark star.

She looked at me out of the corner of her eye and smiled, and me being the goofball I was, waved to her like a kid on a school bus waving to her parents. I might as well have added a "Hidey Ho!" to officially coronate myself as the Queen of the Dorks.

While I mentally chewed myself out, Abraham strolled up to me and gave me a great big smile.

"Brilliant," he said to me.

"You think so? I was so far gone into the music that I didn't get a chance to see other people or gauge their reactions. I was okay then?"

Abraham pointed to the fishbowl wineglass resting on top of the piano. It was jammed with money, most consisting of one hundred dollar bills.

"There's a direct correlation between audience appreciation and the tips you receive. I'd say you impressed my patrons tonight. The tips are all yours. I will also cut you a modest check for your wonderful work. But first, there is someone that I'd like you to meet."

He took me gently by the hand and led me to the table where the black-haired woman sat. A glass of dark red wine rested in front of her.

"Aria, it is my pleasure to introduce to you Calisto Tremaine, of the esteemed Tremaine family," Abraham announced. "She was the one who recommended your talents to us."

There was a familiarity to Calisto's face but I couldn't recall ever meeting her before. Would she be offended if I didn't have a clue who she was? I couldn't possibly pretend to know her. My abilities to tell a lie were as proficient as a hole-punched condom.

"I'm honored," I said, extending my hand out. I figured a good old-fashioned handshake was a safe way to start things off.

Calisto grinned, rose from her seat and returned the handshake. She had a firm grip.

"I'm a big fan of your music," Calisto said, gesturing for me to sit in the empty seat at her table.

I sat down.

Seeing that we were both settled in, Abraham gave us a polite nod. "Well if there's nothing else needed of me, I'll help the others with the cleanup."

"You do realize that's what hired help is for," Calisto said. "You should sit back and relax once in a while."

Abraham smiled. "Believe it or not, I find doing dishes quite soothing."

"You're the poorest rich man I know," Calisto said.

"Wealth is not measured by one's assets, but rather one's reverence," Abraham said. "Do those words sound familiar?"

"How could they not?" Calisto smiled. "I've always been daddy's little girl. You know that."

Abraham bowed politely and then headed back to the kitchen, leaving me alone with my mysterious fan.

"Some wine?" Calisto asked, gesturing to the half-filled bottle on the table. "It's a vintage 82 Bordeaux. You'll love it."

"I can't really say I'm a wine connoisseur," I replied. "Something so expensive might go to waste on my primitive taste buds."

"Nonsense," Calisto said as she poured some of the rosy liquid into an empty wine glass on the table. "It's a travesty for a single girl to drink alone. You're obliged to have a drink with me."

I grabbed the glass, shrugged, and took a healthy swig, downing it like I would a beer. It probably wasn't the proper wine-drinking etiquette seeing as how my chugging display caused Calisto to start giggling.

"You're supposed to appreciate the wine, not inhale it like tequila shots," she said.

"Sorry," I muttered. I felt her judging me, which was item number two on the list of things that vexed me.

"Don't worry about it," she said. "Maybe all the wine snobs are fools and don't even know it. Who has the right to determine how one enjoys alcoholic beverages anyway? To tell you the truth, I never had the palate for wines either. All vintages taste the same to me." Calisto stared at her glass, shrugged her shoulders and said, "Fuck it, why not?" She downed the rest of her wine in a single gulp.

"Fuck traditions," she laughed, slamming the glass down on the table when she finished. "Someone always ends up breaking it anyway."

I liked her already.

"You probably have a lot of questions for me," Calisto said, pouring another glass.

"I sure do," I replied.

"You probably want to know how I heard of you and your brilliant piano skills."

"Yes."

"And why I suggested for you to play at the China White tonight."

"Yup."

"And maybe who I am, besides this lonely girl sitting at this table downing a whole bottle of wine by herself."

"Of course."

"Well too bad," Calisto laughed. "None of that matters. What does matter is if you want to make some more money."

"Like another gig here?" I asked.

"Not exactly," Calisto said. She glanced around the room, making sure no one else was listening in on our conversation. "What if I told you that I'm looking for a pianist for just one night at a very exclusive party?"

"Sounds pretty intriguing," I replied.

"When I say exclusive, I mean that no one else can know about it. I'm talking cloak and dagger secrecy here," Calisto said. "Can I trust you not to say a word of this to anyone else?"

"Say a word of what?" I played along. "We're just sitting here enjoying a nice glass of wine from what I can tell."

Calisto smiled. "I'm part of a very secretive club whose members are very influential and powerful people. Don't ask me to name any names or go into further details, but I can tell you this: if they like you, they can seriously make your career. You can have your pick headlining Vienna, the Metropolitan Opera, or Carnegie Hall. I'm sure you get the picture."

She definitely knew how to throw a good sales pitch.

"Go on," I said. "The wine has made me very impressionable to your sweet talk."

"In three days, my organization is having a..." Calisto seemingly paused, trying to find the right words for it. "...celebration. It's possibly one of the biggest events our secret little organization has had in the past decade. I've been tasked to take care of all the little details, including entertainment. Aria Valencia, I'd love for you to play at this very important and very *hush, hush* event.

It sounded almost too good to be true. There had to be a catch.

There *always* was a catch to these things.

"I don't want to sound like an ungrateful skeptic, but why me?" I asked. "I'm just a nobody who knows how to hammer out a few good pieces on the piano."

Calisto laughed. "You're modest to a fault. A few months back I heard you practicing in the university concert hall. You were playing Liszt's Hungarian Rhapsody number two, a piece that has great sentimental value to me. You played it with such a passionate fire and beautiful grace that the music resonated from the auditorium and straight into my heart, holding me like a mother holding her newborn.

"My father was a huge Liszt fan and listening to you play the rhapsody took me back in time, when I was still a little girl. I remembered sitting in my father's lap one night and listening to that beautiful piece, just before his unfortunate death. It was the last moment we shared together as father and daughter. Your music unearthed that precious memory for me, a gift that's absolutely priceless. I've been a huge fan of yours ever since."

I was taken aback by her story. "You actually liked my version of the Hungarian Rhapsody?" I asked. "I thought I was playing it like shit. Hell, I still don't have it all figured out. My fingering is still a bit stiff on some parts of the song."

"It was beautiful Aria; absolutely beautiful," Calisto replied. "I know this will sound a bit stalker-ish but sometimes I listened to you practicing from outside the hall. I've also attended a couple of your recitals that you had for your classmates. Creepy isn't it?"

I was flabbergasted. I actually had a fan, and she was a woman of impeccable taste.

"It's not creepy at all," I replied. "I'm thrilled that someone appreciates all my hard work. Sometimes as an artist it's hard gauging your own performance. It's great to have a little validation once in a while."

"So here's the deal," Calisto said. "I want you to play for us at this celebration. I'm willing to pay you ten thousand dollars for a single night's worth of music."

I choked on my wine.

"Aria, are you alright?" she asked.

When my airways were finally cleared of fluid, I responded. "Did you just say you'd give me ten thousand dollars for a single night?"

"Yes," she confirmed, "Ten thousand dollars. It's a very good offer. Try finding that kind of money without having to take your clothes off in some sort of fashion."

I had to be dreaming. I should have been ecstatic, jumping on the tables while doing fist pumps, but once again the skeptic in me strangled my excitement.

"If this party is as important as you say it is, why don't you get someone famous, like Marc-Andre Hamelin or Krystian Zimmerman?" I asked. "I'm seriously a peasant who can barely afford a Kit-Kat for lunch."

"Because I don't want either of those two," Calisto replied. "I want you."

"And these guests of yours won't be disappointed that an undiscovered nobody musician will be playing at this grand event?"

Her smile was sly and full of mischief. "Here's the beautiful thing," Calisto said. "I've already made you a star in this inner circle of ours."

"I don't follow."

"I created a story about you, one that may be on the fictitious side," Calisto said. "Right now you're known as the Golden Virgin, a mysterious pianist who lives a life of chastity so that your music is as pure as your heart."

"But I'm not a virgin," I said.

"Just pretend."

"I dunno," I replied. "I've never been a good liar."

"When's the last time you had sex?"

16

It was a rather bold question to ask. I was fairly private when it came to my personal life and felt uncomfortable discussing it with someone whom I met ten minutes ago. I was also embarrassed to admit that my sex life was as dry as a sand dune over the past two years.

Having no money didn't exactly give me the freedom to go out and meet people worthy of dating.

"I guess it was an intrusive question to ask," Calisto said, after a brief moment of awkward silence. "I'm fairly open about my indecent escapades. The last time I had sex was yesterday with a Chilean carpenter who was installing hardwood floors in one of my condos. He looked like Johnny Depp with muscles. I came twice that night."

"Uh…"

"I thought I'd share that with you, just so you understand that my question to you had no cruel intentions behind it."

Oh, what the hell. What harm was it in telling Calisto about my dismal and chaste personal life.

"Two years," I said.

"Two years?"

"Yes."

"Perfect. You're practically chaste anyway. I'm sure you'll play the part of the Golden Virgin well."

"So this story telling of yours, does that make you a habitual liar?" I asked. I was always cautious around storytellers. I hated being the fool.

"No," Calisto replied. "It makes me a habitual marketer."

"I see."

She must have noticed the look of disapproval on my face. She immediately took my hands and gave me a pleasant, and strangely hypnotic, smile.

"So Aria, it all comes down to this," Calisto said. "For ten thousand dollars, will you play at our exclusive party?"

I didn't have to think long nor hard about it.

"Yes," I replied. I needed to take every opportunity I could get. Also ten thousand dollars would cover my rent for the year along with supplying me with some much-needed groceries.

"Excellent," Calisto said clasping her hands together. "Now remember, you mustn't breathe a word of this to anyone else."

"I swear, not another soul will hear about this," I raised my hand in the air, as if I were pledging my allegiance.

"Good," Calisto said. "The punishment for violating the sanctity of our little secret is death—to you and the person you divulge to."

I couldn't help but laugh at the amusing cliché.

"Sadly, I wish I was joking," Calisto replied. Her words sent an instant shiver up my spine and for a moment, I couldn't help but wonder what I was getting myself into.

CHAPTER TWO

The black limo pulled up in front of the sad little shanty that I called home. I was surprised to see Abraham, dressed in a splendid slim-fit tuxedo, step out of the driver's side door, greeting me with his trademark smile.

"You're my chauffeur for the evening?" I asked.

"Indeed," he said, opening the backseat door for me like a true gentleman. "I'm a jack of all trades: restaurant owner, respected socialite, and for this evening, your personal driver."

"Well if anyone's to drive me to my potential career suicide, I'm glad it's you," I said. Since this morning, I've had some issues with my confidence.

It went missing.

I was as jittery as a pornstar in church. I blamed Calisto and her "make or break" line that echoed in my mind over and over again.

If they like you, they can make your career. You can have your pick headlining Vienna, the Metropolitan Opera, or Carnegie Hall.

That was a lot of pressure placed on one single night. What if I screwed it up?

When I was a child, my worst fear was having rotten produce tossed at me after a poor piano recital, which was absurd thinking about it now. Who brought tomatoes and lettuce to piano recitals in the first place?

The more plausible scenario was that someone would hate my music and spread the word of how shitty my performance was to the musical mavens and crush my dreams of selling out concert halls.

I'd rather have the tomatoes.

The thought of failing tonight made me want to drop to the sidewalk and curl up into a fetal position.

"You shouldn't doubt your talents," Abraham said as I entered the limo.

He closed the door behind me. As he entered the driver's seat, he continued to cheer me on. "You're one extraordinary pianist. I'm sure you'll have no problems captivating this crowd."

However, his words escaped my ears as my attention was focused on some disturbing details inside the limo. The first thing I noticed was that the rear windows were tinted black from the inside, restricting any view to the world outside. Also there was a partition between the front seats and the back, which separated me physically from Abraham.

I felt claustrophobic and feared that I was a prisoner in this luxurious motorized prison.

"Hey Abraham, not to sound ungrateful for the ride, but to be honest the lack of natural light is freaking me out a bit," I said.

"I do apologize for that," Abraham replied through a speaker in the roof. "Did Calisto inform you that tonight's event is a very private affair?"

"She did," I replied.

"Unfortunately the location of the celebration must be kept secret as well," Abraham said. "You will notice that there is no cell phone reception available in the limo either. I do understand how this may all be a bit unnerving and if you wish, I can inform Calisto that you've changed your mind about tonight's performance. I'm sure she can find a suitable replacement."

Common sense should have told me to leave the vehicle, head back up to my apartment, and find a less shady way to make some cash. But I was a desperate girl and the potential to make ten thousand dollars for one night's work was way too good of an opportunity to pass up. I was flat broke once more after paying my tuition with the tips from China White and still needed to cover rent. Common sense had gone fishing tonight. I'd listen to it when I wasn't down to my last nickel.

"Can I trust that you won't kidnap me and sell me to some European sex-slave ring Abraham?"

"On the soul of my daughter, our organization will not harm you in any way, shape, or form," Abraham said without hesitation.

"Well then, let's get this party started," I said.

"Excellent. I do believe that tonight's event should open many doors for you in the near future."

The limo began to move as I held my breath and prayed that I was making a good decision. Over the past four years, I had a tendency to make poor ones, and it was only in hindsight that I realized what an idiot I was at times. I wondered if this was going to be one of those instances.

The quietness of the car ride made me nervous so I decided to start some conversation.

"You have a daughter?" I asked. I had read up about Abraham after the gig last Saturday and there was never any mention in old news articles about his family.

"I *had* a daughter," Abraham replied. I could hear the sadness in his voice and immediately felt bad for asking. I decided to change the subject.

"There are some wild stories about you on the internet. Are there any truths to them?"

Abraham chuckled. "Like all competitive business owners, I became a victim of slander," he replied. "When the China White first opened, it was considered one of the premier dining establishments in the city. My chefs, flown from all parts of Asia, were instructed not only to create food but also to create art. My restaurant was the talk of the town and I worked very hard to maintain that sense of grandeur for the China White. Of course, success has its price and I soon discovered the mean spirit of competitive business. I was accused of many things: participating in wild male orgies in the back of my kitchen while patrons feasted on their suckling pig. Apparently I also practiced pagan voodoo and sacrificed virgin blood to demon gods, and probably much worse."

"That's so juvenile. Is everyone still in high school?" I remarked.

"Sadly in life, progress in money and power leads to regression in common sense and decency," Abraham sighed. "It's a flaw in this little thing that we do. I was hit with these ridiculous accusations, which I took great offense to—not because I was accused of being a homosexual Satanist—but because I took immense pride running a spotless, sanitary kitchen. I would never allow a single drop of body fluid to defile the sanctity of my restaurant's cooking space.

"So I went to war, fighting against the issue that offended me the most—having a dirty kitchen. As for being a gay Satanist, I couldn't care less. Call me a homosexual demon worshipper if you want, just don't insult my spotless kitchen."

"A true gay and religious activist," I laughed.

"There are much worse things people can read about me," Abraham said, in almost a whisper.

I decided not to press him on it.

"It seems like you folks love your stories," I said. "Calisto created one about me, being some virtuous girl who uses her Golden Virgin powers to create beautiful music."

"Storytelling is a very powerful skill," Abraham said. "Empires are built and destroyed from the simplest of tales that seep through people's ears and entrench themselves inside a person's heart."

"What's the difference between stories and lies?" I asked.

There was a long pause. "Stories serve a higher purpose," he finally replied.

"Are you sure about that one?" I asked.

There was another long pause. "No."

Well this topic wore out its course; onto another one.

"Tell me about the guests at this exclusive event," I said.

"It's a secret," Abraham replied, a hint of amusement in his voice.

"Well when I get there, I'll see the guests anyway. What's the harm in giving me a little spoiler?"

"Did Calisto not share with you the details of tonight's events?"

"Nothing much, except for that it was top secret."

"Perhaps that's for the best. I wouldn't want to spoil anything for you either. It makes things more exciting that way."

"Who are you people?" I boldly asked. "I'm almost convinced you guys are twinkling vampires with all your secrets."

Abraham made no reply.

"You're not vampires are you?" I asked.

There was still no reply. Suddenly I began to panic. Oh God, what if they were some crazy sect of blood suckers, ready to feast on my not-so-virgin blood, transforming me into one of their kind? Call me odd if you will, but vampires didn't do it for me. I found their pasty white demeanor creepy as hell.

"I want to suck your blood," Abraham's voice echoed through the speaker in a cheesy Transylvanian voice, followed by a hardy laugh.

"You jerk!" I shouted. "You scared the hell out of me for a second."

"Not to sound insulting but aren't you too old to believe in monsters?" Abraham asked.

I sighed. "Well you can't blame me for being paranoid. Everything about this event is so secretive. For all I know, this could be some kind of serial killer soiree."

"As I said before, I swear on my daughter's soul that no physical harm will come to you tonight," Abraham said. "There is no hidden agenda aside from you blessing us with your beautiful music."

At that point, I should have sat back and relaxed, but I was too inquisitive in nature. I continued on with my questions.

"Is this organization of yours legal?" I asked.

"Do you have skeletons in your closet?" Abraham asked me.

"Well yes," I said. "Doesn't everyone?"

"As does our group," Abraham replied. "One collective skeleton buried six feet under." There was finality in his voice that told me yet another topic of discussion was over.

I felt like a terrible conversationalist along with the gnawing suspicions that I was into something way over my head.

The remainder of the drive was in silence, though at one point Abraham did ask me if I enjoyed Jazz music. I told him I did and all of a sudden, the eclectic sounds of Miles Davis filled the limo, which, along with the champagne I discovered in the icebox, calmed me a little.

Eventually the limo rolled into a stop and I felt my composure under attack as my nerves melted into puddles of overwhelming anxiety.

Abraham exited the limo and opened the rear door for me.

"We're here Aria," he said with a pleasant smile. "Tonight your life is going to change forever."

CHAPTER THREE

Yup, I was definitely in way over my head. I realized this the second I stepped foot inside the stunning mansion.

Everything within was overwhelmingly luxurious. The ceilings were at least eleven feet high with crystal chandeliers hanging from them like long diamond earrings. The glow from the twilight sun flooded the rooms through the tall windows while gentle orange rays glistened against the glassy surface of the indoor pool.

Abraham led me deeper into the estate. Every room we passed by blew my mind with its extravagance—beautiful custom furniture, glorious modern works of art, and elegant vintage décor. I felt like I was in a resort rather than someone's house.

Finally Abraham stopped in front of a room on the second floor. "Here at last," he said as he pushed open the large cream-colored double doors. "This is where you'll change. You can find your complete outfit inside the walk-in closet," Abraham said, "Along with a unique piece of attire that you'll be required to wear for tonight's festivities. There is also a piano in the room if you wish to warm up until all the other guests arrive. If there's anything else you need, feel free to page me on the intercom."

I was astounded by the sheer size of the room. It was larger than most condos or apartments I've seen. At the centre of the room was a baby grand piano; a Yahama from what I could tell.

"You guys sure know how to live it large," I said.

"I do admit, we tend to violate many of the seven sins; greed, vanity, and pride at the forefront," Abraham said, glancing at his golden watch which I figured to be worth more than all my measly possessions combined. "Oh darn, I'm running behind of schedule. If there's nothing else you need, I shall take my leave. I'll have someone send up some snacks and beverages within the hour."

When I was finally alone, I did what any other curious girl would do. I began to touch everything—the glorious bed, the mahogany dresser, the full-body mirror, the bathroom's glistening marble countertops—I ran my fingers across it all just to make sure it was all real.

It was.

I walked over to the piano next and lifted open the cover and pressed down lightly on the 'C' key in the upper octave, allowing the note to echo throughout the grandiose room.

I could seriously get used to this.

I had no idea how I was going to return to my three hundred square foot hovel after spending an evening in this glorious room. Perhaps someday, my music would allow me into the social elite and I too could enjoy the magical experience of both wealth and power.

Glancing into the mirror, I realized I looked like a poor university student with my ripped and faded jeans and ridiculously tacky t-shirt that sported a picture of a giraffe hugging a brontosaurus. God, I must have looked like such a kid.

Despite Calisto telling me to come casually and they would dress me up to the nines for the event; I still wished I wore something more presentable. But the only thing 'dressy' I had was my little black dress that I wore to the China White, which I hadn't washed yet.

I strolled over to the walk-in closet and opened the door. Inside was a lavish golden mermaid gown with an elegant neckline and decorated with intricate beadwork. The dress was radiating with beauty. It was love at first sight and I tore off my ruddy clothes posthaste in order to slip into this outfit made for a goddess.

I was astounded by how well the dress fit me. Every curve was tight as the dress accentuated my best features while hiding the parts of my body I was the most self-conscious of. The dress was almost as comfortable as my yoga pants—though not quite. Along with it came a pair of matching heels, which also fit perfectly. They had my shoe size down pat as well.

Finally, there was a neat felt box wrapped in a dainty silk bow tie, resting on top of the dresser with a note on it.

For tonight, it read.

I shrugged my shoulders and tugged on the bow lightly, unraveling it. I lifted off the cover and gasped.

Inside was a golden Venetian mask, decorated with tiny jewels that formed an intricate pattern. Despite it being a stunning piece of work, it gave me the creeps.

This was what I was supposed to wear for tonight? Was I part of some twisted party worthy of Kubrick's imagination? I couldn't handle something like that.

I paged the intercom, hoping to get into contact with Abraham so I could get some answers from him.

"Yes?" I heard his voice echo from the intercom speaker.

"You gave me a mask to wear for tonight," I declared.

"Indeed I did," he replied.

"It freaks me out."

"Not to worry Ms. Aria," he said calmly. "Tonight's event has a beauty and the beast theme to it. The women are all ravishing beauties and we men are to portray silver-tongued beasts. *All* the guests will be in masks."

"Great," I muttered. His answer didn't make me feel any better. I decided to come out with it. "Is this one giant secretive sex party?"

"Ah," Abraham sighed. "I assure you, there will be no open, public sex. We are simply having a party tonight to celebrate a very important milestone for our organization. You will play the piano, grace us with your musical talents, and entertain us. In fact, you don't even have to say a word to anyone. Your only interactions tonight would be with our marvelous piano, if that's what you wish."

I let out a sigh of relief.

"That sounds good to me," I said. "Thank you for your patience while I act like a paranoid nut. I guess I'm on edge. It usually takes me a while to adapt to new situations."

"Not a problem Ms. Aria," Abraham said. "I always enjoy hearing from you. Your presence is…refreshing."

I allowed Abraham to return to his preparations for the party and decided to calm myself by playing some Bach fugues on the piano.

Everything was going to be fine.

While my hands filled the room with Bach's charming Baroque sounds, I fantasized on how tonight could unfold. I was going to go out there dressed like a Venetian Goddess, play my heart out on the piano, and then sit back and wait for my career to truly begin. It was all going to be a piece of cake.

However, hidden underneath this layer of optimism was the feeling that there was more to this night than Abraham and Calisto led on; that I was going to be a part of something big whether I wanted to or not.

The party started shortly before midnight, which gave me plenty of time to get ready. I started off by waxing and shaving every inch of my body, ridding myself of any stray hairs that weren't on my head. The last thing I wanted was to come out looking like a gold-faced Sasquatch. When I was satisfied with the purge, I proceeded to curl my unruly hair into pretty little locks. Finally I applied a healthy dose of mascara and blush on my face, which was probably a waste of time since it was going to be concealed behind the golden mask anyway.

But just in case.

A few minutes before the witching hour, there was a knock on my door.

"I'm ready to party," I replied.

Abraham entered, dressed in an elegant custom suit that fit snuggly on his thin frame. His graying hair was slicked back and he was clean-shaven. In his hand, he was holding a mask as well.

"Let's see what yours looks like," I said, pointing to his mask. He raised it to his head and slipped it over his face.

"How do I look?" he asked.

The mask was smooth and polished grey and its features reminded me of an elegant looking wolf, both feral and beautiful to look at.

"You look like a handsome wolf," I replied.

"Excellent," Abraham said. "That's what I was going for. I feared my mask strayed from my original design and became too beastly looking."

"You were going for the big, bad wolf look?"

"The wolf is the symbol of my family," Abraham explained, the mask still on his face. "It has become synonymous with the Constantine family name."

"Is everyone's mask at the party going to be unique?"

"Yes," Abraham replied. "Every person tonight will have symbols on their masks that tell a rich story of their family's background."

"What about mine?" I asked as I examined the golden mask again. On closer inspection, I noticed that the patterns formed the outline of twin doves interlocked together. "What do these doves symbolize?"

Abraham smiled. "The doves symbolize your legs my lady," he said, "And to have them intertwined together tells everyone that your legs are closed. This is the myth of the Golden Virgin."

"But I'm not a virgin," I protested. "It's just a bold-faced lie."

"And my family wasn't a pack of wolves either," Abraham

replied. "Remember what I said about stories? Some of the most powerful empires are built through stories."

"You also said that some of the most powerful empires are destroyed through stories."

"Touché."

From downstairs, I heard guests being welcomed at the door. Abraham gestured to the mask in my hand.

"Well Aria, the golden angel of chastity and virtue, are you ready to meet your destiny?" he asked.

"I'm never ready," I replied. "But what other choice do I have but to keep on moving through life?"

"None," Abraham replied calmly as he ushered me through the chamber door and out into the hallway.

By this time the mansion was already filled with a fair number of guests. The men wore full facial masks, painted in dark colors, some resembling animals while others were smooth surfaces with beautiful patterns and symbols etched into them. Meanwhile the women wore simple white masks that covered only the upper half of their faces, some decorated with feathers and jewels and others plain. It seemed like I was the only woman displaying a full mask that concealed my mouth.

For a moment, I was worried that breathing was going to be an issue but the air holes in the mask were crafted in such a way that airflow was not restrictive.

Abraham led me to a wide-open area of the mansion, a circular foyer where all paths converged. It reminded me of the center of a labyrinth, with the exception that instead of a massive man-killing Minotaur waiting for me, there was the most beautiful and rare piano in existence sitting on an elevated circular stage.

The angelic glow from the ceiling lights enveloped the entire stage, accentuating the beauty of the nine-foot Heintzman Piano.

It was so very surreal.

I couldn't believe that I, Aria Valencia whom only four days ago was eating peanut butter and pickle sandwiches—not because I liked them, but because there was nothing else in my fridge—was going to play music on an extravagant work of art valued at over three million dollars.

I almost wet myself in front of everyone. Thank God for my mastery over my urinary tract. They would have had to change my nickname from the Golden Virgin to the Golden Shower otherwise.

A familiar voice echoed throughout the hallways, captivating the attention of everyone in the vicinity.

"What a special night it is for all of us," Calisto said, standing at the top of the banister overlooking everyone. She looked ravishing in a cream colored dress that was embellished with tiny diamonds at the bust. The end of her gown seemed to flow like a river of milk as she strolled down the winding marble staircase, making her way to the ground level.

Whereas all the other female masks (aside from my own) were white in color, hers was black with an exotic flower tattooed onto the left cheek.

"Because of the importance of this celebration, I have flown over the rarest of talents from the most rural regions of Eastern Europe—the small town of Anastasia."

I turned to Abraham and whispered into his ear, "Where's Anastasia?"

"I doubt it exists," he replied. "Calisto enjoys playing games with everyone, stretching her stories to the realms of impossible just to see who she can fool into believing her."

It made me second-guess whether or not she actually did fuck a Chilean carpenter rather than a Chili-eating carpet seller.

"I cannot tell you what a treat it is for the Golden Virgin to grace us with her beautiful music tonight," she continued. "She is a mystical entity that will set the entire music world on fire. She is the start of the new era of provocative classical. To give you some history, I heard a tale just last week from a very reliable source that simply stunned me."

Oh God, I thought to myself. What the hell was Calisto doing? I looked around and saw the entire crowd of faceless masks drawn to her speech like addicts; her eloquent words the opium that seduced them.

"Word has it that a man knocking on death's door, dying from an incurable stage of cancer had the final wish of listening to the Golden Virgin play on his old, run-down, out-of-tune piano," she began. "Being the saint that she was, the Golden Virgin rushed as fast as she could to his home, making it just in time before the cancer stole him away into death's arms. She played for him a heartbreaking song that she wrote for her own father when he passed away. *Taofie Cyhmore Mag-pubr Tynwon* she called it, which translated to 'Breathless' in her native tongue."

The people of Anastasia used too many words, I thought.

"Despite the dismal state of the man's upright piano, the sounds escaping from its wooden husk were never more beautiful. It was as if the winds of heaven were carrying her melody through the old man's ears and filling his soul. For a brief moment, just before he died, he no longer felt pain. He only felt peace. It was her music that ushered him through the gates of heaven and into a life of eternal bliss."

There was a moment of silence as Calisto allowed her preposterous story to sink into the hearts of everyone in the room. I'll give her credit; she definitely knew how to captivate an audience.

"And now, without further ado, I am honored to present to you the lovely and mysterious Golden Virgin," Calisto said, turning in my direction.

All eyes in the room, hidden behind enigmatic masks, fell upon me.

Though I had played to large audiences before and dealt with the pressure of pleasing hundreds of judgmental ears, it felt different this time. First off, I couldn't see anyone's face, so I had no idea what type of response I was going to receive from the audience. Usually I could judge by facial expressions.

Second, if what both Calisto and Abraham said was true, someone here was either going to help me realize my dream of becoming a world-renowned pianist, or obliterate it. It was a lot of pressure and the idea of spending the rest of my career playing drinking songs in local dive bars for pennies was too much to handle.

I needed to dazzle this crowd and give them a performance they'd remember for a lifetime.

As I made my way to the Heintzman piano, I sensed the anticipation from this eclectic crowd, and the excitement of hearing that first note resonate throughout the mansion. They craved to hear the sounds of my playing, and I vowed to deliver it to them.

I closed my eyes and brushed my fingertips across the cool, smooth piano keys, worshipping the craftsmanship of this majestic instrument. As I hit the first note, I heard and felt the perfect balance of sound and weight from the piano. I lost myself to the music, allowing it to touch me like a mysterious lover, the reverberations of the instrument reaching deep inside me as I let loose a long sigh. I released the haunting and pleasurable sounds of Liszt's *Benediction de Dieu dans la Solitude* from the piano and played it with an absolute reverence.

Every beautiful note was a blessing from Franz Liszt's creative genius.

When I was finished, I paused for a moment, and then went into another one of the composer's masterpieces, *Harmonies Poetiques et Religieuses,* using the full range of the Heintzman to weave together sounds of this absolutely stunning work.

A few times I looked up from the keys to see the crowd's reaction, but only saw the chilling sight of expressionless masks gazing in my direction. It was unnerving, and I decided that it was best to focus on the music alone, and not allow the people and the surroundings distract me from the music.

After I finished playing an eight-piece set, I had to stop and take a small break. My wrists and forearms were on fire from the sheer complexity of the pieces and to play another one right away would end up a butcher's mess.

I glanced at the audience, many of them still focused in my direction. I had no idea if people were receptive to my playing, or if they were gawking at me like a sideshow attraction. I was glad that I was wearing this golden mask. At least they couldn't see the nervous expression on my face.

"That was simply stunning," said a voice from behind me. I turned around to see a tall man with blonde hair, his face hidden underneath a red Venetian mask resembling a fox. "Your combination of virtuoso playing and eloquent grace is a marvel to watch. I'm just surprised that I haven't heard of you prior to tonight."

"Thanks for the compliments," I replied. I was excited to hear someone acknowledge my performance. "I've been kind of keeping a low profile lately, you know, preparing for my big North American debut."

The fox's eyes glanced over me. "Your European English sounds very...North American."

"I spent a lot of time studying in North America," I was quick to reply. "I've assimilated the language pretty fast."

There was another long pause from Mr. Fox. "Speak in your native tongue over in Anastasia."

What was with the twenty questions? Why was he so concerned about my background and where I came from?

"Tranqata oblingonata kaliquicky ayamana," I replied, ranting off gibberish from the top of my head.

"Translation?" Mr. Fox asked.

Go away, I wanted to say. However what actually came out of my mouth was, "You're a curious one Mr. Fox."

"Calisto is storytelling again, isn't she?" he said.

Damn it. Was there any point in continuing this ridiculous rouse any longer? I knew that the further down the rabbit hole I went, the smaller the tunnel would become.

"Look," he said. "I personally don't care which way the wind blows and how far the story goes. I appreciate talent, which you have an abundance of. However, there is one aspect of Calisto's story that needs to be proved, and any failure to do so will be a poor reflection on your capabilities as an A-list artist."

"Oh?"

"Play your father's song," the fox said. "Play Breathless."

Perhaps the one thing about Calisto's yarn that had some fibers of truth to it was that I did write a song for my dad shortly after he died.

His passing away wasn't an easy thing to get over. He was the only family I had. My dad was the pillar that held me up when I wanted to crumble emotionally.

I remember on one snowy evening, not long after my father died, my loneliness and depression felt like a gun pressed up against my temple. I decided to head over to the university's conservatory and found myself an old upright piano that was outside one of the examination rooms, waiting to be tossed out the very next day.

It was a little out of tune and missing the F sharp key in the lower octave, but at that moment in time, the piano was perfect for me. This lonely, broken and abandoned instrument was an exact reflection of me, both physically and mentally.

I closed my eyes and my fingers unearthed a simple and sad melody that had long been buried inside me. It was a melody that had haunted my imagination before, but up until then, I lacked the raw emotions to do it any justice. I stored the tune in the back of my mind until the time was right—when I felt the most vulnerable.

I played the song on that old piano with my heart bleeding out into the music while tears streamed down my cheeks. I allowed the world around me to dissolve into nothing, imagining that the only thing left in the universe was that old piano, a heartbroken daughter that played it, and the spirit of her father listening to her one final gift to him.

Since that day, I never played that song again. There were too many raw emotions associated with it and I feared that playing it would tear open deep wounds.

"I don't think I can," I replied to Mr. Fox. "I'm sorry."

The fox shook his head. "Please," he said. "I wish to hear it. It would mean a great deal to me and everyone here as well."

I looked around and noticed that Mr. Fox had effortlessly drawn the attention of the room to us.

"What do you say?" he said aloud to everyone. "Wouldn't we love for the Golden Virgin to bless us with her beautiful tribute to her father?"

The applause and the cheers of everyone provided a definite answer. But I just wasn't ready, was I?

Oh dad, what would you like me to do? I silently prayed to him. That song was like a secret message to my father, one that was meant for his ears only. The idea of playing it for anyone else felt blasphemous.

No. That wasn't true. It was just an excuse I was making. I knew exactly what my dad would have said to me.

"Enchant them all," I whispered aloud. Without another word, I turned my attention back to the Heintzman piano, closed my eyes and allowed the feelings of loss and hurt to overtake me. In my mind and heart, I was no longer at the mansion but sitting in front of that broken old upright on that lonely winter night a couple of years ago.

The music that resonated all around me was filled with pain, as if the loss of my father were still a fresh wound. It would always feel that way.

I played that song with my heart torn apart; the ache of my dad's passing now at the forefront of my thoughts. It sounded sad, lovely, and wounded. As I reached the finale, I realized that I was crying underneath the mask. My fingers fell on the final chord and I held my hands there and allowed the note to linger until it eventually faded away into silence.

The entire room was hushed. The only sounds audible to me were those of my heavy breathing.

I bowed my head, closed my eyes and swallowed hard. I had bared my heart to everyone in this room, and I was met with silence.

It wasn't until Mr. Fox began clapping that I realized that the silence was a result of the emotions everyone felt after listening to my father's song.

Like a musical chorus, the applause started off softly at first but it didn't take long for it to crescendo into cheers and praise.

I felt a tap on my shoulder and turned to see Abraham, still in his wolf mask.

"My heart is breaking with that haunting piece you've just played," he said, "And though you cannot see it, I assure you that I am tasting my bittersweet tears."

"Thank you Abraham," I replied. "I'll let you in on a little secret. This is the first time I've played it for anyone."

"What an outstanding job you've done," he replied, "Simply outstanding."

For the next ten minutes, I was met with continuous adoration and praise. My heart was racing and I felt delighted every time someone showered me with kind words.

"You're a treasure," Mr. Fox said as he took my hands in his. "I would kiss your priceless hands, but alas, this mask stands in the way between my lips and your skin."

"I guess you liked it huh?"

"I won't lie, I'm a cruel and cold hearted man and the emotions I identify with the most are jealousy and greed. But listening to your music, it stirred something inside me," he said. "But don't let these kind words get to your head, Golden Virgin from Anastasia. I see a lot of money being made between the two of us. I'll have someone call you."

"Really?" I beamed.

"Yes. As beautiful as your tune was, nothing sounds better than money raining down from the wallets of the public," Mr. Fox said. "Now if you excuse me, there's a lovely lady in this room that I've had my eye on for a while."

"We're all wearing masks here," I laughed. "How do you know what she looks like underneath?"

"These stupid things are a façade and a novelty. True beauty radiates through a simple piece of dried plaster and can slay a man's heart in seconds," Mr. Fox said.

"You sound like quite the hopeless romantic."

"Once again, you mistake me for being a gentleman. I'm actually a sexual deviant," he replied. "I've been dying to taste her skin again."

As appalling as it sounded, I couldn't help but laugh. Mr. Fox seemed harmless enough, and the fact that he offered me an opportunity had me on cloud nine.

"Well, I won't be a cock block any longer then," I replied. He bowed graciously and made his way through the crowd. I watched him pass by a dozen ogling girls, paying them no attention and finally stopped in front of Calisto and offer her a greeting.

I didn't blame him. Calisto looked absolutely stunning in her dress. For a split second, I almost felt envy for all that she had and all that she was.

I continued chatting with other party guests for the better part of an hour, playing along to Calisto's lies as I practiced my storytelling abilities. I discussed the politics and scandals behind the fictional city of Anastasia. It was actually kind of fun pulling the wool over people's eyes, coming up with elaborate and outrageous stories.

I was ashamed to think it, but I was becoming better at lying.

I was in the middle of telling a story of how the last Mayor of Anastasia was caught in a sex scandal involving transvestite prostitutes and raccoons when suddenly, I heard the heavy chimes of what sounded like church bells.

Everyone's attention was drawn to the origins of the bells outside in the gardens, just beyond the sun parlor and through the towering French doors. The guests made their way outside towards the sound, bewitched by every vibrant chime.

My curiosity was peaked and I fell in line with everyone else, leaving the warmth of the mansion and immersing myself into the cool air of the night. I looked up and saw the stars fill the sky like tiny speckled diamonds.

It was a magical night.

The sweet scent of blooming flowers flooded my nostrils and I was amazed by how enchanting the gardens looked. It was something out of a fairy tale.

I was captivated while continuing to follow the crowd through the spellbinding gardens.

How odd it was that in a matter of seconds something could go from appearing so lovely to so fucked up.

At the centre of the gardens, three women were kneeling on velvet pillows, worshipping a large stone bell, fiery torches to each side of it.

Something strange was going on here.

Calisto stood behind the three women, each one dressed in elegant white gowns, their faces covered with milk-white masks. She was examining them; no different from how I examined a piece of fruit at the grocery store, running her fingers down every curve to check for imperfections.

What was going on here?

Finally Calisto turned to all the guests and addressed us.

"We have all come today to celebrate a very special time for the Midnight Society," she began. "Twenty-three years ago on this day, not only were my brother and I born, but the future of our society as well. Over the past decade, we endured harsh times. We've had our wars with others, but persevered and came out of it stronger than before. We have also lost people close to us…" she paused, "…But I know if my father were still here today, he would tell everyone that the future of the Midnight Society shines brightly with Shadow leading it."

There was a round of applause and acknowledgements to the words she had just said.

I, however, was baffled. What the heck was a Midnight Society?

"Tonight Shadow, the prince of our Midnight Society, will choose one of these three women to stand by his side and continue on with the legacy of the Tremaine family name. Because he considers each and every one of you as a part of his family as well, we are invited here to watch as he selects his mate, a worthy queen that will honor both the Tremaine lineage and the Midnight Society as well."

There was another round of applause followed by a chorus of cheers.

It sounded like this was some sort of arranged marriage.

Calisto raised her hands to the night sky, which silenced everyone. When she was content that everyone was listening, she continued.

"Ladies and gentlemen, I am pleased to welcome my brother, Shadow Tremaine, lord of the Midnight Society."

Out of the darkness of the gardens emerged a tall, muscular man wearing a form-fitting suit, his face hidden behind a solid black mask. His emergence out of the depths of the foliage reminded me of a monster out of a horror movie.

As he strolled towards the three women, I couldn't help but feel that his eyes were focused on me, and that was more than enough to turn my insides into liquid.

CHAPTER FOUR

His presence cast a hush throughout the gardens. Shadow strolled towards the three women on their knees, stalking them with an animalistic grace.

He was ominous, yet electrifying and I found myself trembling just standing in the same vicinity as he was.

"Your bride awaits you Shadow," Calisto said to her brother.

I glanced around and noticed that everyone had their head bowed in reverence of this man.

It was disconcerting and this made me panic.

This had to be a cult; there was no other logical explanation in my mind. Any second now, this Shadow fellow was going to pass out the Kool-Aid and we were all going to drink it and die.

There was still time for me to flee. I could pretend to use the bathroom and then sneak out the window or something. I had no idea where on the map this estate was, but that didn't matter. I needed to escape and I could figure the rest out later.

I looked around to see if anyone else was watching me.

Damn it, indeed someone was. Calisto's eyes were deadlocked onto me.

I panicked and almost let loose a scream, but managed to contain myself. Thank God for the mask I was wearing, which hid the expression on my face.

Calisto smiled and winked at me, which I thought was a bizarre thing to do. I had no idea what was happening or what to expect, but I desperately wanted to be away from here.

Shadow strolled over to the first girl, a fair skinned beauty with silky blonde hair that glowed. She had her head bowed down low, as if she were in prayer.

"Rise," he said in a deep authoritative voice. She did as she was told and rose to her feet. He examined her from head to toe, just before speaking again.

"Why should you be worthy of being my mate?" he asked.

"I am Elizabeth Mayweather, heir to the Mayweather Hotel Empire," she replied. "The Mayweathers have a long and prestigious history with the Midnight Society and to be united with the Tremaines would be a historic moment for two of the world's most powerful families," she explained. "As your wife, I shall be faithful, loyal, and will always stand by your side. I will bear your children in my womb and when it is their time, they will rise up and set this world on fire."

It all sounded like overdramatic nonsense to me.

Shadow looked at her for a moment without saying a word. Elizabeth was noticeably uncomfortable underneath his gaze.

Finally he spoke. "When it's all said and done, will you have said more than you've done?"

Elizabeth looked bewildered. "Excuse me?" she asked.

"Answer my question," Shadow said. "When it's all said and done, will you have said more than you've done?"

"Yes?"

"Unacceptable," Shadow said as he moved onto the next girl, a young Asian woman with long curly hair and almond colored skin.

"Rise," Shadow said as he gently touched the beautiful girl's shoulder. The contact was like a magnetic force that bonded to the woman's curvy body and she rose to her feet effortlessly.

"I'm Elena Zhao," she said. "I am the daughter of Yuen Xi Zhao and heiress to the Zhao shipping corporation, the most powerful business entity in all of the East. My father's fortune is worth well over one hundred and fifty billion U.S. dollars and for the Zhao and Tremaine family to merge together would create an everlasting dynasty of wealth and power. However wealth is only a fraction of what I can offer you. I am skilled in the arts of pleasure, taught to me by the exotic mistresses of rich and powerful men. I can pleasure you in ways that you never thought possible..." she paused and smiled wickedly. "I will stimulate all five of your senses. You will feel my sensuous touch upon your body, taste the sweetness of my skin, hear the cries of pleasure as we unite together as one, smell the scent of our lust, and see every act I perform with only the intentions of fulfilling your deepest desires."

Shadow stared at her for a moment before finally replying.

"You trained yourself to be a whore."

The look of shock on the perfect little Asian princess's face was priceless. I let loose a snort, which caused the woman to the right of me—a snooty blonde in a white swan-decorated mask—to turn around and shoot me an angry glance with disapproving eyes.

Once again, I was thankful for my golden mask, which hid my childish grin.

"It was him," I whispered, pointing to a large bellied man standing on the other side of me, who was fixated on the spectacle. The swan woman shrugged and turned her attention back to Shadow, who had already moved onto the third prospect.

He took one glance at her and immediately shook his head.

"You're better off staying where you are," he said. "I don't want to breathe the same oxygen as you, unless I wish to decimate my brain cells."

This guy was turning out to be a real dick.

"You're going to have to make a decision," Calisto said frowning. "You'll have to choose your lady tonight."

43

"All three of these women are a disappointment," Shadow said. "I can't allow any of them to share the Tremaine name."

The spectators erupted into whispers and I was surprised that there was genuine concern that Shadow had spurned all three women.

"What's the big deal?" I asked the swan woman. "There's plenty of fish in the sea. Why can't Shadow go back to the pond and cast in another line?"

"The ritual of selecting the first lady of the Midnight Society is both a historic and sacred event," she replied. "On the twenty-third birthday of every society's leader, they have to choose their soul mate, a woman worthy to inherit their powerful family name. It's a tradition that's been kept since the dawn of our organization almost two hundred years ago." And then she gave me a disdainful stare. "I don't care how good your music is or how closed your legs are, you don't deserve to be here."

"Thanks for making me feel welcome," I scowled.

The swan woman ignored my sarcasm and began complaining aloud to no one in particular. "What a cluster fuck tonight has been. But what else can you expect from Shadow. He's reckless and disrespectful when it comes to sacred traditions of the Midnight Society."

"Well can you blame him?" I asked. "You folks are practically forcing him into an arranged marriage."

"Those three women are the best that the Midnight Society has to offer," the swan woman replied. "They were handpicked by the Council of Seven and for Shadow to insult all three is a slap in the face to our organization and the family name's of those women. Shadow made three powerful enemies tonight."

"So why's he your leader then, if he's such a shit disturber?"

"It's in his blood. He was born into it."

"Give me a break," I said. "This is America. The idea of kings and queens is a foolish fantasy. Is democracy dead in this little

Midnight clubhouse of yours?"

I had received some dirty looks in my days but the one that Swan Girl gave me then was straight from the bowels of the filthiest sewer ever seen.

"Sometimes, we need people to make decisions for us," she spat. "People in general, especially the lower class like you, are too stupid to make the right choices."

This girl was really getting on my nerves. Justin told me once that swans, despite their beauty, had the heart of the devil and now I agreed with him.

I was about to unleash a verbal assault on swan woman but I suddenly noticed that everyone's attention was focused on me.

"I choose her," Shadow said.

My heart turned into lead and sunk like an anchor; deep into the murky ocean that was my stomach. Did I just hear him correctly?

"I choose the Golden Virgin," Shadow repeated.

The lord of the Midnight Society had chosen me—nobody special—to be his bride.

Ignoring the gasps of everyone around me, I allowed two words to escape my quivering lips.

"Oh shit."

CHAPTER FIVE

"I don't think you understand how this works," Calisto said to Shadow. "The Golden Virgin is not a member of the Midnight Society. She's not even a member of high society; not yet anyway."

Shadow shook his head. "You wanted me to make my decision Calisto, and I did. The Golden Virgin is who I have chosen."

"I think you should listen to your sister," I was quick to chime in. "Really, you don't want to choose me. I'm just a ragamuffin girl who knows how to play a tune on the piano."

"I've heard your story," Shadow said. "It touched me in a profound way. With such an intriguing and mysterious history, how can I not choose you to be my eternal soul mate?"

I could sense a hint of sarcasm in his voice.

Damn it Calisto, your stupid fairy tale stories about me were causing me a lot of grief. I had to sort this out before things got any worse.

"Look," I began. "The truth of the matter is--"

"The prince has made his choice everyone," Calisto was quick to interrupt me. "As controversial as it may seem, who are we to judge the decision of a Tremaine?"

Furious protests shattered the silence as the guests voiced their displeasure all at once.

"You're kidding me, she's a lowborn!" one woman cried out.

"This will tarnish the Tremaine family name," another man in a monkey mask shouted. "This has to be a joke."

Calisto raised both her hands to silence everyone.

"My brother has made his decision, and might I remind you that he *is* the lord of the Midnight Society. Anyone who opposes this can take it up with him privately if you wish."

Dead silence.

"Wonderful," she said. "Refreshments will be brought out shortly. In the meantime, perhaps the Council of Seven can convene in the study, along with my ever-so-wise brother?"

"How can I say no to my ever-so-lovely sister," he replied with jest.

While everyone was distracted, *now* was a good time as any to escape all this madness. I could scale the walls with some Spiderman shit and flee from this disaster.

"As for the Golden Virgin, we'd love for you to attend our little meeting as well," Calisto said, her attention focused on me.

Shit.

"You know, it's actually getting kind of late," I began.

"Nonsense," Calisto said. "This night just started and you, my little nightingale, are the center of attention. Isn't that what you always wanted? Attention?"

"With a piano in front of me, yes," I replied. "But the last thing I wanted was to get forced into some sacred love bond."

"Don't you worry about that," Calisto said. "We'll sort that all out. By the way, there's a group of lovely people that are dying to know more about you and your music. Why don't I introduce you to them?"

"Can I go home first and meet them over a cup of coffee later on in the week?"

"They're here for one night only," she replied. "It'd be a

wonderful opportunity for you."

They had no intention of letting me go.

I was screwed.

"I'm stuck here aren't I?" I stated.

"It's really for your benefit."

Calisto strolled up to me, taking my arm in hers, and began leading me back towards the estate. Trailing behind her was a pair of large, muscular men in white owl masks, whom I assumed would snatch me up like a rag doll if I attempted to make a run for it.

The feeling of dread was poison in my veins and I wished that I hadn't come here in the first place. How stupid could I possibly be? I was lured into a spider's web with the promise of money and fame.

Ugh.

"I think we're going to become very close friends," Calisto said with a wide grin on her face.

That was funny, because I was thinking that by the end of the night, I was going to end up six feet under somewhere. I was scared shitless, but the only thing I could do at this point was play along until I could figure out a plan to get myself out of this mess.

Calisto led me into a large study, one of the typical manly ones you saw on television and in movies. Moonlight flooded the large bay windows, casting a cerulean afterglow against the tall oak bookcases, filled with leather tomes, stretching from floor to ceiling. Oil paintings of medieval knights and their insignias lined the walls, each piece exhibiting the European flavours of chivalry and romance.

At the centre of the study, seated around a circle in large leather armchairs, were six well-dressed men, still donning their Venetian masks. I felt some relief when I recognized Abraham's wolf mask along with Mr. Fox, whom I had chatted with earlier in the evening.

"Abraham!" I practically leapt at him. "What's going on here?"

"Don't be alarmed Ms. Valencia," he said in his same reassuring tone of voice. "We'll have this sorted out before you know it."

"You're having quite the eventful night," Mr. Fox said with merriment. "You went from being no one, to a music star, to a princess all in one night."

"I seriously don't know what's happening here," I announced to everyone in the room. "I just want to go home. Look, keep the money you owe me, just let me go."

I was a sniveling mess. Between the walk from the gardens back to the estate, I had imagined hundreds of horrific scenarios.

I saw myself lying naked on top of an altar, ready to be sacrificed to some pagan cult god; or being auctioned off into some slavery ring and dragged over to Europe to be used as a sex puppet for the rest of my life. Or what if I was in some serial killer's den and I was going to be chained up, tortured, and killed in some basement dungeon? All the possibilities paralyzed me and I broke out into a cold sweat.

Calisto led me to the centre of the circle and sat in the seventh empty seat. Everyone was watching me with penetrating stares, their expressions hidden behind those damned masks. At least I was wearing one as well.

Shadow stood by the large bay windows, staring out into the night as if he couldn't care less of what was going on in the room.

One man, wearing a red mask with a black scorpion pattern on it, broke the silence with his acidic tone of voice. "Take off your mask."

This mask was all I had to hide myself from these people. With the mask off, they could see the fear and desperation on my face, things that any demented predator probably got off on.

I shook my head. "No."

"You've got nothing to hide from us honey," Calisto said sweetly. "My friends just want to see what a pretty girl you are."

I felt my last bit of strength in me erode away, like stone pillars crumbling into dust. I was at my wits end.

"Please don't kill me or sell me into slavery," I blurted out, resisting the urge to fall to my knees and beg, figuring that once I was off my feet, they weren't going to allow me to return to them.

There was a moment of silence amongst the circle. I noticed that even Shadow had turned his attention away from the window, glancing in my direction.

And then they all broke out into laughter.

I was baffled.

"Oh dear," Abraham said. "I always said that communication amongst our group needs to be better. I believe you misunderstood our intentions for you Aria."

"You guys kidnapped me," I cried. "And now you won't let me go home. What the hell am I supposed to think?"

"I assure you, what we want is not sinister in nature," Abraham said. "Just like I promised you in the car, you will not be physically harmed."

"You know, if the roles were reversed, I could understand why our little Golden Virgin would be so anxious," Mr. Fox said. "Perhaps if we showed her ours, she'd be more inclined to show us hers."

"I don't want to see anything from you sick perverts," I retaliated. I heard a sigh come from Mr. Fox, and then he slowly removed his mask to reveal a handsome young man in his mid-twenties. He had sparkling emerald eyes and a bright smile that complimented his sun-kissed hair and fair skin. His grin displayed a boyish charm that could melt hearts.

"Lincoln Richards," he introduced himself, "Owner of First Light Media Corporation. I'm sure you watched a movie or twenty produced by my company."

"You've seen me without my mask on already," Calisto said from behind me. Instinctively I turned around. Her mask was now removed and resting in her hand. "Hopefully I don't look a day older since we last met."

Abraham was the next to remove his mask and he smiled at me.

"Cheers," he said.

Sitting next to him was a thin, grey-haired man wearing a red and black kabuki mask. He removed it, revealing a sophisticated looking Asian man in his early fifties. Despite his age, he was still very attractive with a mature and distinguished look about him.

"James Takeshi," he said. "As my name suggests, I own Takeshi Technology."

I was astounded. Takeshi *was* the top brand in entertainment technology, taking the world by storm and driving down the market shares of all its competitors in only five years.

To Takeshi's right was a large man wearing the mask of a golden lion. He removed it, revealing the proud and strong chiseled face of an African American man. He looked at me with intense fire in his dark brown eyes.

"I am Brevin West," he said, with a slight yet traceable island accent, "Owner of the Majestic Glory Corporation, the largest Christian multimedia and business enterprise in North America." He spoke with reluctance in his voice, like his words were being yanked out of his throat. I could sense the distrust he had for me.

The next person to introduce himself was a hefty man in a tight fitting suit, the buttons on his one-size-too-small dress shirt threatening to bust off. He removed his white eagle mask revealing his pear-shaped face and a white, neatly trimmed beard. He was someone who I've seen a couple of times before on television and in the newspapers.

"I'm Senator Donald Huff," he said cheerfully. "It's always a pleasure to see someone ascend through the ranks of the Midnight Society, especially at such a young age."

"A United States Senator?" I asked, astounded.

"I'm sure I don't have to tell you that discretion is extremely important as to who I associate with in my spare time," he said. "Curiosity didn't kill the cat; her purring did, if you know what I mean."

I nodded my head in agreement.

The man in the Scorpion mask was the last of the introductions.

"I'm not taking off my mask until she does," he said in a distinguished British accent.

"Lucien, must you always be so difficult?" Abraham sighed. "We've all removed our masks for our esteemed guest."

"This is all bullshit," Lucien replied. "Shadow is once again playing us all for fools, but you folks are so in love with our fearless leader that you're ignoring this simple fact; the Tremaine's are broken. I've been saying it since the start; we need new blood in the commander's chair."

"One more word out of that shameful abyss you call a mouth, and I'll drive my foot so far up your ass that you'll be shitting out my four inch heel for a week," Calisto threatened. "Nobody insults the Tremaine name."

"Shadow does just by having it," Lucien laughed.

"Respect who you're with and where you are," Brevin said, though it seemed like he spoke more out of duty than belief.

"We've all been thinking it," Lucien said. "But I'm afraid none have the bollocks to bring the matter to the table. Well, after tonight's bloody embarrassment, let me reiterate. The Midnight Society needs new leadership. The Tremaine's are broken. The death of Tristan Tremaine marked the end of the family's power."

Calisto began to rise from her seat, but it was Shadow's thunderous voice that made her sit back down. The beast had woken up.

"Take off your mask," he ordered, as he stood behind Lucien's seat. However Lucien pretended not to notice, and continued his rant.

"Look at this scrawny girl standing before us. She's supposed to be the first lady of the Midnight Society? All of us in this inner circle of ours know that the Golden Virgin is nothing more than a flea in rags. Her story is nothing but a bunch of Chinese whispers originated from the imaginative mind of Calisto," he continued. His scorpion eyes focused in on me. "Tell me you bony little slag, how virtuous are you really?"

Suddenly Shadow erupted and he scooped up Lucien from underneath his armpits, lifted the brat high into the air, and slammed him onto the ground.

"You shite!" Lucien cursed as he sprung back onto his feet. "I'm a fucking Gamble. You do not get to touch me."

"Get the fuck out of here," Shadow said, "Before I make you swallow all of your soon-to-be broken teeth."

"Calm yourselves, both of you," Takeshi said as he rose from his seat. "I swear my dog has more patience and common sense than you two."

"This bloody excuse for a 'lord' laid his hands on me. Tell me James, since when did we start striking each other," Lucien said.

"It was..." Takeshi paused, and then turned to Shadow, "Inappropriate."

Takeshi's words seemed to have affected him as Shadow's shoulders slumped and he retreated back from Lucien, his authority now diminished. I was curious to see the face of the man behind the mask and the whirlwind of emotions he was going through at the moment.

"Leave us alone," Shadow finally said.

"But our business is not finished," Abraham said. "We still need to discuss the selection you've made-"

"We're done for tonight." There was finality in Shadow's tone of voice.

Even though his visage was hidden behind the scorpion mask, I sensed a burning hatred radiating from Lucien that was dark and hideous.

"You've made a big mistake laying your hands on me," he seethed. "I promise you that--"

"Yeah, yeah, yeah," Shadow mocked. "I haven't heard the last of this. You'll make me pay. Throw in whatever cliché you find appropriate. Just stop whining and get the fuck out of here already."

He then turned to everyone else. "Please, just leave me alone. We'll finish this another time."

I watched as the council members left the study one-by-one. I followed closely behind Abraham. However just before I could reach the door, Shadow called out to me.

"Not you Golden Virgin," he said. "It's a nice night out. I'd like for you to take a stroll with me."

It was the last thing I wanted to do. More than anything, I just wanted to go home and forget this night even happened.

"But my ride is leaving," I said, gesturing towards Abraham.

"I'll wait for you dear," the old man reassured me. "Take your time."

I watched helplessly as Abraham closed the door behind me, leaving only Shadow and I alone in the room.

I turned my attention to the towering masked man. Something about the way he stood, his shoulders slumped and his head bowed low, made me fear him a little less. He was no longer the dominating monster I first saw, emerging out of the foliage of the garden. Instead the way he stood reminded me of an emotionally wounded man.

"Why did you choose me?" I asked.

Shadow didn't reply. Instead he lifted his hands to his head and slowly removed his mask, revealing himself to me.

CHAPTER SIX

The man was gorgeous. He had his sister's hypnotic blue eyes and I found myself lost in his gaze, as well as Calisto's skin, though not as pale. His ageless chiseled face was smooth and unblemished.

Shadow was not the monster I envisioned him to be. He was a ravishing angel that for some unexplained reason had chosen me to be his soul mate.

And he hadn't even seen my face yet.

I took off my mask and allowed him to look at me, the fabled Golden Virgin sent from the heavens, as rumor had it.

"Huh," he said after the big reveal.

I was taken aback.

"What do you mean huh?" I asked. "Huh, as in I look like ass?"

"I never said that," Shadow protested. "Don't start putting words in my mouth."

"I take off my mask so you can look at my face, and the first thing you say is 'huh'? Excuse me if I'm not dancing on the clouds at the moment."

"You're very pretty," Shadow said. "I wouldn't kick you out of bed."

What the hell was wrong with this guy? For someone as

handsome as he was, he was terrible with women.

I was starting to feel self-conscious and foolish. This entire night was turning out to be a first degree fuck up.

"Look, I'm tired," I said. "I can see you're having some domestic squabbles in this clubhouse of yours, and you're using me as some strange way to stick it to them. You couldn't care less about me. Am I right?"

"You're not so far off," Shadow said, "with one exception."

"Do I even want to know?"

"Like I said, I think you're very pretty. You have the entire 'don't care about you' part a little off."

"Who the hell looks at a girl for the first time and says 'huh'?"

"It's the opposite of what you think," Shadow said. "When I chose you to be my sham bride, I actually wasn't expecting much."

"Why?"

"As long as I've known Calisto, which is all my life, she has found ways of using strong adjectives to exaggerate both people and situations," Shadow said. "Pretty to her really means 'only a face a mother could love', and drop-dead gorgeous really means 'she's alright'...well you get the idea."

This guy was starting to sound pretty shallow.

"Maybe she sees a person's inner beauty," I said. "You jerk."

Shadow laughed. "Right," he said, "Inner beauty. You haven't heard her insulting people. Look, long story short, when Calisto called you 'lovely', I was expecting worse."

His story seemed plausible, though I had to wonder if Shadow was as gifted a liar as his sister was.

"What now?" I asked.

"I don't know about you but I'm not ready for serious commitment right now."

That was a relief. Neither was I.

I admit Shadow was hot as hell. However it was plain to see that we weren't a good fit.

An upper echelon aristocrat dating a poor college girl was a foolish fairy tale that belonged in a storybook. If there was one thing I was good at, it was being realistic. Too bad though.

The guy was a stud.

A yawn escaped my lips and I glanced at the clock. It had been an extremely long night.

"So you're not ready to get married, and neither am I. How about you get Abraham to drive me home and we'll call it a night?" I asked. "Maybe you can add me on Facebook so I can show everyone how I turned down a rich guy's proposal for marriage, just for kicks."

Shadow gave me a backwards glance.

"I'm joking," I said. "Seriously, I don't even like Facebook. I have no friends."

"Come walk with me in the gardens," Shadow said.

"Right now? Can I take a nap first or something?"

"Do you want some cheese with that whine of yours?"

What a jerk. All the pretty rich boys I met in my life were all the same—all dicks and no substance. Shadow didn't seem any different.

"Fine, I guess I can go for a little stroll. But then you'll have Abraham drive me home?"

"I cross my heart," Shadow replied as he opened the doors in the study, leading to the outside pavilion.

The first rays of dawn's light were peeking over the horizon illuminating the dark sky like the flame of a candle.

Shadow took me gently by the wrist and led me down a cobblestone path towards the gardens, the sweet smells of the flowers overtook my senses.

I opened my mouth to speak, but he quickly hushed me.

"Not yet," he said. "Not here."

It wasn't in my usual nature to be silenced by anyone, but the serious look on Shadow's face was enough to keep me from arguing. He seemed deep in his thoughts, whatever they were.

I tried to keep track of where I was going, but eventually after the fifth—or was it the sixth?—turn off I had given up trying to draw the mental map in my head. I prayed that Shadow's intentions of leading me into this garden maze weren't sinister in nature. Where were breadcrumbs when I needed them?

Eventually we ended up in a secluded spot where a stone bench rested underneath an ancient oak tree, its branches stretching a hundred fingers out into the beautiful orange dawn sky.

We both took a seat, much to my relief. I kicked off my heels, giving my poor feet some temporary relief.

"You probably have a lot of questions," Shadow said.

"Why did you choose me?" I asked, jumping right into it. "Those three girls were on their knees, ready to throw themselves on you. Just to let you know, I'm not one to kneel down for anyone, if that's what you're expecting."

"Those three women were harpies," Shadow replied. "All they wanted was to sink their money grubbing talons into a pound of my flesh."

"Who's to say I'm not the same way?" I asked.

He smirked. "You're not," he said.

"How can you be so sure?"

"You're just not. One thing I'm very good at is reading people."

He seemed confident about himself. Perhaps I could have a little fun with him, ruffle his dark feathers a bit.

"Read me then," I said. Shadow shrugged and looked at me with those hypnotic crystal eyes of his. I couldn't help but feel naked before his piercing stare, but for some reason, I didn't feel uncomfortable. In fact, I almost welcomed it.

After ten seconds or so, he smiled at me, though I noticed traces of sadness behind it.

"We're similar in some ways," he said.

"What do you mean?"

He was about to say something, but then paused and shook his head. "Nothing, don't worry about it."

"Hey, don't leave me hanging like that," I said. "When you start a sentence, you best damn well finish it."

He folded his arms and leaned back against the massive tree trunk and sighed. He looked out towards the sun, which peered back at us, casting a warm orange glow against our bodies.

"They expect me to get married and have an heir soon," Shadow said, shaking his head. "It's not something I want. No offense to you. Out of all the women here, you're the most intriguing."

"Why?" I asked.

"I like your music," he said. "Especially the song you played, Breathless. As corny as this sounds, it stirred some emotions in me that I thought were long dead. It was nice."

I felt my heart skip a beat, but not because I was swooning over his deep voice, handsome face, or muscular build—okay maybe I was swooning a little. The thing that made me flutter high in the clouds was the fact that my music was touching people in profound ways.

Sometimes, being a new independent artist was a lonely job, one filled with many self-doubts. Every little compliment I received was an additional piece of metal added to my criticism-proof armor; toughening up my defenses to the insensitive assholes I called music trolls.

So to hear that my song had an effect on Shadow warmed my entire body, like a fire burning deep within my heart.

"Well, I'm really glad you liked my song," I said.

"I still don't want to marry you though," he quickly added.

Yup, this guy sure had a way with women. But it didn't matter. I didn't want to get married either, especially to the jackass that Shadow was turning out to be.

"No need to let me down gently," I said. "I have no intentions to get hitched either."

"Good," he said. "We're in agreement then."

There was a long awkward pause as we glanced at each other briefly. I wondered what he was thinking.

"Why don't you want to get married?" I asked. "If that's what supposed to be in your cards."

"It's not one of my priorities," he said. "And with the way things are looking, I doubt I'll ever have the time for a relationship in my life."

That was a bold statement to make—an entire lifetime without love. I admit, falling hopelessly in love and being whisked away in a horse-drawn carriage wasn't on my list of priorities either, but eventually someday, when all the stars aligned, I had the desire to meet a perfect guy, experience the entire "on cloud nine" dating thing, and have a meaningful relationship where love meant walking around in yoga pants and leaving the washroom door open while I pissed.

I believed most people felt the same way. After all, who wanted to be alone in this world? This made me curious about Shadow.

"You're not an amoeba are you?"

"What?" he asked me, surprised.

"Like an amoeba, you know, asexual? No desires for women, or men, while floating around in life, hanging low and lazy."

"I like women," he stated. "And I enjoy sex."

"You're not a player are you?"

"No definitely not."

"You don't have to lie to me. You're a man who enjoys the playboy lifestyle too much and when it comes down to it, you just want to have messy, emotionless sex."

"I'm not sure what part of 'no definitely not,' confused you," he replied, before adding "believe it or not, I'm not the one in my family that has trouble keeping my pants on."

Did I sense some annoyance in his feelings towards Calisto's personal life? It was probably best I didn't delve too much into family matters. It wasn't any of my business anyway. In fact, his sex life really wasn't any of my business—though watching Shadow navigate out of my twenty questions minefield was kind of fun. It was good knowing I could hold my own with one of the aristocrats.

"So why not have a relationship then?"

"Too busy," he replied.

"Too busy with what?"

I could tell he was getting annoyed with me. Perhaps I had pushed things too far? I had a tendency to be oblivious to situations at times.

"We need to go on a few dates," he said.

"Excuse me?" I asked, surprised. That certainly came out of the blue. He went from 'I don't want any relationships this lifetime' to 'let's have dinner and a movie.' Maybe on top of being an arrogant, rich prick, he was schizophrenic as well—a mentally unstable heartthrob.

"Look, I selected you as my woman in front of the entire Midnight Society," he said, "So it's expected that we're seen together at least a few times."

"You want to go on pretend dates?"

"Yeah," he said. "Exactly."

"Why should I do this for you?"

"Because I can give you everything you want--a career for starters."

Tempting. But I was still skeptical. "And then what? We get engaged and at the last second I call off the wedding because I got cold feet?" I asked.

"No," he replied. "After the second date I'll tell everyone that I made a mistake in choosing you and I'd rather have you as a close friend."

"Why am I the one who gets dumped? How come I can't dump you?"

"It'll look bad on my family name," he said.

"What about me? It'll look bad on me too," I said. "I have to think about my illustrious career too you know."

"People will sympathize with a heart broken woman," he said.

"Use that to your advantage."

"Ugh. You're such a dick."

"A flaccid one according to you," he smiled. "Apparently I'm hanging around low and lazy."

I couldn't help but snicker also, but I scrunched up my face quickly after, showing him that I was displeased at the prospect of being dumped by a guy I wasn't interested in, despite his hotness.

"Two public dates," Shadow said. "We'll put on a show and when it's all over, I'll give you everything you need to kick-start your music career. And then I can have my life back to normal."

"What's normal?"

"You're very inquisitive."

"All part of my beautiful personality," I said.

"It's annoying."

I shot him a dirty look.

"So do we have an agreement?" Shadow asked.

"How do I know that after two dates, you won't become infatuated with me and then force me to marry you?"

"I'll draft up a contract, if that will make you feel any better."

I eyed him suspiciously.

"A contract?"

"Yes, those pieces of paper with written agreements on them that we both have to sign afterwards."

"I know what a contract is," I said. "It just seems so…business-like."

"I do run a business empire in my spare time," Shadow said. "A contract will protect both of us."

After giving it some thought, I finally agreed. "Draft it up," I said.

We headed back into the estate in silence, which was good. It gave me time to process all the strange events that had occurred overnight.

My music was a sensational hit amongst the rich and powerful, I was chosen to be the bride of some 'Lord of the Midnight Society,' I was going to go on two dates with him only to be dumped afterwards, but it would result in a blossoming music career.

"Wait," I said. "You're going to help me with my career because you like my music, and not because I'm going to go on two dates with you, right?"

"Yes," Shadow replied. "You're very talented. I believe that you can do great things with those fingers of yours. You just need a little help to reach your goals."

I was satisfied with his answer, and I smiled at him.

"Thanks Shadow," I replied.

"Two dates," he repeated.

"Alright already," I said annoyed. "Draft it up and I'll sign on the dotted line. Man you're like a broken record, you know that?"

"Just confirming our agreement," he said. "The human mind remembers things through repetition."

"Why don't you just tattoo it on my forehead," I replied. "Two dates."

Shadow seemed to ignore me as he found himself a piece of paper and pen. He began scribbling onto it, and then set it aside and began working on another piece of paper.

When he was finally done, there were two handwritten contracts in elegant neat writing lying on the wooden oak desk.

"Read it through," he said.

There was a lot of technical and legal mumbo jumbo that I was oblivious to. I skimmed through it briefly, searching for the few key words I was looking for.

Finally on the last line, Shadow had written:

After the second public meeting between Aria Valencia and Shadow Tremaine, the two shall agree to mutually terminate their courtship with one another. Shadow will provide Aria with assistance in furthering her career as a classical pianist through his vast resources (excluding money and personal time) and Aria Valencia will agree to cease any contact with Shadow Tremaine. These conditions are firm.

I looked over to Shadow, who casually handed me a pen. "The contract is broken only when both parties decide to dispose of it. As long as one person is holding onto it, it's binding," he said.

"You have yourself a deal," I said as I wrote my name onto both copies of the contracts. Shadow did the same, before extending his hand towards me.

"Deals should always be solidified with a handshake," he said.

I shrugged my shoulders and reached for his hand, taking it in mine. His grip was firm but gentle. There was a lot of strength contained within that muscular body of his and I pitied whoever was responsible for stirring the demons buried inside of him.

However there was also tenderness to Shadow, and for a brief moment, I wondered what it felt like being held within his massive arms.

I had to stop fantasizing about him. No good would ever come from being with this guy.

Shadow was gorgeous. Shadow was mysterious. And Shadow was dangerous.

"I'll have Abraham pick you up on Saturday then," he said in a business-like tone. "Wear something nice."

"Okay," I said dumbly. I was still enthralled by the strength of his touch.

"And you can let go of my hand now," he added.

How embarrassing. I released my puny grip from his large, strong hands.

"Right," I replied. "Saturday sounds good."

Shadow raised his arms to the ceiling and stretched while rotating his neck from side-to-side. "Great," he said in between a yawn. "Well if there's nothing else, I'm exhausted. You must be pretty tired yourself. I'll buzz Abraham to give you a lift home."

He was right. I was ready to collapse onto my single bed back in the shack I called home.

"Well, I guess this is goodbye now," I said, adding, "it was a pleasure."

"I'd love to hear you play again sometime," Shadow insisted. "Maybe you can on one of our dates."

I smiled. "That depends on how the dates go. I don't play just for anybody you know."

"Right." He shrugged, turning his attention to the outside of the bay window, peering out into the morning light. There was an unmistakable sadness hidden deep within him.

Perhaps we weren't so different after all.

It was almost noon when Abraham dropped me off in front of my apartment. I was wiped.

"I shall pick you up on Saturday evening, say around five p.m.?" Abraham asked.

I nodded wearily.

"Make sure to check your bank account as well. Your payment should be there already."

"But I never gave you guys my bank account number," I said.

Abraham grinned and waved farewell. "I'll see you Saturday," he said as he rolled up the window of the limo.

I watched him drive off into the distance, leaving me alone with my thoughts.

Who the hell were these people?

I dragged my tired ass up the rotting wooden staircases of my apartment, still wearing the evening gown they gave me. It was too good for this hovel.

It took me a good minute of fumbling around for my keys before I let myself into my apartment, stumbling in wearily like an impeccably dressed zombie.

Bleary eyed, I flipped open my laptop and checked my bank account. Last night I had exactly $4.36 to my name. Now there was $11,004.36.

Not bad for two night's work.

If I wasn't so tired, I would have screamed to the heavens in pure ecstasy, but instead, I let out a yawn and said, "Sweet."

I collapsed onto my bed not bothering to remove the dress. The last image I had before drifting off into a deep sleep was the brooding look of Shadow's face, just before I left him alone in his study.

Who are you Shadow? What ghosts haunt your thoughts? Two intriguing questions which I hoped to unravel on our future dates.

But first, sweet precious sleep.

CHAPTER SEVEN

I woke to the sounds of the Muppet's *Mahna Mahna*, my cellphone ring tone, which normally put me in a cheerful mood. However seeing as how I slept only for an hour before it ripped me away from my sweet slumber, the song pissed me off.

No I couldn't blame the happy tune. It was whoever was calling me that was the culprit. I reached for my phone and looked at the name on my call display.

Justin.

I put my phone on mute and tossed it back onto my night table, rolled over, and went back to sleep.

I was bailing on musical history class, and like an overprotective brother, Justin was probably trying to figure out where I was.

I'll meet up with him later tonight and grab whatever notes I missed from class. But for now, I wanted nothing more than to be seduced by my warm duvet and Mr. Sandman's dreams.

Justin opened the door to his condo, dressed in torn jeans and a white tank top.

He greeted me with a boyish "kiss me beautiful" type of grin, like he always did.

"I missed you in class today," he said.

"I noticed," I replied. "You called me five times in the span of five minutes."

"I was wondering if you forgot about our test today," he said. "I guess you did."

Oh shit! There *was* a test today on Schubert's Erlkonig. It was one of the more interesting topics in music history, and one that I read up a great deal on. It would have been an easy way to boost up my average in the course, which was presently suffering because of my dick-faced professor who didn't agree with a few of my essays.

"Fuck," I cursed.

"Yeah," Justin said. "It was on a topic you liked as well. Where were you anyway?"

"Come on, let's go grab some food at the Brickstone," I said. "I'll fill you in on the way there."

"I was in the middle of making dinner, but I guess I can save it for tomorrow. Just let me get my wallet," Justin said as he headed back inside.

"No way, you bought me lunch last time. Let me at least get your burger."

"Are you buying me dinner?"

"Yes."

"Is this a date?"

I saw the twinkle in his eye and regretted my offer almost immediately.

"No," I replied. "I'm just paying you back. I don't like being in debt to anyone."

"You don't have to do that," Justin said.

"Yes I do. Now no more debating," I said. "I'm starving."

I was hesitant to tell Justin the truth, especially seeing how clandestine last night's celebration was, but I was going to explode if I didn't spill my guts to someone about it. Justin was my closest friend and I trusted him with just about any secret.

After having Justin swear an oath of eternal secrecy, I filled him in on last night's events. As I listened to the words coming out of my mouth, I was beginning to realize how preposterous it all sounded: masked aristocrats, the Golden Virgin, secret societies, fucked up rituals, arranged marriages, and a dating contract. The only thing I left out were the names revealed to me.

Justin stayed quiet the entire time. I wouldn't be surprised if he thought I was crazy.

When I finally finished spinning my yarn, I looked at him and shrugged my shoulders.

"Well?" I said. "Sounds crazy right? Am I going nuts?"

"You shouldn't go on those dates," he replied. There was anger in his voice along with resentment.

"Why?" I asked, but secretly I already knew the answer. It was a mistake to tell him about the dates.

For a second, I felt guilty that I was letting him down.

"Just don't go," he replied.

"I have to. I signed a contract remember? And I'll be fine. Who knows, it might even be fun, mingling with the rich and famous."

"What if I don't want you to go?"

I met his question with a shrug. So this was it; the relationship talk. I knew this day was coming at some point. I had tried so hard to put it off, but I knew I couldn't run away from the inevitable forever.

"Aria…" Justin began.

"Look Justin, you're an important part of my life," I said. "In fact, you're the only friend I have in this lonely place."

"I can be more than that," he said, reaching for my hands. I pulled them back and saw the look of hurt on his face.

"Why not?" he asked.

"I just don't want any relationship right now."

"What about later on?"

I shook my head, "Eventually yes," I said and paused before adding. "But with someone else."

If this were a street fight, those words were the knockout punch. Justin looked at me like I had stabbed him, tears welling up in his eyes.

"I...I love you Aria."

Ugh. I brought this on myself. Justin needed to know how I felt. I had been stringing him along for far too long now, all because I was a lonely, selfish girl.

"Justin," I began, "I told you this many times, you're important to me. But I've always seen you like the brother I never had. To start dating you would be..." choose your next words wisely Aria, "...like incest."

Legendary failure.

"The thought of us together disgusts you that much?" he asked.

"No," I said, "that came out all wrong. God, I'm terrible at expressing myself sometimes."

"No," Justin said, the look of hurt evolving into anger now. "I think you made it loud and clear. Well, I wouldn't want you to feel like being with me was some forbidden taboo. We're done here."

He turned around and stormed off. I wanted to call out to him, but stopped myself. Emotions were at a peak, and nothing good would come out of anything he or I said right now. I'll text him in a few days. Hopefully he'll have cooled off by then.

I watched as Justin—my only friend in the world—disappeared over the horizon. Like everyone else in my life, he left me alone and feeling miserable.

But telling him the truth was the right thing to do; the *only* thing to do wasn't it?

CHAPTER EIGHT

After mutilating Justin's heart with my brilliant 'feels like incest' explanation, I felt awful. I could have sat around feeling miserable about the entire thing, but I decided to do something for myself instead, just to take my mind off things.

It's been so long since I had a 'me only' day.

With my freshly stocked bank account, I headed over to the mall to buy some new clothes, which was a long time coming.

I only had three pairs of jeans, which all had holes in various locations and not being able to afford a new pair, I ended up becoming quite skilled in the art of sewing up the gaps.

With some newfound financial flexibility, the thought of retiring my jeans and wearing a brand new pair delighted me.

I decided to spoil myself and purchase a pair of designer skinny jeans that was one hundred and thirty six percent over my usual budget.

With my credit card in hand, I strolled up to the cash register of the trendy boutique to ring in my purchase. However after inserting my card through the chip reader, the foggy-eyed cashier pulled out my card and returned it to me, smiling while shaking her head.

"Shit, am I maxed out again?" I asked.

"Your money is no good here."

"What do you mean?" I asked. "Like you won't take my business?"

She chuckled. "Enjoy the jeans," she replied as she placed them in the shopping bag and handed them over to me.

"Just like that?" I asked incredulously. "I get to walk out of here without paying a cent?"

"Yes," she said, still maintaining her glowing smile.

"You're not entrapping me or anything? The second I walk out of the store, security's not going to drag me back in and search me?"

"No, your purchase is valid."

She rang up a receipt in the cash register and handed it over to me.

"Just to ease your worries," she said.

I grabbed it, gave her my thanks, and walked out the store, stunned. Did that just happen? For me to walk out of a store with a three hundred dollar pair of jeans without dropping a cent was too good to be true.

Oddly enough, the same thing occurred when I tried to purchase a tall Americano at Starbucks. My credit card went inside the chip reader and the barista took my card out and handed it back to me, along with my drink, without any purchase confirmation.

"Enjoy," he said.

Holy shit! Was it possible that my credit card had become the holy grail of unlimited shopping?

I needed to test this theory. I went to Michael Kors next and purchased a large Hamilton canvas tote handbag valued at five hundred and fifty dollars, followed by a cotton linen parka from Burberry priced at eight hundred and fifty bucks, and topped it off with a pair of Jimmy Choo pixel high heels costing six hundred bucks. Total value of purchases: two thousand bucks.

Total amount I was charged for these items: zero.

I was on cloud nine.

My shopping spree continued on for another two hours, until the mall's closing. I had a grin that stretched across my entire face knowing that I had just restocked my wardrobe and jewelry collection with designer purchases.

Hunger soon gnawed at my stomach and I decided to treat myself to a special dinner.

As I sat at Omakase Japanese Restaurant, dining on pieces of raw fish that cost four hundred dollars per plate, I could only speculate on my recent fortunes.

No doubt, Shadow and this clandestine Midnight Society had a role to play in all this. As I looked at my piles of shopping bags—filled with dresses, shoes, sunglasses, etcetera, etcetera—with insuppressible glee, common sense snuck up from behind and struck me like a slap across the backside of my head.

By accepting all of these items, I had put myself in debt to these crazy people. I was blinded by my shopping frenzy and during those three hours of euphoric bliss, I had lost my mind.

"Fuck, fuck, fuck," I cursed aloud, drawing the attention of all the rich patrons in this overpriced—but incredibly delicious—restaurant.

"Is the sashimi to your liking?" the old sushi master asked, a dumbfounded look on his face.

"They own you too, don't they?" I whispered as I dropped my chopsticks onto the table. "By eating these delectable pieces of raw fish, I'm handing my life over to your organization."

The old master, whose wrinkles reminded me of a prehistoric turtle, looked at me, puzzled. Eventually he let out a deep sigh.

"There is an ancient Japanese proverb--" he began.

"Blah, blah, blah," I said as I quickly pulled out my debit card that was linked directly to my bank account. There was no way I was going to add more to my tab owing to the Midnight Society, which was to be paid for with my soul.

"Your money is no good here," turtle face replied.

"Charge me for this meal," I cried out in desperation. "Please."

"You are our guest here today. Your presence brings our restaurant great honor."

"No, there's nothing special about me. I pull up my pants the same way you do so let me pay for this freaking meal," I demanded.

He shook his head.

I was about to lose it.

"Please I insist," I tried one last time.

"When royalty dines in a peasant's house, the peasant does not charge the queen," he replied.

Royalty? I'll show them royalty. I decided to go off the rails. I picked up my bottle of sake and dropped it to the floor.

"Let me pay for that," I said.

"No."

Argh. At this point I was seriously considering taking out the bottle of overpriced perfume I purchased and spraying the entire sushi bar with it, defiling the sanctity of their kitchen with the scent of perfume. However I had caused enough damage here for one day.

Feeling rather ashamed, I reached down to pick up the broken glass from the shattered bottle of sake. A waitress was already there cleaning up the mess.

"Don't," I said. "I got it."

"Please, do not concern yourself," the waitress remarked as she placed the last of the broken pieces on an empty tray and headed to the back of the kitchen.

"I'm really sorry, I didn't mean to be such a jerk."

"No apologies needed," old master turtle said.

I gathered up my shopping bags and stood up, suddenly aware that all attention in the restaurant was focused on me.

"I still owe you," I said as I headed for the exit.

"No you don't," the old man replied. "And please do come again."

"That'll be twenty-four dollars," the cabdriver said as he dropped me in front of my apartment.

I was shocked.

"Really?" I asked. "You're going to charge me?"

"Well yeah," the cab driver said, shooting me an awkward glance. "Why are you surprised?"

I was ecstatic as I reached into my pocket and yanked out two twenty-dollar bills.

"Thank you!" I exclaimed as I thrust the cash into the palm of his hand. "I'm so happy you're charging me. Please, keep the change."

"You're fucking crazy," the cabdriver said, just before cracking a smile. "But I like your generous ways."

"You're sweet," I replied as I got out of the cab.

Just as the taxi pulled away, a black limo pulled up beside me. The passenger side window slowly scrolled down revealing Abraham's weathered features.

"Is it Saturday already?" I asked. "I didn't know the universe decided to remove Wednesday, Thursday, and Friday from the weekly calendar."

Abraham laughed warmly. "Actually, I'm here to drive you home."

"I am home," I said.

"To your *new* home," Abraham corrected me, as if I was to know this tidbit of knowledge. "All your belongings have been moved to your new penthouse condo down on Fifth Street."

Did I hear him correctly? "What?"

"You now live in the Penthouse suite at the Luxe down on Fifth Street," Abraham repeated.

This had to be a joke. "Abraham, I can't afford a condo there, let alone a parking spot."

"It's all been taken care of Ms. Aria."

I shook my head. "Abraham, thank you for the gifts and all, but I really can't accept any of it."

Abraham tilted his head towards the piles of shopping bags in my hands. "It looks like you already have," he pointed out.

"Uh yeah…" I began. "I kind of lost control."

"What are you afraid of Aria?" Abraham asked.

"I don't want to be owned by anyone," I replied. "Not by Shadow or the Midnight Society. I haven't earned any of this stuff and I don't want to be in debt to anyone."

"We'll never ask for you to pay this stuff back," Abraham said. "Accept it as a gift."

"You know the saying 'if it's too good to be true?'"

"I am aware of Shadow's arrangement with you. After two dates, the fictional relationship between Shadow and yourself will end. I also understand that these two dates will take up a lot of your time and efforts. Consider all these gifts as payment for your time."

"In exchange for two dates, you're giving me a condo," I stated. "That's way too much."

"The Midnight Society offers exceptionally competitive rates," Abraham said.

I stood on the sidewalk dumbfounded—shopping bags in hand—and stared pensively at the ground. I was still unsure about any of this. I just didn't trust the Midnight Society and whatever games they had me involved in.

"I feel like an over-priced escort," I finally sighed.

"Nonsense," Abraham said. "You won't be required to have sex with anyone."

I had the mental image of Shadow pressing his massive, rock-hard body against my naked flesh and it sent shivers all over my body. I guess that wouldn't have been *so* bad.

"Right," I said.

"So Ms. Aria, I guess the question for you now is, do you intend to spend the rest of the evening standing on this shady street with your expensive clothes, enticing savage criminals to rob you of all your gifts? Or will you get into the car and allow me to drive you to your new four thousand square-foot condo?"

He made a good sales pitch.

I opened the passenger door to the limo, tossed all of my bags into the backseat and got in.

"Home Jeeves," I said.

"Please don't call me that," Abraham said, pleasantly. "I'm not a butler."

"Sorry."

"All is forgiven," he said cheerfully. "Your new home awaits my princess. Welcome to the world of the social elite."

CHAPTER NINE

I had to be in a dream. The condo—my new home—was simply stunning. It was a four thousand square-foot urbanized wonderland filled with expensive and stylish furniture, marble floors, crystal chandeliers, and a view to the city that took my breath away. The best part was the brilliant D-274 Steinway piano sitting at the centre of the living room.

I felt like a queen sitting high on her throne above the clouds.

"I'm absolutely speechless," I gasped. "This is seriously all mine?"

"Yes," Abraham replied.

"What about yearly taxes on this thing? I can't afford it you know."

"All the maintenance and condo fees will be taken care of," Abraham said.

"Until the end of time?"

"Yes, until the sky falls and the earth swallows us whole."

"Wow."

I rushed to the piano like an excited schoolgirl on Christmas morning. The sounds from it were majestic, echoing throughout the penthouse suite, creating a full, rich sound.

"We had some of the city's top acoustic engineers in to calculate the optimal spot for this piano," Abraham said.

"You're kidding, right?" I asked.

"It's true. Shadow wanted everything absolutely perfect for you."

I raised a brow. "You know, Shadow is spending quite a bit of money on a girl he plans on dumping in a couple of weeks."

"What can I say? He's a gentleman about it, as long as you don't break his heart."

"Like that's going to happen," I snickered as I rose from the piano and examined the few books I owned neatly lined up on the bookshelf. "He doesn't even want a relationship." There was a brief silence. "So you guys moved all my stuff?" I asked, changing the subject of conversation.

"Yes," Abraham said. "It's all here."

"You moved my underwear as well?" I asked, feeling embarrassed that they may have seen a couple of pairs of granny panties that I owned.

"*I* didn't move it," Abraham stated. "Shadow had a few of his maids from his estate come down and pack, move, and unpack all of your belongings. It didn't take too much time."

He paused for a moment, glancing at his watch. "Well, I best give you some time to settle into your new home," he said. "On the fridge is a list of numbers should you need anything. There's a personal chef, a personal maid, a gym trainer, a chauffeur, and whatever else you desire."

After he left, I spent the next three hours running around my brilliant new condo squealing like a complete idiot.

After I was done, I grabbed my phone, wanting to call Justin to tell him how kick-ass my new place was. However I remembered he was pissed at me. I stared at the limited list of numbers on my phone and realized that there was really no one I could call to share my excitement with.

What good was having all this amazing stuff if I had to experience it alone?

I decided to head to the gym in the condo and work out. Aside from playing piano, exercise was another quick pick-me-up when I needed an immediate injection of endorphins to combat the blues.

Dressed in my ratty pair of jogging pants, and an old t-shirt displaying the ravenous mug of the Cookie Monster, I entered into the exercise room, found a treadmill, and attacked it.

While I ran, I couldn't help but wonder if Justin would ever forgive me. Even though it's been only a day since he stormed off, I missed him already.

Of course now that I had money to spare, I could go out and try to meet some new people, but who was I kidding? I liked having Justin around. He never judged me like others did.

I could come to class dressed like a donkey's ass and he'd still chat me up like a normal human being without second glancing me.

But I had to let him go. It was the right thing to do, wasn't it?

I felt my legs begin to seize up and I stopped the treadmill. Sweat dripped down my face, which I wiped away with my t-shirt.

The exercise didn't help my mood much. Not only was I still pissy, but now I was a sweaty mess as well.

As I stepped off the treadmill to get some water, I noticed that three other girls in the gym were staring at me. They were all dolled up in expensive yoga pants while plastered with makeup and they stared at me like I was the creature from the black lagoon.

Seriously--it was a fucking gym. They could at least try to break a sweat.

I scowled at them and they immediately broke out into gossipy whispers, which was irritating.

I snapped.

"What the hell are you looking at?" I asked.

One of them, a snooty little Barbie girl with a condescending smile shook her head. "Nothing sweetheart," she laughed. She had a familiar voice. "I'm looking at absolutely nothing. I love your outfit by the way. I heard Sesame Street is *in* this year."

"Apparently so is dressing up like a whore," I retaliated. Perhaps that was a little harsh.

"Bitch," the blonde said, looking aghast. She spat in my direction and then headed for the exit, her little minions hot on her heels.

Great.

Less than five hours in my new condo and I've already made enemies, which was the complete opposite of making new friends.

As I strolled towards the elevators, I noticed that everyone who passed me by glared at me like I was some disgusting sweaty pig. Was this what it was going to be like living here? To have judgment cast on me by these rich bastards every time I set foot outside my condo?

I entered into the elevator, which to my relief was empty.

Now, more than ever, I missed Justin and how normal I felt around him.

When the elevator doors opened again on my floor, hot tears were streaming down my sweaty face.

I tried texting Justin a few times throughout the week, hoping to hear from him, just to make sure he was okay.

Okay that was a lie. I missed him and his friendship.

Even though I crushed his heart, I just wanted the small glimmer of hope that one day he would speak to me again, despite me deserving nothing less than the finger from him.

I became a slave to my phone, frequently checking to see if there was a text back.

None.

I felt myself sink into depression.

Justin didn't show up to lectures either, which was strange. He was the model of punctuality and discipline when it came to classes. If the world was burning all around us and the skies were raining blood, he'd still be sitting in his seat during lecture time.

I spent the next few days going to class, and then going straight to my condo and locking myself away from the rest of the outside world. I didn't want anyone to see me this miserable.

Tonight, I ended up lying on my couch, watching episodes of shitty reality shows in front of a seventy-inch television while devouring an entire Hawaiian pizza.

I felt like I was going through a break up. I wondered if this was what the rest of my life was going to be like, living life in solitary like a spinster, avoiding human interaction like a plague.

I missed my dad. I missed Justin. I missed talking to someone-- anyone about my day and listening to theirs in return.

I just wanted to feel like someone cared about me. That someone out there still loved me.

Tomorrow was my first date with Shadow, and unexpectedly, I was looking forward to it. I desperately needed company.

I closed my eyes and crumpled into the couch, feeling like an empty husk.

My last thoughts before I drifted to sleep were of Shadow and his beautiful eyes filled with the same overwhelming loneliness that I felt now.

CHAPTER TEN

Why was I feeling nervous? It was ridiculous for me to feel this way, especially since my date with Shadow tonight was nothing more than a glorified show for all the snooty bastards to see.

But I'd be lying if I said I wasn't looking forward to it; and the anticipation made me nervous. I had really misjudged just how much I relied on Justin's friendship over the past few years and the loneliness I now experienced left me feeling empty and the guilt from our confrontation gnawed at my conscience.

I spent at least three hours on my appearance, enhancing every one of my facial features with makeup I had just bought.

I also invested a good amount of time on my hair, trimming every loose strand and running it through the curling iron, transforming my straight, boring locks into soft voluminous curls.

Finding the perfect dress to wear was the hardest decision. It seemed a lot easier when all I had in my closet was one little black dress. In a matter of days I acquired an extensive collection of evening wear and finding the right one was a time-suck. Eventually, after much deliberation, I settled on an elegant midnight colored cocktail dress that was sexier than the usual stuff I wore.

I was applying a few finishing touches to my makeup when I

heard a knock on my condo door. I opened it and Abraham greeted me.

"Looks like you've become my own personal chauffer," I said.

"I find these little car rides of ours enjoyable. Your company always brightens my day," he replied. "I must add that you look absolutely brilliant. Shadow will fall head over heels for you tonight."

"I doubt it," I laughed, "This date is all a song and dance, remember?"

Abraham put his index finger up to his lips, hushing me. "Let's just keep that our little secret."

The limo pulled up next to Starfall Supper Club, a prestigious dining establishment that boasted being one of the highest peaks on our urban landscape. It offered a breathtaking panoramic view of the city's sparking lights.

When the doors of the high-speed elevator opened at the top floor, I saw Shadow standing by the north window with a drink in hand, and staring out into the skyline.

He looked handsome wearing a dark suit, and his black dress shirt unbuttoned at the collar. He *was* the cliché of tall, dark, and handsome.

I strolled over to Shadow and hid my excitement to see him—or anyone for that matter.

It's been a long, lonely week.

"Hey there," I said, sneaking up behind him.

He turned around and smiled as he did a glance over on me. "You look stunning," he said.

"You look…" I paused, "…huh."

Shadow laughed. "Not going to let me forget that one, are you?"

"Not a chance. You know the saying about a woman scorned?"

"They need to get over it?"

"We'll work on your manly charms a bit later," I replied. "But how about you buy me a drink first?"

He nodded and led me over to the island bar situated at the centre of the room.

"What can I get for you?" the bartender asked, a kindly looking grey man with a genuine smile that seemed to light up his eyes.

"What does the lady want?" Shadow asked.

The bartender shook his head and laughed. "A true gentleman with a woman as lovely as this should already know what the lady wants before coming here."

I liked the bartender already. I made a mental note to leave him a generous tip.

Shadow looked at me with his brooding eyes, as if peering deep into my soul. I gave him a funny look that shouted 'what the heck are you doing?'

After analyzing me for a few seconds like a lab specimen, he finally said, "The lady will have a gin and tonic."

"Vodka soda with two limes," I corrected him. I turned to Shadow and grinned. "Nice try Sherlock."

"Deduction was never one of my strengths," Shadow said. The waiter brought back my drink and set it down in front of me.

"Can I pay for this?" I asked.

"What do you think?" Shadow replied.

I sighed, reaching into my purse and pulling out a ten dollar bill. "At least let me leave a tip."

Shadow shrugged and watched as I pushed the bill towards the bartender, who took the tip and nodded graciously.

"You're most kind," he said, before walking away to serve another couple at the far side of the bar.

"You see how happy he was receiving my tip?" I said, feeling good about myself. I hated not having to pay for stuff, as odd as that sounded. Everything I owned, before this Midnight Society business happened, was stuff I purchased with my own money. Sure, my clothes were bought from thrift stores and my handbags and sunglasses were cheap knockoffs from Chinatown, but at least I earned them.

The last thing I wanted in life was to be in debt to someone.

Just as I finished that thought, Shadow snickered.

"What?" I asked. "Do you find something funny about me leaving the hardworking bartender a tip so he knows that he's appreciated?'

"No," Shadow said, "Of course not. It's just that he makes about five thousand bucks a night working here and if you take a peek over at the couple for just a moment, you'll see why I'm laughing."

My eyes followed where he was pointing to, and sure enough I saw a swanky-dressed patron across the bar pull out a hundred dollar bill and hand it over to the bartender as tip.

"Oh God," I said. "I must look like the biggest cheapskate ever.

"Don't worry about it," Shadow said. "Collin's a good guy. He knows that you're not swimming in green."

"I honestly thought that giving him ten dollars was more than generous. I mean, that's ninety percent more than what I usually tip a bartender at the Beer Dome."

"This isn't a university bar," Shadow said, "But as I said, don't worry about it. Collin isn't one to judge people by the tips they give."

"I'm still embarrassed."

"Come on," Shadow said gesturing towards an open table situated by the window. "Let's have a seat."

I looked outside.

The city skyline was astonishing, lit up by thousands of shimmering blue lights that reminded me of moonbeams reflected on crystal waters. Cars sped across the highways like dancing fireflies. I was staring at a stunning urban wonderland from high above.

"The view always gets me every time I come here," Shadow said. "It's funny how some things can take your breath away no matter how many times you see it: our city lights on a moonlit night, the streets of Paris during an afternoon sun shower, the sun rising above the falls of Plitvice Lakes in Croatia." He paused and looked at me before adding, "A beautiful woman who takes your breath away."

I couldn't help but blush, though I managed to refrain myself from giggling like a stupid schoolgirl.

"Are you trying to flatter me?" I asked. "I thought this date was all for show."

"What makes you think I was talking about you?" Shadow teased.

I decided to steer the conversation to matters of more importance. "I received all your gifts and I'm grateful, I really am. However I can't accept any more of these freebies," I said.

"Here we go," Shadow sighed.

"What?"

"The song and dance that you girls like to give," he replied. "About how it's an equal opportunity world and how you're independent and don't want handouts."

"Well yes," I replied. "That's exactly it."

"Heard it all before," Shadow sighed. "Look, if it makes you feel any better, you're earning all that stuff right now."

"How? By going on a date with you?"

"Yes," he said.

"What do I look like? A high end escort?"

"I never said that."

"But that's essentially what I'm doing, isn't it?"

"No," Shadow said. "I don't go on dates with hookers. That's the difference."

I needed him to understand the type of person I was.

"I've always had to work for everything I own, and though it's been difficult to...eat this past semester, I could at least hold my head high and say that I've never accepted anyone else's charity."

"What's wrong with charity?"

"There are other people in the world that need it more than I do."

Shadow sighed. "Do you want the stuff I've given you or not?"

"I want to earn it."

"I already told you, you're earning it now."

"No," I demanded. "I want to earn it in some other way, and if you can't think of any other means, then I'm going to have to hand you back the keys to the condo."

Shadow looked at me with a pensive look as he took a sip of his drink. "You're being serious?"

I reached into my purse and grabbed the keys and access card and set them on the table.

"Those are yours until I've figured out a way to earn them," I replied. "That's the way things will have to be with me."

Shadow looked at the keys and pass card with a furrowed brow.

"Huh," he muttered.

"Again with the *huh*?" I replied.

"You're a stubborn one."

"I don't want to be your trophy-two-date girlfriend," I replied. "I earn whatever you give me, period."

Shadow leaned back in his chair and rubbed his chin. "Okay," he said with a glimmer in his dark eyes. "There is one thing I'd love from you."

"Choose wisely," I said. "Otherwise this vodka soda and two limes are going right in your face."

"Relax," Shadow said. "What I want is nothing sexual in nature."

"Good," I said with a stern nod. Though I had to admit, I was slightly disappointed. I had hot flashes picturing his naked body on top of me. However I wasn't the type of girl to accept bribes for the prize in between my legs. Sex without feelings was pointless to me.

"There are five piano pieces that have always infatuated me," Shadow said. "I would love an original recording of all five pieces from the Golden Virgin."

"That's it? That's hardly worth the price of a condo."

"Wait until I tell you what the pieces are," Shadow said as he grabbed a napkin and removed a pen from his side pocket. After he finished scribbling on the napkin, he handed it to me.

"Ravel's *Gaspard de la nuit*, Boulez's *Second Sonata*, Stavinsky's *Three Movements from Petrushka*, Prokofiev's *Eighth Sonata*, and Beethoven's *Sonata Hammerklavier*," I read aloud. I set down the napkin and gave him an evil scowl. "You're kidding right?"

"No, I want for you to perfect these five songs and record them. Not one mistake allowed in the recordings."

"You picked the five fucking hardest pieces in all of piano. People spend years trying to master one of them," I said.

"You have to admit, my request is equal to the worth of a condo, isn't it?"

He was right, it was. I was still surprised Shadow was so well versed in classical music to be able to choose the five toughest songs to master technically.

"So we have a deal?" Shadow asked, extending his hand towards me.

"Deal," I replied. I was intrigued by this arrangement. Those pieces had always been on my list of songs to learn and perfect. I had attempted *Gaspard de la Nuit* once before but my fingers weren't as well trained at the time, and I ended up giving up. I was now three years wiser and more confident in my abilities. If mastering this song along with the others would pay for the condo and my single-day lunatic shopping spree, then so be it.

"Call Abraham whenever you're ready to record the songs and he can arrange a time at Lincoln's studio."

I couldn't help but smile when Shadow mentioned Abraham's name. I was curious about their relationship. It seemed like Abraham was always there to do whatever Shadow requested, despite not being under his employment.

"I've been meaning to ask you about Abraham," I said. "He's not your servant, he's not your butler, but he'll clearly do anything you ask of him. His loyalty to you is astounding."

"He's been a good friend to my family over the years," Shadow said. "I can never repay him for all that he's done for my sister and me."

"He loves you. You can tell just from the way he talks about you," I said. "He's very fatherly. I miss having someone like that in my life."

Every time I thought about dad, the pipes attached to my tear ducts threatened to burst. I had to get a grip. Unleashing waterworks on our first fake date was inappropriate.

As I glanced over at Shadow's face, I noticed his eyes were glistening, sympathetic to the strong emotions I was feeling. He too had lost his own father, and I was being a fool by digging up sad memories.

"I'm sorry, I didn't mean to sour the mood of our date," I said.

"It's alright," Shadow replied. "Sometimes you can't help but think about the past."

I decided to divert the conversation away from our fathers and the pain that went along with their memories. "Tell me how you got to know Abraham?"

The sadness on Shadow's face faded away as he spoke affectionately about the man. "For generations, the family names of Tremaine and Constantine have been linked closely together, though not as friends but as rivals. The Midnight Society had always been ruled by either a Tremaine or a Constantine."

"That's another thing I wanted to ask you about, this entire Midnight Society business. Who are you people?"

Shadow shook his head. "You know that saying ignorance is bliss?"

"What if I don't want to be ignorant?"

"Do you want me to continue my story or are you going to interrupt me with questions I'm not going to answer?"

I sighed. "Fine, continue."

Shadow downed the last of his drink and leaned back in his

chair, his dark alluring eyes fixated on me. I felt exposed underneath his gaze and grabbed my vodka soda, taking a healthy swig. I was starting to regret that this date was a façade. "Now where was I, before your premature interjection?" Shadow asked.

He was an egotistical blockhead.

"The Midnight Society was ruled by either a Tremaine or a Constantine," I reminded him, doing my best to hide my annoyance.

"There have always been political rivalries between our families within the Society, stemming way back to when swords and steel were still in fashion," Shadow continued. 'The family who sat on the Midnight Society's throne had control of the world. Our organization anointed Kings and Queens, influenced wars, and placed key figureheads into the public eye. We were the secret empire that governed the civilized world and the head of the Society had the absolute authority over all.

"Every five years, an election was held to see who would lead the organization—either a Constantine or Tremaine, which sets the stage for the next part of my story. Eighteen years ago, my father and Abraham were campaigning to determine the next leader of the Midnight Society. From what I recall, it was a close and heated race. Both my father and Abraham were influential powerhouses and both had all the qualities of great leaders. It was like choosing between Winston Churchill and Abraham Lincoln—two extraordinary men but, unfortunately, one seat at the head of the table."

"So did your families hate each other then?" I asked. Shadow shook his head.

"No, despite centuries of rivalry between the Constantine's and the Tremaine's, there was mutual respect. In fact, my sister and I often played with Abraham's only child, Julia. With our father gone during these year-long campaigns and our mother taking care of the Tremaine corporations, Calisto and I bonded with Julia, who suffered from abandonment as well," Shadow said. "Some of the fondest memories I have are exploring our family estate with Julia, getting ourselves into all sorts of trouble and keeping it a secret from everyone."

Shadow stared into the remnants of his drink as he took a deep breath before releasing a hushed sigh.

"Julia loved the daffodils that grew in our family's garden. She always pissed off our personal landscapers by stealing the heads of the flowers," he chuckled.

"So where is Julia now?" I asked, despite knowing the answer. Abraham had mentioned his daughter was no longer a part of this world.

"This is where the story of our families takes a tragic turn," Shadow said. "On Julia's fifth birthday, she was kidnapped, raped, and murdered."

CHAPTER ELEVEN

The revelation was horrifying. It was always a tragedy for a parent to outlive their child, but to have your own child experience something so violent...so traumatic—I couldn't even imagine what Abraham must have went through. When I had asked Abraham about Julia, he became distant. Now I knew the reason why.

"What happened?" I asked. My heart sank into my stomach and hot tears collected at the corners of my eyes knowing Abraham suffered through such a tragic event.

"Three days before the election, Julia disappeared from her home late in the evening. She was playing outside on their large family estate and when the servants went outside to call her in for supper, she was gone," Shadow said. "The Constantine estate was searched thoroughly but there was no trace of her. She had vanished."

He paused and looked into his empty glass. "There was a mutual agreement between Abraham and my father to suspend the elections until Julia was found. Using the vast network of the Midnight Society, almost every police officer in the city was tasked to find her. It was a grueling search and emotions were running high. Everyone clung onto that small glimmer of hope that she would be found, alive and well, including Calisto and I."

"Two days later, her body was discovered in an abandoned shed on the farmlands in the outskirts of the city," Shadow swallowed hard. "I remember eavesdropping on a conversation my father had with my mother the night Julia's body was found. I'll never forget what he said—'I never knew a human could scream like that,' referring to Abraham after seeing the body. That night was the first time I ever saw my father cry."

"Shadow..." I began to say, but I found that all words escaped me at the moment.

"When the autopsy report came back, they said that her larynx was crushed and she had been sexually violated by a metal instrument. There were no traces of any DNA, which made it difficult to identify the sick piece of shit that raped and murdered her.

"My father agreed to suspend the elections completely until this matter was dealt with. He vowed to hunt down Julia's killer and make him suffer for what he did to the Constantine family. My father led his own personal investigation into Julia's murder and it became an obsession for him.

"Weeks later, another tragedy struck the Constantine family. Abraham's wife was suffering from depression, wracked with guilt over her daughter's death. One night, she took her own life. Abraham found her in the bathtub, wrists sliced open with a steak knife, her eyes open and still red from tears.

"This was enough to drive Abraham to madness. For the next six months, he was a recluse. He didn't leave his house. He was horrified and devastated. Lord only knows what went through his head during this time—what ghosts haunted his thoughts.

"My mother and father were there every night to check on him, worried that Abraham would follow in his wife's footsteps. Understandably no one could help ease his pain.

"Meanwhile, the investigation continued. Nine dark months passed without a single break. My father was giving up hope. His obsession to find Julia's killer was taking a toll on both his physical and mental health. He had trouble sleeping, and often spent long, bleary-eyed nights staring at Julia's picture and scouring over case files, which he had scrutinized thoroughly. As well, he had grown distant to us, his children.

"I suspected that he was afraid to look at us, terrified by the idea of us becoming victims like Julia."

"Please tell me this isn't one of those unsolved mysteries," I said. "Poor Abraham."

Shadow nodded.

"Nine months after Julia's body was discovered, there was another rape, a seven year old girl similar to Julia's physical profile—brunette hair, blue eyes, delicate white skin. Luckily this girl managed to escape, scraping some of the bastard's skin underneath her fingernails during the initial struggle. The girl's physical descriptions of the man fit the picture that the criminal profilers painted: a forty-year old white male, heavyset and with a speech impediment. The sick fuck tried to rape her with a brass cane. The DNA results lifted from underneath the girl's nails confirmed his identity as well.

"His name was John Taluzzi, a contract worker that did yard maintenance for not only Abraham's estate, but my father's as well. When my dad found out, he used all his influence down at city hall to persuade the police to turn a blind eye to this pedophile while the Midnight Society extracted its own brand of justice on him."

"Why not let the police handle it?" I asked. "Send this degenerate to prison where he'll never bother anyone again?"

"The system is flawed," Shadow spat. "They protect child molesters in prison, giving them private cells so that the other inmates can't get to them. Tell me this; in what lifetime do these sick pieces of shit deserve to be protected?"

I had no answer for him.

"My father, along with some of the more unruly members of the Midnight Society, hunted Taluzzi down, beat him senseless, and brought him to an abandoned factory where he was chained up like a dog. They tortured the pedophile some more, until he finally confessed his crimes. The filth described every detail of Julia's rape to my father."

"The Midnight Society tortured him?" I asked, frowning.

"Yes," Shadow replied, his voice full of conviction. "He deserved far worse than he received. Julia was innocent. Julia was a ray of light in a grey, overcast sky. Julia was the first person outside my family to care about me."

"I'm sorry Shadow," I said. "Sometimes it's hard to dig up the past. You don't have to finish the story if you don't want to."

Shadow shook his head. "It took a long time for me to get over Julia's death, but knowing that John Taluzzi was captured and dealt with helped me through the grieving process. I'm thankful that the demons that haunt me now don't include Julia's restless spirit. Sometimes, only death can make things right."

"It's sad that you think like that," I said, disagreeing with Shadow's skewed sense of justice. It had always been my belief that no single person could make the decision to end a person's life, no matter how much they deserved to die. Law and order just didn't work that way.

"The legal system has failed too many times," Shadow said, swirling a single drop of whiskey inside the empty glass before setting it down on the table. There was a brief pause while he collected his thoughts. "When Abraham was told that his daughter's killer was caught and chained like an animal, he finally decided to leave his house for the first time in over six months. I still have the newspaper clippings with photos taken of him stepping outside. His hair and beard, once a chestnut brown, was now grey and brittle. He looked frail.

"I'll never know what happened that day in the abandoned factory. I do remember my father coming home and telling my mother that it was finally over. It is every father's right to avenge the murder of their child, and he was glad to give that precious gift to Abraham."

"Abraham killed that man, didn't he?" I asked, despite knowing the answer already. I just couldn't picture that sweet old man harming anyone. However I could sympathize with the rage he must have felt towards Julia's killer.

Shadow ignored my question and continued on with his story.

"With Julia's death finally avenged, it was inevitable that the lingering question about the Midnight Society's leadership would resurface. When my father met with Abraham to discuss reopening the elections, Abraham responded by withdrawing his right to the Society's throne. He told my father that with Julia and his wife's death, the Constantine line was coming to an end. From that point on, the Tremaine's would have complete leadership over the organization and that Abraham would stand by my father's side as his trusted advisor, his loyal friend, and as his brother. We were the only family he had now."

I was flabbergasted as I took in the entire story.

"I guess that explains the bond between Abraham and yourself," I said.

"He's family to me," Shadow replied. "It's just unfortunate that it took the death of Julia to unite the Constantine's and the Tremaine's so closely together."

"You were five at the time. How do you remember all the details?" I asked.

"I found the case file when I was nine and read every word in it and studied every picture. It's impossible to keep secrets buried within the organization. Someone *always* has a file of secrets to share." Shadow rose from his chair, picking up his empty glass. "You look like you can use another drink," Shadow said. "How about we have one more and then we head out for dinner. We have reservations at one of the most exclusive restaurants in the entire city, the Black Swan. Everyone's talking about it."

"It's not on the tip of my tongue," I stated.

"Anyone who pays six figures in taxes is talking about it," Shadow corrected himself as he walked over to the bar. He waved Collin over and placed his order.

As we waited for our drinks, Shadow turned to me and whispered into my ear, his gentle breath sending shivers throughout my body. I felt myself go wet as I breathed in his scent.

"Everything I told you about Abraham, keep it to yourself. Though everyone knows about his past, we've kept it long buried. The old man seems happy now, though you can still see that from time-to-time he feels the hurt all over again."

I nodded, "Of course."

Collin returned and handed me vodka with two limes.

"You remembered," I smiled at Shadow.

"Some things I can never forget," he stated. Though his voice was calm and playful, he looked at me with dark, haunted eyes.

I knew he wasn't referring to my drink.

CHAPTER TWELVE

The drive to the Black Swan was made in silence, but not the awkward kind where I usually struggled to think of things to say. It was a comfortable silence where I sat back in the luxurious leather seats of Shadow's silver Aston Martin DB9 and enjoyed the fiery sounds of Miles Davis's trumpet resonating from the car's crystal clear speakers.

I still couldn't get Shadow's tale out of my mind. It made me see Abraham in a different light—a loving father who lost his only daughter.

I suddenly had the urge to find the old man and give him a giant hug, but that would violate the promise I just made to Shadow.

Instead I closed my eyes and freed my mind from all negative thoughts.

It was a perfect night.

I examined Shadow's profile as he drove, his pensive eyes fixed on the road. He was stunning to look at and the mystery surrounding him was nothing short of intriguing.

I really had to stop thinking about Shadow like this. I had convinced myself that there was no meaning behind these dates. The contract I signed proved that much.

"Are you cold?" Shadow asked, breaking the silence between us. I shook my head.

"Usually I hate the cold, but for some reason tonight, I find the air invigorating," I replied. "Why? Are you cold?"

Shadow shook his head. "I'm never cold."

"You're one of *those* people. Don't tell me you enjoy long winters."

"I'm impartial to it."

"Man, I absolutely hate snow," I said. "Find me a warm place to be and I'm there in a heartbeat."

"Like a destination resort?"

I shook my head. "Too typical," I replied. "I'm not a fan of lying around while the sun bakes my skin. Give me exploration any day."

Shadow cocked an eyebrow and smiled. "So you like adventure?" he stated in a playful way that had me wondering what his version of adventure meant.

"You bet. There's so much history and so many interesting places to discover in the world that I just can't see myself lazing around a beach all day."

"Any place in particular you dream of visiting?"

I shook my head. "I try not to think about places I want to visit. Vacations have never been in my budget."

"You have at least ten thousand in the bank from the gig at my place," Shadow pointed out.

"No," I replied. "I need to pay of my debt and that money's going to have to last me for the rest of my University studies. Food and tuition don't come cheap."

"I can make some calls at the University," Shadow said. "The Midnight Society has strong influences there."

"Don't you dare!" I snapped. "It's bad enough I owe you for the condo. I'm not going to owe you for my tuition as well. It's something I need to do on my own."

Shadow shrugged. "Suit yourself. But the offer is always on the table."

"I don't even see the table," I said. "I will support myself through my studies, thank you very much. I don't need a sugar daddy paying for me."

Seconds later we pulled up to the Black Swan. The establishment was a lavish affair, its patrons dressed in expensive outfits that were typically seen on a red carpet.

Inside, extravagant chandeliers hung from the ceilings that were decorated with beautiful murals that belonged in old European churches. The antique tables were hand carved with the highest degree of craftsmanship, intricate patterns decorating the rich wooden surfaces. Three-storied windows lined the walls of the room, offering a spectacular view of the tranquil night sky.

A waiter dressed in butler garb greeted us with a wide smile and led us to our table, though hidden underneath his pleasant demeanor, I sensed he was looking down on me, for whatever reason.

Maybe he could smell the scent of student poverty.

When Shadow and I were both finally settled in, I couldn't hide my excitement of being able to dine in such a magnificent looking place. Sitting inside the Black Swan, with its renaissance architectural influences, made me feel like I was on a European vacation as the queen of fine dining this evening.

"This is amazing," I said. "This place is like a natural treasure. I can hardly believe it's only a restaurant. Just look at the building and how everyone's dressed in this place."

"The food here has been the talk of the town," Shadow said. "It's one thousand dollars for a three course meal. I hope it's good."

It wasn't.

The appetizer was four paper-thin slices of raw beef, decorated with some fancy looking leaves and served in an over-sized bowl that gave the illusion that I was getting a substantial sized meal. As I stared at the two hundred dollar dish, all I could think of was, *where's the damn food?*

"What is this?" I asked, pushing the tiny portion of food—that could barely feed a gnat—around with my fork.

"I believe it's beef Carpaccio," Shadow said, placing a thin slice of raw meat on his tongue and chewing it.

"Are we suffering from a famine or something?" I asked. "Did they also forget to cook the meat first before serving it?"

"Raw beef is considered a delicacy."

"It's also considered a way to grow worms in your intestines," I stated. "How does it taste?"

"Try it yourself."

"No thanks," I announced, pushing the appetizer away from me. I try to keep my stomach insect free."

Shadow shrugged and reached for my plate, scooping the meat onto his own. "All the more for me."

"I wonder if they can bring some bread over here," I muttered, suddenly noticing that my stomach was growling at me.

Shadow finished the last of the appetizer and set his fork down.

"The main course should be coming over pretty soon," Shadow said. "I assume that primitive roar I'm hearing is your stomach?"

I nodded. "I hope they bring out the food soon before my stomach decides to revolt and devour the rest of my body."

Just as I finished my sentence, our waiter came by our table and set down two massive plates in front of us.

More disappointment.

"You have to be kidding me," I sighed. At the centre of the plate was a tiny speck of food, hidden within a forest of leaves and grass, which served more as décor rather than anything edible. The waiter informed me that the meal was wild goose.

"Great, you brought the goose's egg. What about the rest of it?" I asked.

The waiter shot me an insulted look. I immediately wanted to eat my words as my eyes adverted from his gaze while he replied to my comment.

"We aren't exactly the McDonalds down the street, if that's what you seek. However this city's elite are very satisfied." Those simple words were like a slap to my face and suddenly, I felt very aware that I didn't belong here. I was, and would always be, a poor college girl, no matter what fancy clothes I wore or whom I associated myself with.

There was something about being put down by a person in customer service—who's only task was to make an individual feel welcome—that felt degrading.

Shadow leaned back in his chair, stared at the waiter with his fiery eyes and spoke.

"Here's what's going to happen," he said calmly. "You're going to apologize to my lovely date for your idiotic remark. The exact words you're going to say are 'Ms. Valencia, I'm sorry for being the world's biggest asshole. I beg for your forgiveness.' Now, after you apologize to her, you're going to head into the kitchen and remain there until we finish our meals so we don't have to see you again."

"Sir, you must be joking," the waiter said.

"No, I'm not," Shadow replied. "If you don't do as requested, I guarantee you that you'll never find a job in this city again. Hell, let's make it this country. However, I don't take pride in being cruel and vengeful so I'm giving you the opportunity to set things right. Apologize to my date and then get out of my sight and all will be forgotten. Does that sound good?"

The waiter opened his mouth, but failed to produce any meaningful words from it.

"It looks like you're tongue-tied. Let me help you out a bit," Shadow said. "Let's start off with 'I'm sorry Ms. Valencia...' I'm sure the rest will start to flow."

The waiter turned to me, wide-eyed and ashamed.

"It's okay," I said.

"I'm sorry Ms. Valencia," the waiter began, "I am the world's biggest—' but before he could finish, I cut him off.

"It's fine." I knew the feeling of shame, and that was punishment enough for the rude waiter. There was no further need to publicly degrade him. "Just go."

The waiter turned to Shadow, who nodded with approval.

"The lady has forgiven you," he said.

Once the waiter was gone, Shadow rose from his seat and motioned for me to come with him, which I gladly did. I held him by his large, muscular arm and together, we strolled confidently out of the Black Swan.

Once outside, I turned to Shadow and smiled.

"You're quite intimidating when you want to be," I said.

Shadow shrugged. "You still hungry?"

My stomach growled again and I nodded. "Yeah, let's get something to eat. You have any suggestions?"

"To tell you the truth, after the waiter mentioned there was a McDonald's down the road, I've been craving a Big Mac. I haven't had one of those tasty sandwiches in five years," Shadow said.

"You're joking, right?"

"Not at all; are you too good to stroll through the golden arches?"

"I do like McNuggets," I laughed.

And that was how we ended date number one, filling our bellies with cheap, greasy fast food.

After Shadow finished the last of his meal, he leaned back in the round metal seat, looked at me and grinned.

"What?" I asked while my mouth was still full of processed chicken.

"I had a good time tonight."

I was surprised. You'd think that discussing Abraham's tragic past and making a scene at one of the top dining establishments in the city was enough to put a downer on the entire evening. But here Shadow was, smiling.

It was infectious, and I couldn't help flash my pearly whites in return. I hoped I had nothing stuck in my teeth.

"Yeah, it wasn't boring, that's for sure," I replied. "So what do you have in store for date number two?"

"I have something in mind."

"So what is it? I hate surprises."

"Everyone loves surprises."

"I don't," I stated.

"Too bad," Shadow said. "I'll make the arrangements for our next date."

"It better be a good one then," I teased as I finished the last McNugget. "Examinations are around the corner and I'm dying for a little bit of excitement before then."

"If excitement is what you want, I'll make it happen. I just hope you can keep up with me."

He was flirting. A thrilling rush swept through me, and without realizing, my smile widened. While sitting in this fast food restaurant with the secret king of the world on our non-date, I came to a sudden realization; maybe Shadow was right. Maybe we weren't so different.

"Honey," I said in a half-joking tone, "Whatever pace you set, you'll find that I have no trouble keeping up for the ride."

"Challenge accepted," Shadow said.

His usual hard eyes sparkled with a child-like excitement, like stars reflected against the ocean.

CHAPTER THIRTEEN

Reading was another simple pleasure of mine, one that allowed me to escape into worlds that were much more interesting than my own. I had to admit though, ever since meeting Shadow, my life was far from boring.

Just fresh off my date with him, I decided to unwind by spending the following sun-filled day on the patio of my favorite coffee shop, whisked away in the arms of a sexy book. As I sipped on my Americano and lost myself to an adjective-laced sex scene, I was abruptly interrupted.

"I saw you last night."

It was Justin.

I was at a loss for words. I had tried texting him for over a week and each one of my messages was met with silence. I missed his friendship terribly.

"Justin," I said, surprised. "I haven't spoken to you for so long. Please, sit down?"

He looked at me with sour eyes and shook his head.

"I saw you last night," he repeated himself. "You and your date, that rich guy, were at McDonalds."

"You were there too?"

Justin shook his head. "I was coming back from the bar and I saw you through the window. Not a place I expected a loaded man to take a girl on a date."

"I guess I didn't mingle too well in the classy restaurant," I said, smiling.

Justin glared at me, angry at first, but the look of hurt that followed made me want to reach out and hug him. It was quite the dilemma. How do you console someone when you were the person that hurt them in the first place?

"I'm sorry Justin," I began, but he was quick to cut me off.

"No, don't," he said. "I really can't talk to you right now."

He walked away from the table, breaking off a piece of the happiness I felt earlier this morning, dragging it in the dirt behind him.

I noticed a few awkward glances from the couple sitting at the table next to me. Typically, I would make some rude comment or snarl at them like a wild jungle cat, but I was in no mood for a fight today. Instead, I picked up my coffee and took my reading to the park across the street from the coffee shop.

I settled myself on an empty park bench, cracked open my smutty book and tried to lose myself in a world far away from my emotional problems.

However, my encounter with Justin left me frazzled and no matter how hard I tried to concentrate on the words in my book, I just couldn't do it.

And then I received my second visit of the day.

"You're the Golden Virgin," a voice said with a noticeable British accent that sounded familiar. I looked up from my book and saw a thin man in a beige suit and white dress shirt, his short blonde hair slicked back to one side, his face dressed with a neatly trimmed beard. He looked at me with dark eyes that were filled with venom. Tucked underneath his arm was a large envelope.

"Do I know you?" I asked, feeling rather uncomfortable

underneath the man's gaze.

He sat down next to me and lit a cigarette, not bothering to look at me, as if I were insignificant in whatever world he was living in.

"We met before," he said in between drags. "Though last time, we were both wearing masks."

"You were at the party," I deduced.

"Yes, a rather dreadful affair and a complete waste of time," he snickered. "Shadow made a mockery of the entire ritual by choosing you."

"Thanks."

"In addition, that primitive ape who sits on the throne decided to lay his hands on me."

Inside my head, all cylinders were firing as I realized who he was. I said his name aloud. "Lucien."

"So virgin, which I highly doubt you are, what makes you so special and deserving to be chosen?"

"I'm not special at all," I replied truthfully. "I shit the same way everyone else does."

I saw Lucien crack a slight smile, but quickly suppressed it by taking a generous puff of his cigarette.

"You're out of your element," he stated. "You don't belong in our organization and the fact that you've been chosen for such a prestigious position taints the blood of the Midnight Society."

"Since when is marriage considered a position?"

"Don't be naïve. For centuries marriages were about forging alliances and building empires, not some trivial act of love."

"You must have a hard time with dating."

"I've looked into you, Aria Valencia. You're nothing more than a lowly arts student," Lucien continued. "There's no such thing as the Golden Virgin. Calisto was spinning tall tales again. You have no influential bearing on our society."

"And what makes you so high and mighty?" I asked. "You're probably some over-glorified suit and tie guy, running some boring business where you spend your days crunching numbers in a cubicle while talking to other equally boring business people. How do you enrich the little people in any way?"

"I own Kingdom United, the world's most famous football club, or known to you American Neanderthals as 'soccer.' I unite my city and give them something to cheer for each and every week."

I shrugged my shoulders. "Okay, that is pretty cool. But you're still a dick."

"Let me give you some simple advice," Lucien said, his eyes directed on me for the first time during the conversation. "Stay away from Shadow. He is possessed by demons from his past that have driven him insane. The man's a sociopath and the darkness that controls him is like a flesh-eating disease, one that will consume anyone close to him."

"That's rather dramatic."

"I love the Society," Lucien said, "And it saddens me to know that the destruction of our organization is imminent under Shadow's leadership. He will burn it to the ground like the mad Emperor Nero, and the rest of us will crumble like ash."

"Sounds like a sad story," I said in a mocking tone. I always hated the melodramatic types, making everything sound more Shakespearean than things really were.

"Of course you don't take me seriously," Lucien muttered. "What else can I expect from an arts student? Someone who chooses your area of studies can't be taking life seriously."

I had enough.

"Look, are you going to sit here all day and play guidance counselor?" I raised my sexy novel to his face. "I have some erotic smut that needs to be read, and no offense, you're killing the mood."

"Stupid girl," Lucien said as he rose from his seat, just before handing me the blank envelope, which was resting on his lap the entire time.

"If it's naked pictures of you, I don't want it. I get nauseous when I stare at assholes for long periods of time."

"I'm giving you the opportunity to discover the mystery behind Shadow," Lucien replied. "He's an emotionally unstable man, and the information in this envelope will unlock his troubled past. I think you'll find it a much more fascinating read than the filth you American's pass as literature these days."

"Are we done here?" I asked, annoyed.

Lucien flashed me a sly smile. "If you have any common sense, I won't be seeing you ever again," he said, just before adding, "Virgin," mockingly.

I watched the bastard stroll away from me at a casual gait, hands buried in his pockets while whistling a cheerful tune. I was left alone with my erotic book in my hand and the mysterious envelope in my lap.

Whatever was inside was probably poisonous propaganda with the sole intention of soiling Shadow's reputation. The best thing for me to do was to set the envelope on fire. Extreme measures, yes, but logical at the same time.

Everyone deserved to have his or her personal skeletons buried and laid to rest, Shadow included.

Who was I kidding?

"Fuck," I muttered as I gave into the temptation and ripped open the envelope, uncovering the mysterious contents inside.

CHAPTER FOURTEEN

I had done my due diligence on Shadow before our first date.

Google didn't provide much information, aside from him being a reclusive billionaire and owner of the Tremaine estate along with his sister Calisto. I did manage to dig out an obituary for both his parents; the circumstances of their deaths were unknown.

On the pixelated screen, he seemed like any other rich and powerful businessman—boring.

In person however, Shadow was an enigma.

Curious to learn more about this mystery man, I scanned through the contents of the envelope that Lucien gave me.

It was a full transcript of a session between Shadow and a psychiatrist.

I was intrigued.

"This is wrong," I muttered to myself. "I should respect his privacy." I continued reading it anyway.

From the files of Dr. Frederick Rosenburg, Professor of Psychiatry at the University of Morality, Moral City.

Subject: Shadow Tremaine. Age thirteen, suffering from severe posttraumatic stress disorder.

Dr. Rosenburg: Hello Shadow. How have you been?

Shadow: Fine.

Dr. Rosenburg: How have classes been at the Academy?

Shadow: Good.

Dr. Rosenburg: No troubles with the other students?

(silence)

Dr. Rosenburg: Your headmaster contacted me the other day telling me that you've been in several fights recently. Do you want to talk about them?

(silence)

Dr. Rosenburg: Okay, we don't have to. Is there anything you want to discuss? It's been a while since our last meeting and I'm sure there must be a lot of things on your mind.

(silence)

Dr. Rosenburg: How has your sister been doing?

Shadow: Good.

Dr. Rosenburg: She's been doing well in her classes it seems. I'm also hearing that she's making quite a lot of friends. Are you happy for her?

Shadow: I guess so.

Dr. Rosenburg: Wouldn't you like to make some friends yourself? Some people you can talk to and play with?

Shadow: I have no time for friends.

Dr. Rosenburg: Of course you do Shadow. You should be out playing sports, reading books, going to movies.

Shadow: A waste of time.

Dr. Rosenburg: What would you rather be doing?

Shadow: Finding the person who murdered my parents and setting them on fire.

Dr. Rosenburg: And why would you rather be doing that?

Shadow: Because they deserve to die.

Dr. Rosenburg: The anniversary of your parent's death is coming up in a few days. That day must be hard for both you and your sister.

(silence)

Dr. Rosenburg: Are you upset that your parent's killer hasn't been caught yet?

Shadow: No.

Dr. Rosenburg: Why not?

Shadow: Because I want to find the killer myself and cut off the hands he used to kill my mom and dad. And then I'm going to tie him to a chair, pour gasoline over him, and set him on fire. If the cops catch him, they'll throw him in prison where he'll grow old and die. He'll never get what he deserves.

Dr. Rosenburg: Revenge won't bring your parents back Shadow. You understand that, don't you?

Shadow: Yes doctor. I know my parents are gone. I also know that if this killer is dead too, he'll never be able to murder someone else's parents again.

Dr. Rosenburg: Does it make you sad thinking of hurting someone else instead of enjoying what life has to offer?

Shadow: Life has nothing to offer me.

Dr. Rosenburg: Life has plenty to offer you Shadow. Can you close your eyes Shadow, just for a moment?

Shadow: Why?

Dr. Rosenburg: Trust me.

Shadow: I don't trust anyone.

Dr. Rosenburg: I'm your friend Shadow. You can trust me.

Shadow: Would you still be my friend if you weren't getting paid a thousand bucks every time we meet?

Dr. Rosenburg: Please. Close your eyes.

Shadow: Fine.

Dr. Rosenburg: Good. Now I want you to picture yourself standing on the top of a green, grassy hill. There's a gentle breeze blowing as the warmth of the sun's rays shines down on your skin. Far off in the distance is a beautiful blue ocean, the sounds of water bringing you both peace and tranquility. As you stand there, I want you to picture the fresh smells of—

Shadow: This is a bunch of crap.

Dr. Rosenburg: You were doing so well.

Shadow: No, I wasn't. What you don't realize is that every time I close my eyes, the only thing I can picture are my parents, lying on the floor, blood draining from my father's open neck and the multiple holes in my mom's body. Their blood mixed together looks like red, rusted paint. Their eyes are both open. They look terrified. I always thought my father was never afraid of anything, but the truth is, my father was afraid of dying. I saw it on his face.

Dr. Rosenburg: Are you afraid of dying Shadow?

Shadow: I'm afraid of dying before I catch the fucker that ruined my life.

Dr. Rosenburg: Your life isn't ruined. Just look at your sister. She's doing very well for herself. I want you to use her as both inspiration and means of support.

Shadow: My sister never saw my parent's bodies. I was the one who discovered them. But I'm glad it happened that way, and that Calisto doesn't know the horrors surrounding their death. Did you know the cops said that my dad was stabbed in the throat first and as he was dying, the killer tried sawing off his head with the knife? That was why my dad's head was tilted back at such a weird angle.

Dr. Rosenburg: The police should never have told you such a thing.

Shadow: I'm a Tremaine, doctor. If I want information on something, I'll find a way to get it.

Dr. Rosenburg: Perhaps we should increase the frequency of our sessions.

Shadow: Why? So you can double the money you earn? I don't think so.

Dr. Rosenburg: Shadow, I'm here to help you. I want you to get better.

Shadow: I don't want to get better. I want to stay angry so when I find this guy, I can torture him. I want him to suffer and I want him to burn.

Dr. Rosenburg: Violence will solve nothing. Let's revisit your past week at the Academy. Your headmaster said you beat up one of your classmates the other day.

Shadow: He said something about my mother.

Dr. Rosenburg: And hitting him was the first thing you decided to do?

Shadow: No. Telling him to shut up was the first thing I decided to do. When he refused, I decided to kick his ass.

Dr. Rosenburg: And what did that solve?

Shadow: He stopped talking about my mom on account of his broken jaw. I'm also pretty sure he won't do it again.

Dr. Rosenburg: It looks like we have a lot of work to do still over the coming months.

Shadow: No, we don't. This is our last session.

Dr. Rosenburg: Only your guardian can make—

Shadow: I always liked puppets, doctor, because you could make them dance and move whenever you wanted them to.

Dr. Rosenburg: I don't understand.

Shadow: My guardian agrees with me. This session is finished now and forever. Please, enjoy the BMW that's waiting for you out on the driveway.

End Transcript.

Holy shit.

I was stunned. No wonder Shadow was brooding all the time. I thought of the way he described the torture of Julia's killer, almost like he wished he had participated. After picking my jaw off the park ground, I rushed home and looked up any information regarding the murders of Tristan and Sienna Tremaine.

There was no mention of it anywhere. It was like that part of their history was erased from the archives of the Internet.

As I sat there staring at the transcript while trying to digest the information from it, my cell phone rang.

It was Abraham.

"I hope I'm not disturbing you Ms. Valencia," he said cheerfully.

"I wasn't doing anything important," I lied. Snooping into Shadow's life was very important. "I'm just sitting around reading slutty books."

"Well, I won't bother you too long then. Shadow has requested that for your next date, you pack three nights worth of clothes and also suggests they be garments that you don't mind sweating into."

"What?"

"I'm only the messenger," Abraham said. "And perhaps you should bring a couple of those slutty books as well. It's about a sixteen hour flight time to the destination of your next date."

"You're kidding right? Where are we going?"

"That my dear, is a surprise," Abraham said before adding, "Just make sure you have all your hepatitis shots."

CHAPTER FIFTEEN

Cambodia. We were heading to Cambodia, which I realized after boarding one of Shadow's private jets.

Abraham sat in the aisle adjacent to me, newspaper in hand, busy skimming through the headlines.

"I can't believe I'm going to Cambodia," I said with excitement. "I have to admit, I don't know much about the country."

Abraham set the newspaper down on his lap and looked at me thoughtfully.

"It's a beautiful country, with many ancient temple ruins that will take your breath away. However it has a tragic past," he sighed. "In the late seventies, a guerilla army under the leadership of a mad man named Pol Pot took control of the kingdom of Cambodia. During this period, they murdered over two million people, specifically targeting anyone who showed any forms of education or intelligence."

"That's insane; two million?"

Abraham nodded. "Pol Pot was insane. It's funny how the leadership of one man can destroy a once promising nation, crippling it for many years after. To this day, Cambodia still struggles to recuperate from the Cambodian holocaust."

"All it takes is one crazy man," I agreed. I suddenly thought of Shadow and the interview I had read.

"Despite the tragedy that occurred over thirty years ago, the country itself is simply stunning. There are many ancient ruins to explore, situated deep in the jungles and exotic foods that will stimulate your palate. It's also the Cambodian New Year this weekend and the streets will be filled with celebrations."

"How do you know so much about Cambodia?" I asked.

"I travel there frequently," Abraham replied. "I've been trying to bring work to the country for some time now. I want to expand their knowledge of business and technology. Cambodia can't live off of tourism alone to sustain itself."

"You're such a good guy."

"I do what I can," Abraham replied. "I have over forty years of bad karma to make up for. Take this old man's advice, live a life you can look back on and not regret a single thing. Don't end up like me, spending the twilight of my years making amends for the sins that'll haunt me until the day I die."

His words resonated with pain and I thought of Julia, his only daughter murdered by the hands of a pedophile. I wanted to say something to comfort him, but making any mention of her would break my promise to Shadow about keeping my lips sealed.

So instead, I nodded in agreement.

"I must excuse myself," Abraham said with a smile. "I'm absolutely exhausted. I stayed up late finishing a series of books about a boy wizard that were absolutely fabulous."

"You're living life with a young heart," I laughed.

"Absolutely," Abraham said. "Now pardon me while I rest my weary bones. There are sleeping compartments in the back of the plane, should you wish to nap. As soon as our other tardy passenger arrives, the flight will take off."

I watched as Abraham strolled through the curtains to the back of the plane. I had nothing but time to kill. I had my books in my bag, but was too tired to read, so instead I placed my headphones in my ears, closed my eyes, and allowed the music to take me away.

Two songs later, I heard a cheerful voice overpower the sounds of my music.

"Aria! Or should I call you the Golden Virgin? What a pleasant surprise."

It was Lincoln Richards, sporting a handsome grey jacket. He held a thin laptop in his hand. I pulled the earphones out of my ears and smiled.

"Lincoln," I said, "Or should I say Mr. Fox?"

"What classics are you listening too? Chopin? Mozart? Some Berlioz maybe?"

"Calvin Harris," I replied. "Love his bright, blasting beats."

"And here I thought you were a classical music snob," Lincoln laughed. "I tried for a while to sign Mr. Harris to my record label but alas, he slipped out of my fingers."

"I enjoy all types of music, well maybe except country. Something about the twang that annoys the shit out of me," I said. "Why don't you sit? No offense but having you standing over me for the duration of a sixteen hour flight is rather unsettling."

Lincoln sat down in the same seat Abraham was in moments ago.

"Seat's warm," he noticed.

"Abraham went to the back to take a nap," I replied. "What brings you on this flight? Are you going temple exploring as well?"

He shook his head and smiled. "I explored all the temples a couple of years ago. It was grueling but very rewarding as well. I take it you'll be meeting Shadow in Siem Riep?"

"Where?"

"It's the more touristic centric region of Cambodia."

"Oh," I replied. "Right; I don't know too much about the country aside from some crazy guy named Pot Pie who murdered millions of people."

"Pol Pot," Lincoln corrected me. "I guess Abraham gave you the twenty second verbal wiki."

"He did," I replied. "So what are you doing here? Are you going to be a third wheel on my date with Shadow?"

"Tempting, but sadly there's work to be done," Lincoln said. "I'm helping Abraham with some accounting issues before he can get his Cambodian businesses up and running."

"So you're one of the good guys as well."

"Hardly," Lincoln smiled. "But I have a hard time saying 'no' to the old man. After that it's off to Japan for some Society business with James Takeshi, whom you met at Shadow's birthday party."

"Right, he was the owner of Takeshi Electronics."

"One and the same."

I paused for a moment, wondering if Lincoln would answer some burning questions I had about the Midnight Society. Ah fuck it; what did I have to lose?

"Who are you people?"

"We're businessmen," Lincoln replied.

"Why do I feel like the entire suit and tie image is a mask you wear," I said. "I want to know more about the Midnight Society. Every time I ask Shadow or Abraham, they refuse to give me any information about it."

"And what makes you think you can get information out of me?" Lincoln asked.

"How about a good, old fashion barter?" I suggested. "I offer you some sort of payment and in return you provide me with the information I want."

Lincoln chuckled at my proposal. "Sorry, not to sound like I'm on a golden horse, but I don't think there's anything of value that you could offer me in exchange. I swore a blood oath never to divulge any secrets to outsiders, and I take that blood oath very seriously."

"I can give you information."

Lincoln tapped his temple with his index finger and smiled. "There's not much information that I haven't digested already. I do have a good memory."

"It's not information you can get from reading a book," I said. "I know that you have a thing for Calisto. At Shadow's birthday party, I saw the way you hovered around Calisto for most of the night. I also know that she's not your typical girl that you can easily figure out."

"I guess I'm not as subtle as I thought myself to be," Lincoln sighed.

"So here's the deal. I'll get closer to Calisto, find out what she wants in a man, feed you this information, and in return you answer my questions about the Society."

Lincoln thought for a moment. "Three questions only," he finally said.

"Agreed," I nodded.

I extended my hand out to Lincoln and he gripped it with a firm handshake.

"Great. So I have my first question," I said. Lincoln looked surprised.

"Now?"

"Yes. Consider it a deposit. If I'm going to be a spy, I'll need some payment up front."

Lincoln shrugged his shoulders. "Fine. What's your question?"

"Why does Lucien hate Shadow so much?"

"You couldn't ask an easier question first?" Lincoln said, more as a statement than a question.

"I want to know the dirt behind those two."

"You swear that any secret information provided to you will never leave your lips?"

"I swear," I replied.

Lincoln leaned back in his seat and thought about it for a moment.

"I've always believed that the order of balance in the universe required both harmony and conflict," Lincoln began. "There is one person in everybody's lives that's destined to make you happy and on the flip side, there's also one person whose sole purpose in life is to torture you."

"Who gives you grief?" I asked.

Lincoln smiled. "Why that's a silly question. Isn't it obvious? It's Calisto," he said. "Some people fit in both categories."

"I don't get it, if she causes you so much suffering, why do you want to be with her?"

"I'm a glutton for punishment," he replied.

"Guys are fucking weird."

"Is it any different than a girl going for the sexy and dangerous bad boy instead of the safe, intelligent Poindexter?"

I thought about Justin, the very definition of safe and stable and placed him next to Shadow.

Shit, he was right.

"Anyway, it looks like I've gone off topic," Lincoln said. "Similar to royalty, membership into the Midnight Society has always been passed down by lineage, with a few exceptions. The children are involved within the society at an early age—participating in functions, learning about the organization, and meeting others their age. Shadow and Lucien started hating each other while they were still learning to walk. Every interaction they had with one another was just another brick laid on the foundation of their hatred."

"But two people don't just start hating each other for no reason. There must have been a spark," I said.

"Children are stupid and petty," Lincoln said. "They start fights over idiotic things like broken toys and stolen candy."

"But to have a feud originate at childhood and then carry over until now is ridiculous. There has to be something recent that you're not telling me."

"Lucien grew up with complete devotion to our organization.

It's hard to find someone who loves the Midnight Society more than he does. The Gambles have always lived and breathed the ways of our organization."

"And that's why he hates Shadow?"

"Shadow is the undisputed leader of the Midnight Society," Lincoln said. "But he doesn't take his duties very seriously."

I paused for a moment, reflecting on the fateful night that Shadow had chosen me to be his life mate. Compared to the three other women, who practically threw themselves at his feet, I was undeserving of this 'honor.' I could see how it was insulting for everyone who bought into this ritual.

However I still felt there was something that Lincoln wasn't telling me.

"There's got to be more," I replied. "This hatred is deep."

Lincoln shook his head. "What more is there to say?"

"I'm not satisfied."

"It's been a longtime since a woman has said that to me," he smirked.

"Do you want my help or not?" I asked. "I could easily plant seeds in Calisto's mind to place you in the dreaded friend zone. Once there, there's no getting out."

Lincoln raised a brow. "Did you just threaten me?"

"I suppose I did."

"Perhaps you do belong in the Midnight Society after all," he laughed. "You're not going to let up on this are you?"

"I will when you tell me the truth."

Lincoln sighed. "Fine. Shadow got drunk and fucked Lucien's sister about four years ago."

"That's why?"

"Yes."

"How's that such a big deal?"

"Clearly you're not an older brother," Lincoln said.

"They were teenagers," I said. "Teens make stupid decisions.

Hell I had some sexual encounters in high school that I wish I could take back."

"Do tell," Lincoln grinned.

"That comes with a price too you know."

Lincoln shook his head. "I always found that Lucien had an unhealthy obsession with his sister," he said. "It was borderline taboo."

"Gross," I said. It wasn't a stretch though picturing Lucien in the creepy and obsessive older brother role.

"Are you satisfied now?" Lincoln asked.

"Are you lying to me?"

"No."

"Fine. I'm content. The next time I see Calisto, I'll see what information I can dig up."

"Excellent. During our next meeting, I expect a plethora of inappropriate information about her," Lincoln said. He picked up his laptop. "Anyway, I have quite a bit of work to do on Abraham's accounts before we land."

"Lame," I said.

Lincoln smiled as he rose from his seat. "I didn't want to steal you away from Calvin Harris for too long," he said, just before making his way to the back of the plane as well.

Alone again.

At least I had my music, my slut books, and my anticipation to keep me company.

It didn't take me long to drift off into sleep once we were up in the air. I dreamt of an intense hot sun ruling over a majestic foreign kingdom, and Shadow--naked, holding me in his arms.

CHAPTER SIXTEEN

It was a long sixteen hour flight. After we landed, I desired sleep. I had smuggled in an hour or two of rest but I was worn out from travelling and needed another few hours to recharge my batteries.

By the time we reached the hotel—a charming European inspired Villa on beachfront property—it was roughly 5 A.M. Cambodian time. I collapsed onto my bed, not bothering to change, and closed my eyes. Just as I began to fall asleep, there was a knock on my door.

"You're kidding me," I muttered. I trudged towards the door slowly as if I were wading through molasses.

When I opened it, a young Cambodian man greeted me. He looked to be in his late teens and was full of enthusiasm as he spoke.

"Tut-tut driver," he beamed.

"What?"

"I'm tut-tut driver," he repeated. "Mr. Shadow sent me to pick you up."

"You're kidding right? Do you know what time it is?"

He looked at his watched before replying. "Five fifteen."

"That was a figurative question. Anyway, I'll go after I get seven hours of sleep," I replied. "Can you come back around noon?"

"Noooo," he replied, his gentle voice full of concern. "Mr. Shadow made me promise to take you to Angkor Wat before 6:00 A.M. I can't break promise to him. He very good to me. Give me and wife a job."

"You're married?" I was shocked. He looked as if he hit puberty two minutes ago. "How old are you?"

"Twenty-Seven."

"Must be the Asian gene," I surmised. "Look, I know you made a promise to Mr. Shadow but I made a promise to my pillow to spend some quality time with it. I hope you understand."

The tut-tut driver shook his head. "Please, it's very beautiful."

"What, Mr. Shadow? Yeah, he's definitely not hard on the eyes."

"No, Angkor Wat is very beautiful. We go see now, yes?"

"I'm sure it is very beautiful, but we can go later in the afternoon, yes?"

"No."

I let out a huge sigh. "You're not going to let me sleep, are you?"

He nodded. "I let you sleep later. For now, we go to Angkor Wat. Shadow waiting for you there."

"Fine," I gave in. "But next time you see Mr. Shadow, you tell him that Aria said he was a dick for dragging her ass out of bed so early in the morning."

"Okay," he nodded.

"On second thought, don't say that. Just wait for me while I get ready."

"Temperature today will be very warm. Dress with more skin. I'll wait for Ms. Aria at front of hotel," he said before taking his leave.

I closed the door and stared at my bed, tempted to dive into its sweet embrace. However if I did fall asleep again, the tut-tut driver would only be pounding away at my door again ten minutes later.

For a moment, I considered scaling the window ledges from the outside and breaking into a different room so I could have an affair with another bed. It probably wasn't worth the effort.

I sighed.

When I finished changing and wandered into the lobby, sauntering like a tired creature out of a zombie flick, the tut-tut guy was waiting for me by the entranceway, still smiling.

"Tut-tut ready," he said as he gestured for me to follow him. I had to admit, I was curious to know what a tut-tut was.

"You wait here and I bring it over," he said as I waited in the hotel veranda. It wasn't long before he pulled up in a vehicle that looked like the combination of a rickshaw and a Vespa scooter.

"That's a tut-tut?" I asked.

He nodded. "That's *my* tut-tut," he said with a sense of pride. The vehicle clearly meant a lot to this guy, despite it looking like an unregulated death trap. "Please enjoy yourself."

"I'll try," I mumbled as I sat in the vehicle.

Soon we were speeding away on the winding roads of the Cambodian streets, the darkness of the night melting away into a pale morning gray. I was amazed at all the beauty of Cambodia but saddened by the poverty as well. For every temple that we passed, I saw whole families sleeping on the streets.

It didn't take long for my fears of sitting in the tut-tut to fade away. It was actually quite fun. In fact, there were quite a few of these tut-tuts on the road, which made me feel a bit better.

Eventually we reached our destination. I was completely blown away by the wondrous sight of Angkor Wat.

Standing against the backdrop of the early morning dawn was a majestic stone palace, hand crafted by the gods themselves. Five tall towers, the heads shaped like lotus blossoms, stood erect behind smooth stone walls, like mountaintops peeking through an ancient fortress.

A moat surrounded Angkor Wat, reminiscent of an old medieval castle, the dark waters deterring unwanted visitors from its surreal realm.

I felt as if I were standing at the nexus of the universe and behind Angkor Wat's sacred walls were all the mysteries of the world, woven into one harmonious tapestry.

"Beautiful isn't it?"

I spun around to see Shadow standing behind me, looking like a bronze Adonis, his smooth skin tanned from the Cambodian sun. His muscular frame was practically bursting out of his black, ribbed tank top. His bulging shoulders reminded me of boulders while his six-pack protruded through his tank top. He wore cargo shorts that hit his knees, his muscular calves on full display. My mind diverted to my naughty dream of him on the plane and immediately I felt myself blushing.

Shadow took a step closer to me, his dark eyes tracing the curves of my body as he placed his strong hands on my bare shoulders. I felt the heat radiating off his body and I instantly felt wetness in between my legs. My stomach was fluttering and my heart was pounding like a jackhammer. I was breathing hard and struggled to maintain my composure.

He leaned closer to me as his breath glazed the side of my cheek. I was entranced by everything about him: his heart-stopping good looks, his hard sculpted body, the mystery behind his haunting past, and the excitement of his unpredictable future.

"You're missing the sunrise," he said in a soft, yet commanding voice, just before he turned me to the direction of Angkor Wat. I was captivated by the miracle before me.

Emerging through the five towers of the temple was the orange sun which casted its warm glow over its majestic kingdom. The sky was a canvas of ambient yellow light, which grew brighter as the sun made its ascension into the heavens.

Perhaps the most brilliant thing about this breathtaking scene was the reflection of the temple cast against the still waters of the moat. I was staring at an endless world where the sky and the earth met in a seamless union.

"See pretty lady," the tut-tut driver said, "I knew you would like."

I nodded, my eyes still transfixed on Angkor Wat. I was afraid that the second I looked away, it would vanish forever, like a forgotten dream.

"The City of Temples," Shadow said, unveiling his knowledge of the holy place. "It was built to look like Mount Meru, home of the Hindu Gods."

"Mister Shadow remembers the history I tell him yesterday," the tut-tut driver said with excitement.

"I was trying to impress the lady," Shadow sighed.

I turned to him and grinned. "Failure on your part for taking credit for someone else's knowledge, though you do get full points for bringing me here. I've never seen anything like it. It's stunning."

I felt myself tearing up at the thoughtfulness of Shadow's gift. I couldn't help but wonder what dad would have thought of Shadow if I had brought him home to dinner one night.

"You're going to love it here. It's your idea of a perfect vacation," Shadow said. "There are ruins to explore, hot sunny weather, and friendly locals."

The tut-tut driver tilted his head towards me politely.

"What's your name anyway mister driver?" I asked.

"Narendrapong," he replied, "But you can call me Johnny."

"Huh?"

"He's a fan of Johnny Depp movies," Shadow explained. "Most tourists have trouble pronouncing his Cambodian name so he decided to take on something more American."

"Pirates my favorite," he said, flashing me two enthusiastic thumbs up. "I also like his Scissor Hands."

"Well Johnny," I said. "I'm really happy you dragged my whiny ass out of bed so I could experience this. I'll always remember this sunrise. Thank you."

"We're not done with Angkor Wat yet," Shadow said as he took my hand. A warm sensation from his touch radiated through my entire body like the burning sun.

"Come on, let's check this place out," he said.

"What?" I was surprised. "You're telling me we can go inside?"

"Of course, it's one of Cambodia's main tourist attractions," Shadow said before turning his attention towards Johnny. "We'll probably be inside for a couple of hours."

"Yes sir," Johnny said. "I'll be right here when you are done."

Shadow looked at me with warm affectionate eyes. "Well, if you're ready, let's begin our second date."

"Let's," I agreed.

The insides of Angkor Wat were just as beautiful as the outside. Shadow guided me through the different galleries, scaling across flat sandstone tiles and pointing out the intricate stone carvings that lined some of the walls.

"What are these?" I asked, gesturing towards a pair of naked women sculpted into the walls.

"They're called Aspara," Shadow replied, "Otherwise known as nymphs or dancing girls."

"Strange things to have on holy temple walls," I commented.

"They apparently help ward off evil spirits and demons from this place."

"By giving them a lap dance?"

Shadow shrugged. "They actually seduced them into having sex, believe it or not."

"Interesting."

Shadow gestured towards another wall where a mean son-of-a-bitch was carved into the stone. "And here are the Dvarpala. They're demonic temple guardians used to fight off other demons."

"Was this all part of the same history lesson Johnny gave you yesterday?" I teased.

"Perhaps."

We continued our exploration through the rest of the temple. I felt like an overstimulated kid, climbing over rocks and balancing on stone walls, while forgetting about all the stresses in the world.

Shadow seemed to enjoy watching me navigate through broken stone piles that littered the ground.

"You look really nice," he said, the first compliment he gave me today.

My gaze danced across his large, sweaty body—admiring the raw strength that he exuberated—before finally settling on his eyes.

It was one of those romantic stares that you read about in books and saw on television, where everything around us faded from existence and we were the only two people left in the universe.

Shadow broke our staring contest; his eyes working slowly down my body, and then up again before settling on my lips. I practically whimpered when he licked his lips, and I imagined how soft and hard they'd be all at once—how they would feel on me.

Damn, I was so turned on.

"Hey look where we are," Shadow said, pointing to the large, magnificent tower that stood over us like a silent giant. He was diving right into another little history lesson instead of diving into me, and I did my best to hide my disappointment.

"It's lovely," I said. It really was.

"It's the main tower of Ankor Wat," he said. "The temple of Vishnu."

"How many times have you been here, to Cambodia?" I asked.

"A few. Cambodia is one of those places that has both captivated and broken my heart."

"I noticed the poverty."

It was sad.

"Have you set up business's here, like Lincoln and Abraham?"

Shadow shook his head. "Between those two, they can create a sound business infrastructure that can last this country a lifetime. I don't have the expertise like they do. Instead, I just contribute money wherever I can."

I nodded.

We spent another hour exploring the temple ruins before hunger and thirst finally settled in. I was also a sweaty mess and was beginning to feel self-conscious of my appearance.

"I must look disgusting," I said as I tugged on my shirt collar in a hopeless effort to cool myself down."

"I'm not any better," he said. Beads of sweat glistened across his bare shoulders and traces of it soaked the collar of his tank top. There was something about a sweaty, physical man that did it for me.

I prayed that I wasn't blushing right now.

"Besides, I like a girl who doesn't mind getting wet," he said with mischief in his eyes.

Shit. If I wasn't blushing before, I most certainly was now and damn it if I wasn't picturing every way of getting wet with him.

"I need some water," Shadow said. "If we're ready to leave this place, we can head back to the tut-tut."

"Water would be amazing."

Johnny was where we had left him. In addition he had brought us a cooler filled with water, juice, and a few snacks.

Shadow grabbed a bottle of water and handed it over to me. He took one for himself and drained it in a matter of seconds.

After we were both rehydrated, Johnny handed me what looked to be a bamboo stick.

"What's this?" I asked.

"Tasty treat," he replied as he showed me how to peel back the layers of bark, revealing sticky rice and black beans inside.

"I've never eaten anything out of a stick before," I laughed as I took a cautious bite. It was delicious. I began to devour the bamboo sticky rice like a starved animal.

"Hungry?" Shadow laughed peeling back one of his own tasty bamboo treats.

"This is orgasmic," I said.

"First time I ever heard of a woman getting off from rice."

I was going to make a witty comeback, but decided to use my mouth for eating instead.

After we were finished with our snack, we sat in the cool shade of the tut-tut while relaxing and sipping water; the two of us alone. Johnny had left to go find some lunch of his own.

"Thanks again for bringing me here," I said. "This trip has been incredible so far."

"There's a lot of Cambodia left," Shadow said. "This is only one of many temples to explore as well as more foods to taste. There's deep fried spider if you're feeling adventurous enough."

"You're serious? They eat deep fried spider here?"

"It's more of a novelty for tourists than anything," Shadow replied "It's not considered one of the basic food groups for locals."

"I think I'll pass on the deep fried spider. Everything else sounds amazing. For a fake date, you've really outdone yourself."

"Think nothing of it," Shadow said. "I love this place too. My dad took me here when I was still a little kid. I remember how speechless I was when I saw the temples for the first time—though I was probably too busy complaining about the heat at the time to appreciate the serenity of Angkor Wat."

"Did your dad take you here for a trip?"

Shadow shook his head. "Business," he replied, as his thoughts seemed to trail off into the past. "Everywhere he took me was always for business."

"You never made the coming-of-age trip to Disneyland?" I teased.

Though my words were meant to be a joke, they seemed to have touched Shadow deeply.

"You know my dad never took me to a park, not once? Or played catch with me or read me any bedtime stories?"

"You're probably exaggerating," I said. "He must have spent *some* quality time with you."

"Oh, don't get me wrong, he did spend time with me, but most of that was spent teaching me about numbers, strategy, and business. I remember one afternoon going over to the Constantine house when I was eight and listening to Abraham read to Julia *Where the Wild Things Are*. I was captivated both by the story and the fact that Julia got to experience something fun with her father. I got home and my dad started drilling me on Gaussian distribution formulas. Did you know by the time I was seven, I could already do advanced Calculus equations? I was a freak."

"It sounds like you were quite the brainiac."

Shadow practically scoffed at what I said.

"With all the neurological enhancement pills and vitamins I was taking at the time, I'm surprised I can't read your thoughts right now."

I want you to fuck me until I can't stand anymore.

I turned away for a moment and faked a cough while breaking eye-contact with him just in case he *did* have some voodoo ability to read my thoughts.

"Growing up, people always thought I had it easy. After all, I was the future of the Midnight Society; an anointed prince. They believed that anything I wanted came to me at the snap of my fingers. What bullshit," Shadow's jaw was clenched. "What they didn't see was my father pushing me to my limits, both mentally and physically. I was never allowed to cry, since it was a sign of weakness. I was never allowed to complain because endurance was a way to build both strength and character. Even something that should have been fun like soccer matches were a point of stress for me. I always had to be the best player on the field and my team always had to win, otherwise I risked disappointing my father."

"That's horrible. Every kid should be allowed to enjoy their childhood. Those memories are so very precious." I paused. "Did your father push Calisto just as hard?"

Shadow shook his head. "She got off easy, being a girl. While I was reading books about chaos theory and memorizing political platforms, she got to bake cookies, play with dolls, and go to the zoo."

"What about your mom? Did she agree with what your dad was doing?"

"She worked me just as hard. After all, she bore the Tremaine last name and the prestige associated with it. Every Tremaine male was forced to live up to the family legacy; weakness was never allowed," he sighed. "There's a legend about our family. Back in the seventeen hundreds, there was one Tremaine baby boy born with a birth defect—something as trivial as a cleft lip. Because of this, the baby was a symbol of weakness, and because of this small defect, they delivered the baby to an orphanage and stripped all records of his birth from the history books."

"That's awful. How can a mother carry a child for nine months in her stomach only to dump it away after first glance?"

"This is the world I live in. The Midnight Society only cares about strength and power and they don't mind deception in order to obtain it," Shadow said.

"Do you want to leave the Midnight Society?" I asked.

Shadow shook his head. "Tell me about your father," he said, abruptly changing the focus of topic. "What was he like?"

A wide smile crept across my face as I thought about him. "He was everything to me," I said. "He was my inspiration to become a classical pianist."

"Did he push you to have piano lessons when you were young?" Shadow asked. I shook my head.

"No, I asked for them," I replied. "I have pictures when I was still in diapers and my dad sat me on his lap in front of a piano, my whole fist trying to push down on the keys. I was inspired at a very early age."

"Did your dad play the piano?"

"Occasionally he played a few rudimentary songs like Fur Else and a couple of Beethoven's and Bachs," I replied. "He taught me up to a certain level but when I got into the more complex pieces, we had to hire a piano teacher. The one my dad found was quite the piece of work. He was a Russian psychopath."

"How so?"

"Well for one thing, he told me to start lifting weights so I could build strength in my puny little arms," I laughed. "Keep in mind I was fourteen at the time. However he was a good teacher and many of his unconventional techniques got me to the level I'm at today. He didn't come cheap though. My dad's teacher's salary couldn't cover food, mortgage, and the Russian so he had to take a second job teaching night classes."

"Your dad sounds like a good man," Shadow said. "I would have loved to meet him. I always have high regards for a man who takes care of his family."

"I'm sure your father did the same."

"My father worked hard to obtain power for our family name. Your father worked hard to make you happy."

"Do you resent your dad?"

Shadow shook his head. "No, I loved him and respected him very much. But sometimes I wish…" his voice trailed off.

"You wish what?"

"Never mind, it sounds childish," Shadow said.

"I won't laugh, I pinky swear," I said, extending my finger out to him.

"Now *that's* childish," Shadow smiled.

"No it's not. The pinky swear is the most sacred and holy of promises. One can never violate the sanctity of the pinky swear unless they wish to be cursed for the rest of eternity."

Shadow shook his head. "You're pretty weird sometimes."

"And you're not?"

Shadow shrugged his shoulders, and then hooked his pinky finger into mine. "While my father was alive, I had to work my ass off and struggle to meet his expectations. And now with him dead, I'm working hard and struggling to fulfill his legacy. However Tristan Tremaine never once tried to make the slightest effort to fulfill the expectations I had for him as a father."

"And what was that?"

"I would have loved for him to take me to a movie—just once. Or bring me to the park for an ice cream cone. I just wanted a dad I could hang out with," he said. "Does that sound foolish?"

I shook my head. "It sounds sad."

"When I was a kid, I kept thinking that once I was old enough and achieved all those goals he set out for me, he'll finally be proud of me and then we could finally sit down and watch a movie together and have an ice cream cone at the park," he said. "But that'll never happen. He's dead now, murdered by some sick fuck who's still roaming free out there. The killer stole away from me the only dream I ever had. The only thing I ever wanted."

"Oh Shadow, I'm so sorry," I said.

He shook his head. "I should apologize. Nobody wants to hear a grown man whine about his ghosts."

I wanted to take him in my arms and comfort him, to hold him and give him that safe feeling that my father had given me so many times.

I summoned up the courage to make a move and provide him with a little bit of physical contact. Just as I leaned in closer, Johnny returned from his lunch break.

Damn it.

Johnny hopped onto the Vespa scooter that dragged the tut-tut and then turned to us. "Where to Mr. Shadow?" he asked.

Shadow's eyes, full of grey sadness, glossed over Angkor Wat. Outside he had the presence and physique of a lion, the ruler of this animal kingdom he called the Midnight Society. However in reality he was a wounded animal, seeking solace and affection.

"Take us somewhere beautiful," he finally said. "Take us

somewhere where we can forget all our worries."

CHAPTER SEVENTEEN

We visited four more temple ruins that afternoon. Though not as extravagant as Angkor Wat, each one was just as haunting and beautiful. The one that touched me profoundly was Ta Prohm, where an ancient looking tree seeped through the ruin's walls creating a harmonious union between stone and root.

Two different elements of nature, fused into one to form one of the most breathtaking things I've ever seen.

I turned around and looked at Shadow, who was too busy examining the carvings on the stone walls to notice that I was staring at him.

We were two distinct entities in this vast universe ourselves—Shadow living in a world of money, power, and a haunting past which suffocates him daily. Meanwhile I was a simple girl whose life blood was filled with impossible dreams and musical sonatas. My future terrified me and my past was filled with bittersweet memories.

A week ago, the thought of being in a relationship with this provocative, but ridiculously handsome man was the last thing I wanted. Seeing the symbiotic union between the tree and the temple made me wonder if a love between Shadow and I could be just as beautiful and spellbinding?

I wanted him. God, I wanted him so badly.

I wanted these dates to be more than just a façade.

I wanted these moments we had together to mean just as much to Shadow as they did to me. I wanted him to look at me as I looked at him—as the person who captured his heart.

Who was I kidding? He wanted me as his fake lover, just so he didn't have to commit himself to anyone.

Perhaps this entire date in Cambodia was an elaborate sham, something that the Midnight Society could watch or read about.

Face it Aria, you're just a simplistic girl with a piano, chasing another one of your impossible dreams. To Shadow, I was probably just another news article for the tabloids.

"Are you hungry?" Shadow asked as we left Ta Prohm.

The thought of food made my stomach howl like a wolf, enthralled by a full moon. We had spent almost twelve solid hours hiking, and I'd loved nothing more than to strip naked from the wet clothes that clung to my skin and indulge in a delicious Cambodian meal.

"Let's go back to the hotel and clean up?" I suggested.

"You got it."

It took me about an hour to transform myself from a sweaty, untamed mess into a presentable woman, worthy to take out to dinner. A shower and a glass of wine had me feeling more relaxed, as I waited for Shadow in the hotel lobby.

Outside, the streets were alive with locals running about, wide smiles on their faces as they went about their business.

I turned to Johnny.

"Is it always this busy on the streets at night?" I asked.

"It's the Cambodian New Year Ms. Aria," he replied. "Tonight, there is a big celebration on the streets."

"Oh wow. Shouldn't you be at home with your wife then?"

"I spend time with her yesterday and day before," he said. "Cambodian New Year lasts for three days. She tired from two nights of dancing."

"So you're going to spend the night watching us eat?"

"Depends on what you eat," Johnny joked.

I couldn't help but laugh at his innocent humor. I was going to miss him when I had to return home tomorrow.

"Aria, you look stunning as usual."

I turned around to see Shadow standing behind me, dressed in shorts and sandals and a navy blue short-sleeved collared shirt.

"Fuck," I said. "I'm overdressed, aren't I?" I looked down at my evening gown.

"Of course not," Shadow said. "I'm just underdressed, that's all."

"I had this crazy expectation that you were going to take me to some fancy, over-priced restaurant where they'll judge me for my unscrupulous cheap looks."

"The one thing I love about Cambodia, no one knows who I am," Shadow said. "I don't have to worry about maintaining my appearance. You have no idea how many times back home, I just wanted to walk into a grimy Mexican joint and enjoy a plate of fish tacos and a bottle of Corona."

He licked the top of his full lips. "Anyway, I'm going to take advantage of no one knowing who I am here. I'm going to wear comfortable clothes, eat local foods, and enjoy the street-level atmosphere of the Cambodian New Year."

"Can I change then? I have a casual summer dress back in my room," I said.

Shadow shook his head.

"No." His eyes scanned me from head to toe. "You look very sexy…and very appetizing," he added.

I felt the color of my cheeks flush into bright shades of red. "Okay, I'll keep it on, just for you," I said, my mind floating aimlessly in a sea of his sensual talk.

Once inside the tut-tut, Shadow instructed Johnny to drive us to Pub Street, a popular tourist hang out where they served local food and also housed several westernized bars.

The entire ride over, we sat in comfortable silence. No words needed to be spoken; just sitting next to Shadow was more than enough to make me happy.

Eventually the tut-tut ride came to an end, stopping in front of a two-story restaurant. Instead of the typical four walls you'd see back home, this restaurant was completely open to the outside.

"Call me when finished," Johnny said cheerfully before speeding off like the road runner.

We were greeted by friendly waiters in white dress shirts, who led us up the stairs and seated us close to the main street. With a roof over our heads and the open air, I felt as if I was eating on a veranda.

"You ate here before?" I asked.

Shadow nodded. "I recommend the Khmer curry. It'll blow your mind."

"Is that what you're having?"

"There's this baked fish I've been dying to try here. They wrap it in banana leaves and steam it," Shadow said, glancing over the menu. "As much as I love the curry, I also enjoy a little variety here and there."

The waiter returned with a bottle of chilled white wine and two wine glasses.

"The usual sir?" he asked as he set the glasses on the table and carefully poured the white wine into them.

Shadow nodded, pulling a twenty dollar bill out of his pocket and handing it over to the waiter as a tip. The waiter smiled graciously and then took our food order.

It had cooled down significantly, though the heat still radiated off my body from the intense afternoon sun. A gentle breeze glazed over my body and I closed my eyes, enjoying every second of it.

"It was a good day," I said, my eyes still closed.

"I'm glad you had fun," Shadow said. "This country has a way of mesmerizing a person's heart."

So do you, I thought.

I opened my eyes and reached for my glass, taking a polite sip from the sweet wine. "So do you think Abraham can succeed in stimulating Cambodia's economy?"

"I hope so. He's found the brightest minds in Cambodia already. While Siem Riep thrives on tourism, the other parts of Cambodia suffer from extreme poverty. They're still trying to recover from Pol Pot's madness."

"All it takes is one person to lead a country into its destruction," I sighed.

Shadow nodded. "Funny, I've heard some members of the Midnight Society say that of me."

I saw the opening I needed to inquire more about the organization.

"Tell me more about the Midnight Society," I said, more of a demand than a request.

"Curiosity killed the cat," Shadow said, echoing Senator Donald Huff's warning.

"You never heard that a cat has nine lives?" I replied.

Shadow laughed. "Touché."

"Hey, if I'm supposed to be your Midnight Princess, the least you can do is tell me a little bit about your work."

"You're not my princess anymore after tonight," Shadow said. "Your contract's fulfilled."

My heart sank from his statement, but I hid my disappointment. "I want to know," I said. "I don't like secrets."

"I guess you don't like me then," Shadow said. "I'm full of secrets."

"Let's hear some."

Shadow sighed. "You're relentless."

"Don't you trust me to keep your secrets?"

"The secrets I have aren't trivial, like housewives gossiping about who's sleeping with the pool boy. The secrets I have will get a person killed."

"Try me. I need some excitement in my life anyway."

Shadow reached for his glass of wine, took a big gulp, and set it down again. He licked his full lips and gave me an apprehensive look.

For a moment, I thought he was going to give in and tell me what I wanted to know.

"I can't," he finally said.

"Didn't your mom know your father's business with the Midnight Society?" I asked.

"They also slept in the same bed together," Shadow pointed out.

Then sleep in the same bed with me, I wanted to blurt aloud, but I decided to keep that to myself.

"Anyway, what I do isn't interesting. All I do all day is spin webs of lies. This is the core of the Midnight Society."

"You hate them, don't you?" I asked, "The Midnight Society."

Shadow thought about the question for a moment. "I like certain people inside the Society," he replied.

"That's not what I asked," I said.

"Where do you want to be in five years?" Shadow asked, suddenly changing the topic. He was good at that.

"It's a secret," I said, giving him a taste of his own medicine.

"No it's not. I already know what your goals are."

"If you already know, then why ask the question?"

Shadow grinned. "You have this smile on your face when you talk about your dreams. It's just the prettiest thing to look at. I wanted to see it again."

Damn it. He was sweet talking me again, and succeeding at it.

"How about I make you a deal," I said. "I'll tell you all the things

I hope to achieve in the next five years, and then you do the exact same, truthfully."

Shadow thought about it for a moment before replying, "Okay, deal."

I extended my pinky finger towards him. "Swear it."

"Done," he said as he hooked his pinky around mine and tugged lightly.

I leaned back in my chair, grabbed a glass of wine off the table and took a healthy gulp and looked at him thoughtfully.

"You already know that I dream of being a world famous pianist," I said. "It's a dream that my dad and I both shared."

"Your father wanted to become a pianist as well?"

I nodded. "It's a dream he couldn't fulfill because of me," I sighed. "My mom died of cancer when I was just a baby so all his time was invested into taking care of me."

"I'm sorry to hear about your mom," Shadow said.

"I've seen pictures of her, but I wish I could have heard her voice. She'll always be the woman in the photos that I spent hours staring at; a beautiful smiling woman who succumbed to that fucking disease, robbing her of her life with me way too early."

Shadow was focused on every word I said. I had his undivided attention. It was a welcome change from the other boyfriends I had.

"Being a single parent was pretty much the death of my father's dream to travel the world and perform on grand stages. He always told me that when I had the crowd in Vienna eating out of my hand, then I had finally made it."

"Vienna is a lovely city," Shadow said. "We should go there sometime."

"I thought our dates were finished after this," I said.

"I can make an exception."

I giggled like a school girl, only to realize how juvenile I must have looked. I cleared my throat.

"Growing up, I was always surrounded by pianos. As a side

business on weekends, my dad restored pianos, picking up old clunkers and refurbishing them. He fine-tuned every string until they were restored to their glory again," I said. "I helped him out quite often, handing him tools or helping him with the tuning. Sometimes I even helped restring them. It became a tradition that after every piano was finished, I'd learn a new song on it before it was to be sold."

"What was the first song your dad ever taught you?" he asked.

I smiled. "Twinkle twinkle little star of course."

"Really?"

"No, I'm lying. It was actually Baa Baa Black Sheep."

"Very funny," Shadow said with a smirk.

"It wasn't until I was twelve, maybe thirteen, that I had asked my dad about his passion for music and pianos. It was then that he revealed to me his abandoned dream of playing music for the world to hear. When I asked him why he didn't continue down that path, he always refused to tell me, diverting the conversation to other topics using the same stupid tactic you use.

"My uncle told me the truth one time while drunk. The reason my dad abandoned his dreams was to take care of me. They often say that parents live vicariously through their children. It was true. I decided at that moment that I would fulfill my dad's dream and train to become a pianist myself. I fantasized about sitting in Vienna Music Hall, finishing my encore and the crowd is roaring, giving me a standing ovation. In the first row was my dad, and I'd bring him up on stage, revealing to everyone that this wonderful man was the true inspiration behind the music that they heard tonight." I paused and swallowed hard. "My dad died two years ago from pancreatic cancer. I'll never be able to fulfill that fantasy."

I felt myself getting emotional. Crying was the last thing I wanted to do in front of Shadow. He'd probably think I was unstable.

"I'm sure wherever he is, he'll still be able to see and hear you play in Vienna when the day comes."

"Do you believe in heaven or God?" I asked.

Shadow's eyes diverted to the ground as he reflected on my question. "Not for a long time," he finally said.

"I see."

"I'm sure God comes to those who deserve it. However I don't consider myself one of those people," Shadow said.

"So do you think my dad's watching over me now?"

"I do," Shadow said. "He's probably thinking 'who's this unworthy dipstick sitting in front of my daughter.' That's probably what I'd be thinking if I was him."

"I always believed people from heaven can see deep into people's souls," I said. "I'm sure my dad would have liked you. You seem like a pretty good guy."

"If your dad could look into my soul, then he'd definitely be scowling. I'm fucked up, there's no mistake about that." Shadow leaned back in his chair. "I've heard you play Aria. You have an amazing gift and I'd be shocked if you weren't able to succeed. Everything is in its right place for you."

"I don't know," I said. "The thing about classical music is there's no demand for it. Classical music enthusiasts already have all the music they ever need in their collection. There are only so many variations of Beethoven piano sonatas that can be played, while maintaining the spirit of the original song. Let's face it, I chose a dying breed of business that's highly competitive and could live without another person redoing a famous composer's work. A classical musician is the ultimate cover artist."

"So create your own music," Shadow said. "I heard the song you wrote for your dad. It was brilliant."

"It's not that easy," I said. "The classical music circles are a snobby bunch and they won't welcome a new artist with open arms easily. Take Phillip Glass for example, his music has been the ridicule of the classical elite for years."

"I think it's more along the lines that all the songs he wrote can be played with two fingers."

"That's beside the point. He tried something different with his minimalist style and was ostracized by the very people I need to impress."

"Why do you need to impress them?" Shadow asked.

"Because it's my dream to succeed; it's *our* dream."

Shadow looked at me pensively. "Has your father raised you well?"

"What kind of question is that?" I asked.

"Well has he?"

"Of course he has. My father was the greatest person I've ever known."

"Then technically you have a lot of your father in you, isn't that a fair statement to say?"

"Well...yes I suppose."

I was confused by his line of questioning but allowed him to continue. "Who do you want to impress more," he began, "Those snooty wine drinking, Wagner worshiping mother fuckers who masturbate to the sounds of their own voices," he paused, "Or do you want to impress your dad?"

The answer was obvious. "My dad of course; it's always my dad."

"Then impress yourself," Shadow said. "As you said, there's a lot of your father in you. Compose a song that you're proud of and that's more than enough for you to succeed in this world. Pleasing a bunch of soul-sucking assholes will turn your hard work into a soulless product. However what you're doing is art, and in the end, you—and your father—are the only opinions that matter."

He was right. All this time, I've been killing myself trying to imitate the works of others in order to please a bunch of wine-sniffing music aficionados who knew nothing about me, nor my work. Why the hell was I spending so much time pleasing these people? Why did I need to place my happiness in the hands of others?

"I think you're on to something," I said with a smile.

"Good," he replied. "Now do you remember the agreed method of payment for your condo?"

"Well yeah, you want me to record the most difficult piano pieces ever written," I said, "Which is fair payment. I really shouldn't whine about it."

"I'm going to suggest altering the terms of your payment," Shadow said. "Instead of mastering those songs—which may lead to finger arthritis—I want you to record five original songs for me instead."

"Like a demo?"

"Yes," Shadow said. "Record me a demo of five original songs, written by the Golden Virgin."

"We really have to stop using that nickname. I'm neither golden nor a virgin."

"I like the name," Shadow said. "It has a nice catchy ring to it. It's mysterious and intriguing; perfect for the stage."

"I have issues with the virgin part of it. I'm never allowed to have sex?"

"Not in public."

I couldn't help but laugh. "That's fair I suppose."

The waiter returned, bringing us our meals that looked—and smelled—amazing. I wasn't hungry before but the rich aroma of golden curry was enough to have my mouth screaming for a taste.

I lunged for my fork and was ready to dig in, but paused when I saw Shadow reaching for his wine glass. He raised it in my direction.

"A toast to a great day, and to our second date," Shadow said.

"Can I take a bit of my food first?"

"And here I was trying to be romantic."

"Fine, fine," I said, grabbing my glass and tapped it against his. "Cheers."

I savored every single bite of my meal, the foreign spices of the rich and creamy curry dancing on my tongue—an ensemble of flavors mixed together harmoniously.

Shadow seemed to be enjoying his food as well, taking healthy bites of his fish, which also smelled phenomenal.

As dinner began to wind down, I decided to pick up where our conversation left off.

"So we discussed my five year plan," I said. "Now it's your turn."

Shadow set down his fork and wiped his mouth with a napkin.

"There are two stories I can tell you," he said. "One happy and cheerful—but it would be a lie, which adds onto the other pile of lies I've spun as a member of the Midnight Society—or I can tell you the truth, which isn't pleasant. In fact, the truth may disturb you to the point where you'll never want to see or speak to me again."

"The truth," I said with no hesitation. "I despise lies."

"Okay then," Shadow said as he polished off the last of his wine before continuing. "I'm sure you must know by now that both my parents were murdered."

I nodded. "I wanted to give you my sympathies, but couldn't find the proper time to. I'm sorry."

"It's okay," Shadow said. "Talking about dead parents tends to spoil the mood of a romantic getaway."

"Yeah," I agreed. "I guess we've been talking quite a bit about our dads during this trip."

"Well, they *were* the people that shaped our identities," Shadow said. "Think how drastically different our lives would have been if we were someone else's kid. Everything you and I do, it's because our parents influenced us that way."

"Absolutely."

"For the first ten years of my life, I always knew what my dream was—to impress my father and be a worthy successor to the Tremaine family name. Everything I did was for him; every goal I scored, every exam I aced—it was all done to earn my father's approval."

"Did he ever give it to you?"

Shadow shook his head. "My father wasn't the type to hand out gold stars or pats on the back. To this day, I'll never know if he was proud of me or not," he sighed.

I reflected on my own dad and how he constantly congratulated me on each one of my accomplishments. His encouragement allowed me the confidence to face all my challenges head on and succeed. Listening to what Shadow's childhood was like made me feel sorry for him.

"Have you ever seen something so horrible, you'll never be able to rid yourself of that grotesque image, no matter how hard you try?"

I nodded as I recalled a dark memory of mine. "I was helping out my grandpa on the farm once when I was little. One day, I went out to feed the calves and I noticed one calf in particular was moaning and jerking her head around wildly. I remember walking up to her, only the left side of her face in view. She had looked at me with these wide eyes, terrified, her head swinging from side-to-side as if she were possessed. It wasn't until I drew closer and saw the right side of her face that I realized what was wrong."

I paused, and shuddered at the memory.

"You don't have to tell me the story if you don't want to," Shadow said. "It was more of a rhetorical question anyway."

"Too late now," I said. "I always hated it when someone started a story and didn't finish."

"Don't make friends with writers then," Shadow said. "Many of them tend to start but fail to finish."

I smiled at him. "Storytellers are equally as troublesome," I agreed, before continuing with my memory. "What I saw was something straight out of a horror movie. It looked as if half her face had been chewed off by flesh eating worms; fat bulbous insects that ate away her eyes, the flesh on her cheeks, and her nose. All that was left was cartilage and bone. That's the one image I can never forget, no matter how hard I try."

"Has the image of the worms devouring the calf changed the way you look at the world?" Shadow asked.

"I was twelve at the time. For years, worms and skele-cows haunted my dreams," I said. "But eventually I got over it. However take me to a restaurant and nine times out of ten, I'll still choose chicken over steak."

Shadow nodded.

"This is a lead into your story?"

"Yes," he said, taking a deep breath. "The one image that will haunt *me* until the day I die was opening the door of the study and seeing my mom and dad lying in a pool of blood. My mom had one solid stab wound through her neck, followed by multiple ones all across her body. Meanwhile my father's neck was half sawed off, his head tilted back at an impossible angle."

Shadow swallowed hard.

"I'll be honest with you," I decided to come out. "I already know all this. The other day, while I was relaxing in the park, Lucien approached me and gave me a package. Inside were transcripts of your sessions with your therapist."

I felt guilty keeping this secret until now. I should have told Shadow the minute I received the package, but the mystery behind him was too tempting to resist. And then when I saw him at Angkor Wat, I contemplated telling him then but the beauty of Cambodia had stolen my heart and discussing the murder of Shadow's parents was the last thing I wanted to talk about while we explored the magical Khmer ruins.

"It took him longer than usual this time," Shadow sighed.

"Huh?"

"Lucien's been passing around those files to anyone and everyone who would listen," Shadow said. "Did you read them?"

I shot Shadow a nervous glance. "Truthfully?" I asked.

"I dislike liars almost as much as you do," Shadow replied.

"Yes, I read the transcripts."

Shadow leaned back in his chair and took in a deep breath. "And what do you think?"

"I think you're still a wonderful person and the death of your parents was very tragic."

"Do you know what my first thought was when I saw my dad lying there, dead?"

I shook my head.

"I was angry that he was dead because I could never prove to him that I was a worthy heir to the Tremaine estate, that it was possible for me to grow up into someone he could proudly call his son," he said. "The soulless eyes of my father's, the same ones that looked at me with disgust every time I failed—those dead eyes will haunt me for the rest of my life because they'll never see the man that I would become. I will always be a failure to him, until the day I die."

"That's not true," I said. "You're not a failure. In fact you've become quite the successful man."

"I have none of my father in me," Shadow said. "So even if I'm satisfied with my own accomplishments, I don't think they'll ever be enough for him."

"They never found the killer?"

Shadow shook his head. "It was an unsolved mystery. The Midnight Society was good at suppressing it in the media, allowing us to use our own brand of investigation—and justice when the time came. However the murder was a clean one—no evidence left, no fingerprints, absolutely nothing; only two dead bodies in a pool of blood with no signs of struggle. After five years, the Midnight Society decided to ease up on the investigation, conceding that this was one mystery that would never be solved."

"Fuck that," I shouted. "They need to keep at it. What if the psychopath decides to kill again? There has to be someone who's still investigating their murder."

"There is," Shadow said. "Me."

He broke his gaze away from mine and stared out into the street where a crowd began to form. Music blared from old speakers as people moved to the beats of songs popular ten years ago. There were plastic glasses in hand and many of them were drinking beer distributed from buckets. It looked as if the Cambodian New Year's festivities were just starting.

"I guess this leads back to the original question of what I want to accomplish within the next five years," Shadow said, his eyes coated with a thin layer of moisture. "I want to find my parent's killer and make him suffer. When there's nothing left but a pile of flesh and bone, only then will I be satisfied and perhaps my dad's ghost can look at me and finally be proud of me."

He took a deep breath.

"I want to have a life again," he said, no longer cool and collected. He looked vulnerable now—desperate almost. "I want to start all over again, away from the Society, away from the politics and the lies, and most of all away from all the ghosts that constantly have a grip around my throat. Each and every day, I feel like I'm suffocating and the only way to escape is to disappear and never be found again."

"I'll disappear with you," I blurted aloud. Lord, what a stupid thing to say. I let my emotions take hold of me in the heat of the moment. Seeing Shadow so vulnerable made me want him even more, to take him in my arms and be the one to comfort him and stand by his side while he faced the demons that controlled him. Curse these nurturing instincts of mine. It only made me look desperate for his attention and love.

Just as I was about to crawl under the table and hide from embarrassment, I saw Shadow smile at me—a genuine lovely smile that penetrated through my clothing and bare skin and buried itself deep within my heart.

"I'd love that Aria," he said.

Holy shit! Did Shadow just say he would love to start a new life with me?

"Say that again," I demanded.

"I'd love to have you by my side," Shadow said. "But are you willing to wait for me while I hunt down my parent's killer?"

"I'll wait until the end of the world." I reached out and placed my hand over his. Shadow smiled at the gesture, opening his hand and taking mine within it. It was the perfect moment that was accentuated by the sounds of celebration down in the streets.

After settling the bill for dinner, Shadow and I took to the streets, hand-in-hand.

The music was blaring and the locals were out on the streets dancing as if no one was watching.

"Let's stay for a while," I suggested, as I moved my body to the heavy beat. "I don't remember the last time I heard the Backstreet Boys."

"Yeah, they're a bit dated on their music here," Shadow said. I grabbed his hand and dragged him right into the center of the crowd.

"I have to warn you, I'm not much of a dancer," he pointed out.

"Let me lead then and I'm sure your body will figure out how to do the rest," I said seductively. With the knowledge that he felt the same way I did, it was game on.

I was going to drive this boy wild.

The first obstacle I faced was doing a sexy dance to the tune of Backstreet's Back and its cheesy beat and even worse lyrics. But damned if I was going to let those obsolete boy boppers ruin this moment.

With my back turned to Shadow, I began moving sensually, my body flowing like a gentle wave. I noticed he was keeping his distance from me, clearly uncomfortable with the entire concept of dancing.

I tilted my head back and flashed him a '*I want to fuck you*' smile and said to him, "Don't be shy. You can touch me."

I reached back, found his hands and positioned them around my waist. Feeling his rock hard body against mine was more than enough to make me wet.

"I've wanted to hold you for quite some time now," he replied. "I never wanted to be too presumptuous though."

"You can do whatever you want to me."

I began stroking his crotch with my ass. I closed my eyes and let a soft moan escape my lips as we continued our erotic embrace throughout the song. His fingers splayed across my stomach, pulling me harder against him.

Feeling the hardness of his manhood against my body was driving me wild. I wanted to tear off his clothes and do him right then and there in the middle of the street—not giving a fuck if every Cambodian in the universe saw us getting it on.

I turned around and wrapped my arms around his neck and pressed my body against his, my breasts against his chest. Shadow's jaw clenched and his eyes filled with lust as his breaths grew heavy. I reached down with one hand and brushed his cock lightly.

"Aria…" he moaned.

I didn't let him speak. Instead my mouth found his—finally, we kissed. And it was better than I had envisioned. His tongue explored every inch of my mouth—mine doing the same. He cupped my upper lip with his, just before his tongue found mine again. We embraced each other in the center of the city streets, the locals dancing all around us while we were serenaded with the crooning Backstreet Boys.

It wasn't until the song ended and a new one began that we released ourselves from each other.

"Is that what I think it is?" Shadow asked as he tilted his head towards the direction of the speakers. The notes reverberated through the streets loud and clear. There was no mistaking what this song was.

"It's the fucking Macarena!" I shouted with excitement.

"You have got to be kidding me," Shadow said. "This song is as pleasant as a rusty nail wedged in my ear."

"Yeah, this song sucked major balls at the height of its popularity, but listening to it years later—it's brilliant."

"No, it still sucks major balls."

"I beg to differ. Just look at the crowd," I said.

Everyone on the street had formed into a perfect grid, all performing the ridiculous choreography of the goofy South American song. There was something beautiful about the fact that the locals here were oblivious to how terrible the Macarena truly was. They didn't hear the repetitive beat—reminding me of a rattling air duct—or the man's annoying monolithic droning. Instead, they heard music, beautiful fun music that hadn't been spoiled by American cynicism.

It was a magical thing.

"Let's dance," I said, falling in line with the rest of the locals as I placed my hands behind my head and shook my hips.

"You're kidding, right?" Shadow asked. "This is the most ridiculous song ever."

"Look at the irony of it. We can enjoy one of the shittiest songs in one of the most beautiful countries in the world."

"HAWAAHHH!" everyone turned in unison as we rotated counter clockwise and began the motions of the song again.

"You look absolutely ridiculous," Shadow smiled.

I gestured towards everyone else who had a wide smile on their faces as they moved to the rhythm of the beat. "I see only one odd man out. If we took a video from high above, I'm pretty sure *we* won't be the ones looking out of place."

Shadow turned his head, glancing at everyone around him, before finally giving off a sigh.

"I look like a dick for not participating, don't I?"

"The biggest dick," I replied.

Shadow shrugged his shoulders, fell in line with me and succumbed to the Macarena as well. This was great, I managed to get the leader of one of the most powerful and clandestine organizations

159

in the world to do the Macarena.

Watching Shadow crack a wide smile as he performed the self-depreciating dance routine was fantastic, and what was even more amazing was the fact that he seemed like he was having a lot of fun doing it. It was good to know that underneath the layers of darkness, he was still able to forget about the past and have a little fun once in a while.

Any man that could abandon his machismo and laugh at himself the odd time was definitely one I could be happy with.

As the song finally drew to a close, the streets erupted into cheers and clapping, as if we had finished a live theatre performance. I was caught up in this silly but magical moment, high-fiving the locals and giving others hot, sweaty hugs. When I turned to look at Shadow, his eyes were fixed on me, like I was the only thing that mattered in this universe.

I knew he was going to try and seduce me tonight, and I was going to let him. I couldn't think of anything more I wanted than to feel every inch of him inside of me.

CHAPTER EIGHTEEN

As the door to his hotel room closed behind us, Shadow held me within his strong arms composed of thick-chorded muscle. I brushed up against his tight chest and my fingers found their way to the buttons of his shirt.

I undid each one with my eyes closed, my lips on his. They were gentle butterfly kisses at first that soon became eager. When the last of the buttons were undone, I practically tore off his shirt and my lips found their way onto his smooth body.

I ached for the two of us to be naked, so I could press my bare skin up against his.

My fingers explored every ridge of his chest and down to his perfectly chiseled six-pack abs. He was the epitome of the perfect physical man.

Our lips and tongues danced while our hands explored each other. His fingers moved deftly behind my back and soon, I found my dress slipping from around my breasts and down to the floor, leaving me with only my black-laced bra and panties.

"Christ," Shadow whispered, "You look amazing." His words hit hard, abolishing any possible insecure thought or any part of my mind or heart that wasn't sure how this would end.

"You're not so bad yourself," I said playfully as I pushed him down onto the bed. I wanted control of this alpha male, this secret king of the world.

"Aggressive aren't you?" Shadow asked, lying on his back with pure heat in his eyes.

"You'll enjoy it," I purred as I gently bit his lip. "Trust me."

I straightened myself and undid my bra, taking pleasure in the pure hungry look on his face as I stood bare in front of him. Shadow reached for me, his strong hands cupping my breasts, now full and heavy with need. Shivers ran through my body at his touch and all I wanted was more.

He pinched my nipple lightly and I let out a soft moan as he tugged on it gently, before reaching up and taking it fully in his mouth.

I undid the top button of his shorts, and then unzipped him.

His erection stood tall, pushing from beneath his boxer-briefs. I pulled down his underwear, revealing the full length of his magnificent cock. I gripped it gently in between my hands and felt its warmth as it pulsated beneath my touch.

"You're so hard," I gasped. Shadow grinned and then in one swift motion, flipped me around. I found myself lying on my back with him now on top of me.

"Sorry Virgin, but now I'm in control," he growled.

His hand found the sweet spot in between my legs, his fingers rubbing my mound underneath my panties. Why the fuck were those still on?

Take the damn things off already, I wanted to scream.

As if he were reading my thoughts, his fingers hooked around the side string. Shadow's eyes focused in on me as he ripped them off my body in a seemingly effortless tug.

Fuck!

With my underwear a non-issue, Shadow spread my legs apart

and slipped two fingers inside me and I immediately groaned and threw my head back. As he moved his fingers in and out of me while the pad of this thumb massaged my clit, I shivered and moaned. His touch alone was fucking incredible and I could only imagine what his cock would feel like inside me.

"Fuck me," I practically begged.

"Not yet," he smiled.

His tongue worked wonders around my sex, like nothing I had ever felt before, every gentle stroke driving me absolutely wild. Then his fingers were back inside me and I was lost. I grabbed the back of his head as I shamelessly thrusted my hips to meet his hand.

He made a sexy sound of approval against my clit as I felt the softness of his tongue.

"Shadow…" I gasped. He continued licking every inch of me. I shuddered every time his soft tongue brushed around my clit. As I began to climax, he lifted his head and looked at me.

"Please," I begged. "Fuck me."

"Say it again," he groaned as he hovered over me. I pulled at his massive arms, willing him down on top of me. His solid hard body didn't move. I arched my hips against his erection feeling the delicious friction and screamed with an insatiable need.

"Please…please."

He pushed my legs apart and plunged into me.

His thrusts were slow at first, filling every inch of me, sending my body into a state of bliss.

Shadow leaned down, kissing me with a feverish desperation that I returned eagerly. He gave off a primal scent that was raw and animalistic. It was utterly intoxicating.

He quickened his pace, each penetration fueling me with hot desire. It didn't take long before I felt my entire body seized by an orgasm and I arched my back and allowed the shockwaves of pleasure overtake my body.

"Get on top," he instructed.

I unleashed a deep-throaty moan as I glided down the full length of him and began sliding up and down his hardness.

Shadow's grip on my hips and ass tightened while he told me to ride him harder and faster.

I did.

I felt myself beginning to climax again.

I moaned, shouting out some combination of Shadow's name and something dirty–what exactly I couldn't remember. I was enjoying my orgasm too much to recall anything else but his body, and the electrifying sensation I was feeling.

I suddenly felt Shadow tense up beneath me and he let out a groan of his own, filling me as he erupted.

When he was finished, I collapsed on top of him, and brushed his face with gentle kisses, before planting a long one firmly on his mouth.

He smiled at me and ran his strong hands through my hair, "Well if you were a virgin before, you definitely aren't one now."

I smacked him lightly on the shoulder. "Funny."

"I feel comfortable around you," he said, looking at me with reverence. "It's been so long since I felt some type of peace. It almost makes me want to forget about –"

"Forget about what?" I asked.

Shadow shook his head.

"Nothing, forget I said anything," he sighed.

"Come on you jerk, finish your sentences. Forget about what?" As always, he had piqued my interest, I wanted to know everything about him.

"Forgetting about the vow I made to myself—that I would sacrifice everything and anything to find my parents' killer and ruin that man's life."

"There's something about finding justice that is meaningful and noble," I said. "It can be chivalrous even. But on the flip side, the pursuit of revenge is an obsession that isn't healthy. It can turn even the purest of hearts into hard, black shit."

The look on Shadow's face was an inquisitive one. "I think I know what cliché you're about to lead into," he sighed.

"Can't you find your parents' killer without the entire 'ruining their life' part of it?" I asked.

He shook his head. "An eye for an eye," Shadow said. "And fuck the entire saying of how it makes the world go blind. It'll result in a bunch of eye patches, which I'm okay with."

"I'm sorry," I said sincerely, "I don't mean to lecture you or anything. I just want you to find happiness…to be at peace."

"I've found some of it with you," Shadow said. "I promise, when this is over, I *will* leave it all behind us. Then it'll be just you and me, exploring the world and making love in those places. How does that sound?"

His words moved me like a beautiful song.

"Wonderful," I said as I laid my head down on his chest and listened to his strong heartbeat. "Do whatever makes you happy as long as in the end we wind up fucking on the beach somewhere. In the meantime, I'll wait for you."

"Until the end of the world?" Shadow asked.

"Until the end of the world," I agreed.

We fell asleep in each other's arms and that night, I dreamt of long lost kingdoms, breathtaking ancient ruins, and of a man who climbed up and out of the earth, in search of what he desired most.

When I awoke, Shadow was gone, but there was a note left behind where his warm body had laid beside me.

It read:

Will you go steady with me?
- Shadow

For a man tortured by invisible demons, it was good to know that he was still a goofball.

CHAPTER NINETEEN

I must have had a smile on my face the entire flight back. Abraham couldn't help noticing and commenting on how rejuvenated I looked.

I told him about our dates, the wonderful food, and the Cambodian New Year street party, though I decided to leave out the details about Shadow doing the Macarena. I feared that would tarnish his image as a mysterious, brooding billionaire.

The pleasant conversations with Abraham about my trip and a few long naps made the sixteen hour flight back home feel much shorter.

Soon, Abraham was driving me back to my condo.

"So I take it I'll be seeing a lot more of you and Shadow together?" Abraham asked as he dropped me at the front of my condo.

The smile on my face said it all. "Maybe," I teased.

"That's excellent news," Abraham said. "I had a feeling you and Shadow would fit well together."

We did fit well together, both emotionally and physically. The chemistry we had was enough to turn lead into gold.

"You know, you kind of remind me of someone I once knew,"

he said.

"Oh yeah? Was she smart and pretty?"

"She was the prettiest girl in the world," Abraham said. "No offense Ms. Valencia."

I knew in his heart who he was thinking of—imagining what could have been.

"None taken," I replied, feeling sad for the man. Over the past couple of weeks, I'd grown extremely fond of Abraham and his fatherly gestures. Though he could never fill the void left by the death of my own father, I could still look at him with the same affection.

"Well, you must be tired and it's best to leave you on your way now."

I nodded. "Thanks for the ride. Until next time?"

"Of course."

After returning from Cambodia and experiencing the most wonderful weekend of my life, the transition back to campus life was painful.

The two-hour long lecture on Anton Dvorak and the impact of his music on the twentieth century was as stimulating as a bowel movement and left me feeling drained.

As I sat alone in the library, finishing up my Theories of Harmony assignment, I kept thinking about Shadow and how good it felt being with him. I remembered how sensual his touch was and how amazing our sex had been.

He filled me perfectly.

I couldn't wait for him to return home from Cambodia so I could experience his body all over again. I wanted to taste his lips, to feel his muscles, and to pleasure him like he did for me. Being with Shadow made me feel sexy, which was something I haven't felt for a long time.

He made me feel wanted.

I sat in front of the grand piano in my condo attempting *Gaspard De La Nuit* by Ravel for the fifth time that night. I was growing increasingly frustrated with each failed attempt.

Even though Shadow had relieved me of my obligation to record this song, I still had the burning desire to play it flawlessly. It was my own personal challenge. In order to take my performance to the next level, I needed to master *Gaspard de La Nuit*. Otherwise, I would always see myself as a B-list piano playing hack.

This time, I made it through to midway point before my fingers went off the rails and misfired, creating a few cringe worthy notes amidst the beauty of Ravel's complex melody.

I cursed.

While debating whether I was done for the night or if I should make one last attempt, my cell phone rang.

My phone never rang—not since Justin decided not to speak to me anymore.

I answered it.

"Hey sweetie, what are you up to tonight?" It was Calisto.

"I'm just sitting here on my piano, driving myself crazy."

"Oh?"

"You ever hear the song *Gaspard De La Nuit* by Maurice Ravel?"

"Of course," Calisto said. "It's one of the most complex piano compositions ever created."

"It sure is. I'm trying to master it."

"Any luck?"

"I think I'd have an easier time fitting a tiger in my cootchie than playing Gaspard flawlessly." I sighed.

Calisto laughed. "I love your quirky sense of humor Aria. It's a welcome change from the dry conversations I typically have with my usual girlfriends—which is one of the reasons why I called."

"To listen to me talk about shoving jungle cats into my vagina?"

"No," Calisto said. "I wanted to see if you wanted to go out tonight and part-ay."

"It's a school night though," I said, realizing after the fact how juvenile that must have sounded.

"Nonsense. Classes can wait," Calisto said. "Tonight, you're coming out with me and my girlfriend and we're going to get shit-faced, reject greasy, desperate men that approach us, and get naughty with some swoon-worthy muscle muffin."

I already had my swoon-worthy muscle muffin, and that was Shadow. I kept that thought to myself though, knowing how touchy the subject of Shadow and I shacking up could potentially be with Calisto. After all he was her twin brother.

"So you fuck Shadow yet?" Calisto asked.

"What?" Well that caught me off guard.

"Never mind, it's your private affairs," Calisto said. "I just want the man to be happy, that's all, and if your pussy is what puts a smile on his face, then I hope you throw that kitty at him any chance you have."

I guess that was her strange way of giving me her blessing? "I want Shadow to be happy as well," I replied.

"Great, we're both on the same page. Let's celebrate then. We're going out."

I pressed one of the keys gently on the piano and the note echoed through the condo. "I really had my heart set on staying in and practicing this piece," I replied. "Maybe I'll go out with you next time?"

"Look, it's been an extremely long day in the boardroom handling the family business. Did Shadow tell you that we are in the midst of launching the Inferno, a casino and hotel chain inspired by Dante's works? It'll be a revolutionary experience for all its patrons, and it will be one of the crown jewels of the Tremaine business empire; but before the grand opening, it's been a giant pain in my ass trying to get everything in order. I'm burnt out, I'm stressed, and I need to go out and drink, but most of all, I need some fun people to come with me and you're one of those people."

"Uh…" I began.

"Amazing, we'll be over in an hour for the pre-drinking party," Calisto said. "And don't worry about doing your makeup. I have a specialist that will do it for us while we get some drinks in us."

Before I could protest, I heard a click on her end of the phone, ending our conversation abruptly.

I could see Calisto as being the type of person who didn't hear the word 'No'.

I sighed. I still had a good hour before Calisto arrived and I decided to attempt one more run through *Gaspard de La Nuit*.

About half an hour later and yet another failed attempt, which left me banging my head against the keys, I heard a knocking on my door.

Calisto must have been early.

I rose from the piano bench and headed towards the foyer entrance.

"You're early Calisto," I said as I unlocked and opened the door.

Instead of Calisto standing before me, it was Bitchy Barbie from the gym who had given me attitude the other day.

"*You're* the girl Calisto wanted to invite out tonight?" she said with disdain.

Fuck.

"Well, who am I to judge who Calisto decides to waste her time with," she sighed as she tossed her jacket into my arms and entered my condo like she owned the place.

With her back turned to me, I tossed her jacket outside my door and closed it behind us.

She could pick it up on her way out.

"Nice place you have here," she said as she entered into my living room and plopped down on my couch, making herself right at home. "What sugar daddy paid for this one?"

"No sugar daddy paid for it," I said with half-truths. "I'm earning it."

"I'm sure you are," she made a gesture with her fist and tongue pressed against her cheek, strongly hinting towards the act of fellatio.

However, I could see the lack of common sense in this girl already, seeing as how she raised her right fist and pushed out the right side of her cheek with her tongue.

"Wow, your boyfriend has a right angled penis?" I asked.

"What are you talking about? I don't have a boyfriend," Bitchy Barbie girl said, obviously clueless.

"Never mind," I sighed.

There was a moment of awkward, lingering silence as we both stabbed each other with dagger looks. Despite the soundlessness, I was pretty sure that we were both telepathically screaming the same word at each other.

Bitch, bitch, bitch, bitch, bitch, bitch, bitch, bitch, bitch...

"Well, are you going to stand there like a dumb mute, or are you going to fix me a drink?" she asked.

Actually, a drink didn't sound like a bad idea at all. I needed some liquid Prozac to dull my senses in order to deal with my unwelcomed company.

"What do you want?" I asked.

"I'll take vodka and orange, but not the cheap kind of vodka that a gold digging slag like you probably drinks," she said, not even bothering to look at me. "If it's not at least Grey Goose, I don't want it."

"Don't stress out and give yourself an ulcer," I called out, though secretly I wish she did. "I have Grey Goose."

"Good," I heard her holler from the living room as I made my way into the kitchen and grabbed two glasses along with the orange juice and the vodka out of the freezer. "Make mine a double."

"One double vodka spit-driver coming up," I muttered to

myself. Typically I wasn't this cruel of a person, but I was still jet lagged, and along with the anxiety of waiting for Shadow's return from Cambodia, I had little patience over the past few days.

I should have just poured this bitch the drink she wanted, but instead I decided to muster up as much spit as I could from within my mouth. I even added a bit of hoark for good measure. Her screwdriver was going to be swimming in a sea of my saliva.

After pouring in the vodka, I lifted her glass to my chest level and was just about to spit into it, when I suddenly noticed that Barbie Girl was standing at the doorway to my kitchen.

I felt like a deer caught in headlights, my eyes wide.

She scowled at me, no doubt reading the guilt on my face like a textbook.

I swallowed it all back down, and immediately shuddered.

"What are you doing?"

"Sorry, got the chills," I lied.

"Is that mine?" she asked, gesturing towards the glass I held in my hand.

I nodded.

She snatched it away from me and reached for the orange juice. "I can handle the rest," she said.

After the drinks were made, we both sat back down in the living room, opposite to one another, and sipped our alcohol while staring at each other like two combatants in a squared circle. Neither of us took our eyes off the other, both understanding that the first to break our hateful gaze with the other was the weaker of the two.

After what seemed like hours of me maintaining my death stare, there was a knock on my door, which immediately filled me with a sense of relief.

"I'll get it," I said as I polished off the rest of the drink and lifted my ass off the couch.

It was Calisto, along with a graceful looking middle-aged woman with lemon-colored curly hair.

"Aria!" Calisto said as she embraced me with a warm hug. "How was Cambodia?"

"It was amazing," I said. "I didn't want to come back."

Calisto smiled. "Alas, here you are," she said. "But don't worry, as long as you're in *my* social circle, I guarantee there will be plenty more adventures." She then turned to the woman she brought with her. "This is Kara, my makeup artist. She usually does work for movies and such. I tell you, she can completely transform a person into someone else entirely."

"We're going to be in a movie?" I asked, perplexed.

"You're cute," Calisto said. "Kara's here to do our make up so we look sexed up and ready to conquer the club. After all, there's no point showing our faces somewhere if we aren't the absolute *best* looking girls in the entire establishment."

Kara extended her hand to me. "Aria," she said. "I've heard a lot about you. I have to say, your skin is absolutely divine. You're an absolute natural beauty."

I loved this woman.

"Please, let me take your coats," I gushed, doing my best to give her A-grade hospitality. "I'll pour you guys a drink after."

"Don't bother," Barbie Girl said, as Calisto handed me her jacket. "Her mixed drinks taste like ass."

I rolled my eyes. "You mixed your own drink," I pointed out.

"Whatever," she muttered. "You didn't store your vodka properly or something or maybe your juice went bad. Regardless, your drink tastes terrible."

"It's probably the aftertaste of the right angled dicks you shove in your mouth," I snapped.

Calisto and Kara both gave me a puzzled look.

"Never mind," I muttered.

Kara took her jacket and handed it to me, along with Barbie Girl's which I had tossed outside my door.

"I found this lying on the ground outside," Kara pointed out.

"Oh, geez," I faked ignorance. "No idea how that got out there. Thanks for pointing that out."

"I really love your place," Kara said as both she and Calisto made their way to the living room. "Your style is lovely."

With both their backs turned to me, I opened the door and tossed the Barbie bitch's jacket back outside the door, and then hung up both Calisto and Kara's coats.

"She probably didn't pick out the décor," the Barbie Girl said. "It's probably whatever rich ape that she's sleeping with. Really Calisto, I didn't know you kept such shabby company."

"The ape you're talking about is my brother," Calisto pointed out, "And my shabby company is the Golden Virgin."

The Barbie Girl laughed. "I knew there was a peasant quality about this girl from the moment I saw her at the gym. Even when I was talking to you that night, I knew you weren't worthy of being at the celebration."

"What are you talking about?" I asked. "I don't recall ever speaking with a queen-sized twat at Shadow's party."

"I was the girl in the swan mask, who stood next to you."

Suddenly all the pieces fit together. I should have known.

"Bria, you're insulting my brother and his judgment," Calisto said.

"So what?" Bria said, clearly not caring. "Your brother has always been an idiot, and he knows it. I've told him to his face many times before."

"You only think he's an idiot because he refused to sleep with you that one time," Calisto pointed out.

I snorted. All of a sudden, everything was making sense. Bria was the jealous bitch who couldn't handle the fact that Shadow had no interest in her. Added to the fact that he chose a "peasant" to be his soul mate must have been eating away at her like acid. And the oh-so-sweet icing on the cake was the revelation that the Golden Virgin was the *same* girl, moi, who told her that she dressed like a whore in the gym just last week.

"I don't know what you're talking about Calisto," Bria said, feigning ignorance. "I never wanted to sleep with your brother."

"Yes you did," Calisto said. "He even told me to keep you away from him; that you were like a mad dog in heat."

"Shadow made me cum twice," I announced proudly, deciding that now was a good time as any to rub it in the blonde bitch's face.

Suddenly all eyes turned to me.

Too far Aria, too far, I thought as I saw Calisto raise her brow.

"I'll go make everyone a drink," I declared, as I left the living room and entered into the kitchen, red-faced.

This was going to be an interesting night.

"Your skin is so soft," Kara said as she gently brushed my cheeks with the tips of the makeup brush, applying a thin layer of powder. "Honestly, I don't need to do that much work on you. You have an elegant look—this natural beauty needs almost no work."

"She's not that great," Bria huffed as she sat on my bed and folded her arms.

"Really Bria, give it a rest," Calisto, who was standing in front of my full-length vanity mirror, checking herself out. "I look great Kara, first class work as always."

"You're another easy one Calisto," Kara said. "Honestly, for the amount you're paying me, I feel almost guilty. I don't need to do much with you."

"Nonsense," Calisto said. "I pay you for your artistic vision, not for how much make up you smear on my face. It's those small little touches that really bring out the best in my features."

"What about me?" Bria asked. "How's my natural beauty?"

"Do you mind not sitting on my bed, or cross your legs if you do?" I said. "I'm afraid what toxic chemicals might escape through your vagina."

Both Calisto and Kara laughed at my joke, but Bria sat there in silence, her lips pursed. She was clearly pissed.

I knew I was being cruel, but it was less than what she deserved, right?

After all, I was Shadow's girl now, and I had an image to maintain for his sake. If I was to be the girlfriend of the Lord of the Midnight Society, I couldn't let someone talk down to me like Bria did.

"Did you ever consider dying your hair black, like I suggested Bria?" Kara asked. "I think it'll be quite a good, exotic look for you."

"I did it once in high school but didn't take a liking to it," Bria replied. "With my pasty white skin tone, I got mixed up for Calisto a few times, and we all know that I'm an original."

"More tall tales out of your mouth Bria," Calisto sighed. "No one ever mixed us up."

"Brad did, when he blew you that kiss, which was really meant for me."

"How are you so sure it wasn't intended for me?" Calisto asked.

"Brad was my boyfriend at the time," Bria stated.

"Once again, how are you so sure it wasn't intended for me?" Calisto said with a sly smile.

"Forget it," Bria exclaimed. "Let's just get out of here and go to the club."

Kara applied the final dab of mascara and then stood back and reflected on her work.

"Absolutely lovely," she said. "You're going to kill it in the club tonight."

I took a look in the mirror and was astounded by my own reflection. With only a little bit of makeup and foundation, Kara had made me look like a princess. For the first time, I actually felt worthy to be a part of the upper echelon of society.

"Oh gosh," I said, my breath taken away. "I look…"

"You look the same as you always did," Kara said, "Which is

motherfucking gorgeous. I just brought out a little more of your best features."

I wished Shadow were here to see me like this.

He would fall in love with me.

After regaining my composure, I turned to Kara.

"Are you coming out with us tonight?" I asked.

She shook her head. "My time for partying is long gone," she laughed. "I have a husband and a hyper little boy to get home to."

"As always, the money's been deposited into your account. I'll have one of my drivers take you home Kara," Calisto said as she gave her a hug. "You. Are. A. Godsend."

"It's always a pleasure babe," Kara replied.

Calisto then turned to me. "Are you ready to roll?"

"Yeah," I said. I was filled with enthusiasm. Earlier in the evening I wanted to just stay home and bang on my piano, but now with a dolled up face and a few drinks in me, I was ready to show off the new Aria to the world. "It's been a long time since I hit up a club. I'm excited."

"Well, let's not wait any longer then," Calisto said. "Let's get girls' night started already."

As we headed towards the door, Bria had a look of confusion on her face.

"Has anyone seen my jacket?"

From the second we set foot in the Diamond Lounge, we were immediately treated like rock stars. The club's personal security escorted us to the exclusive VIP area, which so happened to be on an elevated platform right dead centre in the club, overlooking the dance floor. It was as if we were drunken goddesses at the epicenter of the dancing universe and the sea of clubbers—bumping and grinding to the heavy beats of a cute, tattooed blonde DJ—were at our feet, worshipping us.

At first, I sat there in the slick white leather lounge chairs, bopping my head and sipping generously on my vodka. Every time I finished my drink, another one found its way into my hands and I just couldn't say no. Four stiff drinks later, I was standing at the edge of the platform and dancing like it was my first time clubbing—full of enthusiasm and moving like no one was watching.

"Those guys have been checking you out all night," Calisto whispered into my ear as she snuck up behind me and pointed in the direction of two men who were built like trucks.

"They're kind of cute," I said, though I couldn't tell for sure. My vision seemed to have been clouded by the Oval Swarovski Crystal Vodka that clocked in at seven thousand per bottle.

"Let's give them something to watch," Calisto said as she spun me around until I was facing her. Before I could protest, she was dancing with me seductively, her silky body rubbing up against mine.

My first instinct was to take a step back but when I did, Calisto was quick to draw me back to her.

Fuck it. It was time to free myself of my inhibitions.

I followed her lead and moved to the music seductively, following her rhythm. We were two girls in control of our sexuality, and making everyone all around us jealous—including Bria who sat by herself on the couch, staring dully into her drink.

"I think she's bored," I pointed out to Calisto.

"Fuck her," Calisto replied. "I can't babysit her and her mood swings all the time. Take your eyes off of Bria and turn your attention back to Sergeant Sexy and Admiral Arousing."

I did. Both of them were watching us with the intensity of hungry animals, which only served to fuel us even more in our provocative display.

Calisto turned her back to me and brushed up her rear against mine, her arms reaching back and taking hold of the back of my neck. I ran my hands gently down the curves of her breasts, and then held them around her waist. The entire time, Calisto was focused in on the two guys, while the rest of the club focused in on us.

"We're stealing the show honey," Calisto said. "How does it feel to know that at this very moment, all women want to be us and all men want to be *with* us?"

"Pretty damn hot," I replied. "I feel like a sex symbol."

"You *are* a sex symbol," Calisto emphasized. "Make no mistake about it; from this point on in your life, there will be men who will masturbate thinking about you."

"Gross," I said.

"Embrace it. Half the thrill of being a sexual creature is knowledge that someone wants to fuck you—not the act of fucking itself."

"You do know that I'm committed to your brother, right?" I said.

Calisto turned around and faced me again, putting one arm over my shoulder and another around my hip. She used one leg to push apart my legs slightly.

"Don't get me wrong, I expect you to make my brother happy. That's very important to me," she said, "And I know that you'll never break his heart. You're not one to flash your vagina around like a cock-magnet, unlike me. But at the same time no one will fault you if you play the seduction game and steal men's hearts as they lust after you. It's highly addicting."

"No thanks," I said. "One man lusting after me is all I need."

Calisto smiled. "I'm so glad Shadow chose you," she said. "Just between you and me, but I had some strange feeling he would gravitate towards you. You fit his type."

I thought now was a good time as any to keep my end of the bargain with Lincoln and try and steer Calisto's thoughts towards him.

"You never had thoughts of finding one man and settling down with him?"

"Maybe if I'd find one worthy enough," she said, "But for now

I'm perfectly content on tasting a different piece of meat every night."

"What about Lincoln?" I asked. "He seems like a pretty good guy. I saw you guys talking at Shadow's party."

"Lincoln?"

"Yes. He's pretty funny, charming, intelligent, and extremely cute," I pointed out. "I mean if he strolled into the club tonight, I'm sure he'd have half the women eating out of the palm of his hand."

"Granted, Lincoln is quite the fine candidate in bed," Calisto began, "And he does know how to satisfy me, it's the after-sex that puts me off."

"What's the after-sex?"

"He wants me to spend the night, or if I have already, he wants to make me breakfast," Calisto replied.

"What's wrong with breakfast? I eat breakfast. Damn, I don't remember the last time anyone made me eggs and toast."

"I can't explain it Aria," Calisto said. "Believe me, I tried to figure it out before, but I just can't. The more someone pines after me, the more I don't want to be around them. I don't want a man who will look after me—I can do that for myself. I want a man that can break me apart."

"I don't get it," I said.

"Believe me Aria, I don't either."

"So there's no interest in Lincoln then?" I asked.

"I won't say 'never'," Calisto said. "But he's not what I want at the moment—emotionally anyway. Physically, he's a like a roller coaster. You always end up holding on tight and screaming." She winked at me.

The song finally ended and we broke apart our sexy dance. Calisto motioned to the club's private security to bring the two studs over, and they did.

The taller one tried to make friendly banter with me, continuously flirting despite me informing him that I had a boyfriend.

However, he was relentless, proclaiming how he was an all-star defensemen for a hockey team that I couldn't care less about, and how he won something called the Norris Trophy last year. He seemed surprised when I asked him if the Norris trophy was named after Chuck, and if he won it because he punched in the most teeth down on the ice.

I tried to direct his attention over to Bria, who I genuinely felt sorry for. The entire night, she seemed left out and spent most of the time quietly sipping her drink and making herself look invisible.

When I introduced Mr. Hockey Star to her, Bria seemed to perk up, but was devastated when the guy brushed her off and returned his attention to me without even a 'hello'.

"Look Aria, I can feel chemistry between us," he said, as I watched Bria rise from her seat to leave. "Let's just forget about your boyfriend for one night and have a good time. After all, how many girls can say they got to sleep with a Norris trophy winner?"

I was getting fed up. "Look, I don't know where you get this delusional idea from that I'm interested in how many pucks you block with your jock strap or how many hits you deliver on the ice," I said. "But to be quite frank, I have no interest in you whatsoever, so it's best you just leave me alone."

"Why don't you like me?" he asked.

Man, this guy was persistent. I needed to tell him something that would get him off my case for good.

"Because," I began, and I annunciated each of the following words with absolutely clarity, "You're beneath me."

The look of shock on his face indicated that my words had worked, and he rose from his seat next to me and headed towards his buddy, who was busy tangled up with Calisto.

"Come on," the hockey star said. "Let's get the fuck out of here."

"Why?" his buddy asked.

"The girl's a bitch."

"Come on, can't you see I'm enjoying the wonderful company of Ms. Calisto over here?" his buddy moaned.

"Now, now boys, I have more than enough tight spaces to satisfy both of you," Calisto said, as she motioned for Mr. Hockey Star to take a seat on the other side of her. She flashed me a wink, and then began kissing the Norris Trophy winner. Meanwhile, the other guy shoved his hand underneath her dress and cupped her breast while gently kissing her neck.

The security guards at the club seemed to turn a blind eye to the fact that the centre stage was about to turn into a porn scene.

Calisto let out a soft groan as Mr. Hockey Star spread open her legs with his right hand, and then reached down to explore her sex, his mouth still wrapped up in hers. The other guy had already pulled down the top of her dress, exposing her left breast and he began suckling her nipple.

Surprisingly, witnessing this live, sexual display aroused me.

I wanted to reach down and touch myself in order to satisfy the longing ache I felt as I watched the two men ravage Calisto with their mouths and fingers.

Luckily common sense prevailed—along with the unruly feeling that I was being a perve witnessing this carnal act against my boyfriend's sister—and I decided to take my leave. I figured Calisto could manage by herself for the rest of the night.

I exited the club doors and took a deep breath, welcoming in the natural scent of the air outside. I walked towards the edge of the sidewalk, and raised my hand with the intent to flag down a cab.

"We have drivers, you know." It was Bria, who was standing on the corner of the street, huddled up in her jacket, which looked a little dusty from the floor. Her face and eyes were red, as if she had been crying.

I felt terrible. I had said some cruel things to her tonight, which was normally out of character for me.

"Bria," I began, "I'm sorry…"

"Sorry for what," she snapped. "You're Shadow's girl, the woman next in line to inherit the Tremaine estate. You don't get to be sorry. It's your right to trample all over me, if that's what you want. After all, I'm just the stupid bitch with the attitude problem." I heard the self-loathing in her voice.

"Honestly, maybe it's just best that we started over," I said.

"Fuck you," she snapped. "I know you're feeling sorry for me right now. I know you're trying to be the better person, but I don't need your sympathies or your holier-than-thou attitude. I'm perfectly happy if you continue to treat me like shit. At least that gives me an excuse to do the same to you."

"What do you want Bria?" I asked.

Tears were streaming down her face.

"For you to go fuck yourself," she said as she wiped the moisture off her face.

"I've already done that today," I replied. "Now tell me, what do you *really* want?"

She opened the door to one of limos that was waiting outside the club.

"Oh you stupid girl," she said, smiling. "I want what any other girl in this world wants: To be noticed, to be popular, to be loved, to be beautiful," Bria paused, and just before getting into the vehicle, she added, "To be Calisto."

CHAPTER TWENTY

There was nothing more brutal than trying to understand the theories of harmony at eight in the morning while enduring a pulsating hangover migraine.

Today's lecture involved dissonance and its place within modern compositions. Every note that the professor hammered out on the grand piano as an example of unpleasant chords was an assault on my brain and I found myself massaging my temples, like a psychic hack, on more than one occasion.

When it was finally over, I decided to skip the rest of my classes for the day and go home and sleep off this unholy terror.

So this was what being a university student was really like—nights of compromised self-control leading to regretful mornings while sitting through boring lectures.

I wasn't missing out on much.

When I finally arrived back home, I collapsed on my couch, face first, and passed out.

I awoke to the sounds of the doorbell. Bleary-eyed, I glanced at the clock and realized that it was now nine o'clock. I had slept for over twelve hours.

The doorbell rang one final time, and then there was silence.

I forced myself to sit up and stretch. Whoever was at the door could probably catch me another time. I felt like ass and probably looked like it too.

My cell phone, lying on my coffee table, buzzed, indicating that I had a text message. Whoever was trying to contact me was persistent.

It was Shadow.

'Are you home?' his text read. 'I just got back and wanted to see you.'

Oh god, not now. I must have looked like hell and I had dragon breath that could lay waste to an entire village.

However, the thought of not seeing Shadow for one minute longer was too much for me. I desperately wanted to be in his arms again.

'I'll be home in an hour. I'd LOVE to see you then? XOXOXO =P'

My text reeked of desperation but fuck it. I wanted Shadow to know exactly what I was thinking.

'Okay. I'll buy us some dinner while you get yourself ready in there,' he texted back.

Busted.

Fuck how did he know? Oh well, I was starving and dinner sounded wonderful.

I jumped in the shower and cleansed myself of any vodka and sweat residue left over from the club. After I was done, I attacked my face with makeup, doing my best to mimic the styles that Kara had showed me last night.

I wanted to look nothing less than perfect for Shadow.

With my face complete, I finished off my makeover with a pint of mouthwash while slipping into a spring dress that showcased my assets.

In one hour, I had transformed myself from drunken hobo Aria into sexy Aria.

The doorbell rang once more, and I practically threw myself at the door, opening it with the desperation of a deep sea diver surfacing for air.

He looked amazing, as always, wearing a black v-neck t-shirt that fit snuggly against his jacked frame and paired with his ripped jeans, Shadow looked like a model out of a fashion catalogue. His eyes shined as he looked at me.

"Aria, you look…"

But before he could finish, my mouth was already on his, tasting the sweetness of his lips. I wanted to devour him. He returned the kiss, his tongue pushing against mine as they intertwined.

After a long, passionate kiss that left me flush, Shadow pulled away and exhaled, out of breath.

"Missed me much?" he asked.

"Oh yeah," I replied.

I was about to dive in for another kiss, but stopped just shy of his lips as my stomach gave off a rumble that could have been measured on a Richter scale.

We both glanced at my belly for a second.

I was embarrassed.

"You're in luck," Shadow said as he raised a brown bag in his hands that gave off a mouthwatering aroma of cooked meat. "I brought us dinner. I hope veal sandwiches are okay."

I pushed my finger against his lips and hushed him.

"Let's not have words ruin this moment," I said.

My stomach growled again.

"Instead, let's succumb to the allure of your Italian sandwiches."

We sat in front of my kitchen island, the messy but delicious veal sandwiches on our plates accompanied by a glass of red.

"So Calisto told me you girls went out last night," Shadow said in between generous bites. I nodded as I savored the warm, breaded veal in my mouth. I was still a little hung over and it felt so good to get something into my stomach to soak up the alcohol. It was the best veal sandwich I ever tasted—though at this point I could have eaten a crayon and loved it.

I was *that* hungry.

"You enjoy yourself at the club?" Shadow asked.

"Very much," I replied, "Though I could have done without Bria's company."

"Yeah, she's a bit of a head case. I try to stay away from that one," Shadow agreed. "She's rather aggressive in her...advances. But anyway, I'm glad you had a good time with Calisto. It's important to me that you two get along."

"She's a lot of fun," I said. "Calisto really knows how to party."

"It's her form of release from all the stress as a result of the hard work she puts into the family business. She is the main reason why the Tremaine Empire still prospers." Shadow said. "Lord knows I haven't been focusing my full attentions on it. Finding my parents' killer will always be my first priority." He paused to take sip from his wine. "I often feel bad for dumping everything onto Calisto."

"She seems pretty smart and good at what she does," I said.

"Calisto is brilliant. You should see her manhandle investors and executives in the board room. She almost has it down to an art."

"She mentioned you guys were working on a hotel and casino chain?"

Shadow nodded. "The Inferno," he said. "It will be the Tremaine's first big venture into the entertainment business. We used to invest in high tech companies exclusively but with all the uncertainties in the technological sector, we decide to branch out and explore new options—entertainment in particular." He finished the last of his sandwich and wiped his mouth with a napkin. "There's always money to be made when you focus on people's vices."

"I don't know how I feel about having a casino open up in the city," I said. "They tend to attract the seediest types of people."

"It's a genuine concern," Shadow agreed. "But I'm fairly confident we can regulate the hotel and casino in such a manner that it remains exclusive to only the upper class. We're looking to bring in the New Vegas type of crowd while filtering out the rest. Picture it more as a club and hotel, with gambling."

"When's the grand opening?" I asked.

"Construction is almost finished. Calisto has everyone on a tight schedule," Shadow said. "I fear for anyone who misses one of her imposed deadlines. She can get very nasty."

Shadow dumped his empty plate into the kitchen sink, stretched, and then walked towards the grand piano and glanced at the sheet music resting on top of it.

"Gaspard De La Nuit," he read.

"You betcha."

"I thought I released you from the bonds of the torturous task to play this song," Shadow said.

"What can I say?" I shrugged as I dumped my empty plate into the sink as well and made my way over to him. "I'm a glutton for punishment."

"You're a musical masochist," Shadow agreed.

"I've imposed it on myself to master this song," I said. "Only when I have added Gaspard to my performance repertoire can I truly think of myself as an elite pianist, worthy enough of Vienna. Otherwise, I'd just be a hack who just got lucky."

Shadow smirked. "A huge part of show business is just that—getting lucky."

"I want to be better than that," I said. "I *have* to be better than that for dad."

He nodded, understanding where I was coming from. We were two falling stars on the same trajectory. We were both trying to impress ghosts.

"So how's Gaspard coming along?" Shadow asked.

"Terrible," I said. "There are so many hot spots in the song that are finger traps. It's like navigating a spaceship through an asteroid field."

"Like you've done that before," Shadow laughed.

"I've watched enough Star Wars," I said as I rubbed my shoulders while stretching out my neck from side-to-side. "But seriously, Gaspard is becoming a detriment to both my mental and physical health. My shoulder blade feels like it's been stabbed."

Before I could say another word, I felt Shadow's strong fingers kneed through the knots in my shoulders. He did it with such confidence and tenderness that I was immediately delivered into the arms of euphoria.

"Oh Shadow," I moaned as I felt the tension pent up in my muscles loosen underneath the strength of his touch.

"Why don't you get more comfortable and I can service you better," Shadow growled into my ear, gesturing towards the extra-long soft fabric chaise that served as my lounging chair.

My heart skipped a beat and I felt a gentle gush down in my sex.

"My body is yours," I said as I rose from my seat and headed over to the s-shaped chair, one hand leading Shadow behind me.

I slid myself onto the chair and laid face down.

"Do you have oil?" he asked.

"Wow, you mean business don't you?"

"Whenever I do something, I make sure I do it right," he replied, smiling. "Now where's your oil?"

"Bathroom, third drawer," I replied, my eyes focused on his long, dominating stride as he went in search of the lubricant.

Damn, he was gorgeous. I reflected back on the passionate sex we had in Cambodia and felt my nipples turn into diamonds.

"I found it," Shadow hollered from the bathroom. "When I come back out, I expect you to be fully naked."

"What?"

"You don't keep your clothes on for a massage, do you?" he asked.

"Well no…"

"What's the matter? Shy?" he teased.

But that was exactly it.

I was feeling extremely shy.

We shared our first intimate sexual experience together in the heat of the moment. We were in a different country, intoxicated on wine, dancing, and the Cambodian New Year—it was the perfect chemistry for uninhibited, passionate sex. His perception of my body at that time was under the influence of testosterone and lust.

Tonight was different. What if he saw my body again and was disappointed? The magic of that Cambodian night didn't exist in my condo.

The only thing around was me and my imperfect body.

"You naked yet?" he asked.

I was being foolish. He was bound to see me naked again, one point or another. I just hoped that today wasn't the day that the cruel entity known as cellulite decided to pay my ass a visit. I had lasted twenty-two years thus far.

I stripped down to my bare skin—still tanned from Cambodia—and laid on my front on the chaise.

"I'm in the buff," I called out.

There was nothing left to do but wait now, and hope he still liked what he saw.

Shadow came out with his shirt off.

My eyes became hostages to his sculpted body, my eyes zeroing in on the ridges of his incredible abs and perfectly formed pectorals. I had the urge to leap out of the chaise and attack him like a sex-obsessed fan girl, running my hands over every inch of his Adonis-formed body.

How could I—a girl who could barely run one mile without collapsing on the treadmill from exhaustion—be in the same league as Shadow?

"Can you dim the lights?" I asked. Perhaps the darkness could hide my flaws.

"What if I don't want to?" he asked as he traced my body with his eyes.

"Have you ever had a massage with the light fully on?" I asked.

He shrugged, and dimmed the living room lights. Shadow's eyes never once left me while he strolled over to where I lay, stalking me like a panther.

"You look sexy," he whispered.

"You're just saying that," I replied.

"I beg to differ. There are clear indications that I'm very turned on right now." He gestured towards his pants, where I saw a bulge pushing against the crotch area of his jeans.

At that point, I was fully ready to go Tomb Raider and invade the sacred temple that was his body.

Before I had a chance to catch my breath, Shadow was straddling my back as I felt the fabric of his jeans against my bare skin.

A drop of warm liquid fell onto the nape of my neck, and then I felt his palms push deep into the tissues of my muscles, smoothing out the rough knots that had formed from weeks of stress and daily wear and tear.

Every motion he made with his hands was firm, but sensual as well, always kneading in gentle circular motions. Shadow took his time working away at the various regions of my back, starting with my shoulders, and then making his way down—always gentle and never rushing—to my buttocks. As his hands caressed my rear in a sensual manner, I couldn't help but release a smile and a soft sigh from my lips.

Though I loathed having strangers grab my ass, I enjoyed having a lover run his hands all over it.

My reaction to his touch was the indication he needed as he gently pulled my legs apart, opening up the passageway to my sex. I desired for him to plunge into me, fulfilling the ache of emptiness without him inside. I turned my head and caught a glimpse of his muscular frame, working away at my body.

Two fingers gently brushed the outer folds of my vaginal lips and I moaned with anticipation.

Do it already, I wanted to scream, *Fill me with every inch of your cock.* But I held my tongue, allowing Shadow full control to do as he pleased.

I felt his fingers rub the outer regions of my canal. I wanted him so badly.

"Turn over," he instructed.

His wish was my command.

No sooner had I done so, Shadows warm, lubricated hands were on my body, stroking the top of my shoulders and then making their way down to my breasts. He filled both hands with them, and began rubbing the massage oil deep into them while his thumbs played with my erect nipples.

That was more than I could stand, and I immediately lunged for his belt, hungrily undoing the clasp. With a bit of help from Shadow, it didn't take long before his jeans and boxer-briefs were both on the ground and he was naked and on top of me, his hands still focused on my breasts.

I scooped up some of the excess oil, dripping down the sides of the bottles, and I rubbed it into my palms. Then I cupped his massive erection in the palm of my right hand and held it, marveling at its primitive strength. It was pulsating—calling out for me to sheathe it inside my sex.

I began stroking it, the oil allowing my hands to glide over his manhood without friction.

He began groaning and the pace of his breathing became short staccatos.

It wasn't long before he pulled his shaft away from my hands and slipped it deep into me.

"I needed this," he growled.

"Me too," I replied, breathless.

It felt so right to have him slide in and out of me, each plunge a masterful stroke controlled by his primitive, sexual instincts.

I clung onto the back of his hair and wrapped my legs around his waist as he continued thrusting into me, our moans intertwined in a chorus of pure ecstasy.

It didn't take long for the muscles in my sex to clench up as I braced myself for an orgasm that erupted throughout my body, stretching from my curled toes all the way to my mouth, which unleashed a satisfying scream that was guaranteed to wake the neighbors.

Soon after I came, Shadow did as well and the thought of him being pleasured by my body was enough to send me into another orgasmic fit that lasted for a good solid minute.

Eventually I regained my senses after Shadow literally fucked me out of my senses. He lay on top of me, his weight crushing down on top of my slender body, but his heaviness didn't feel like a burden at all.

It felt perfect, like warm armor that would protect me from everything that was wrong with this world.

I smiled.

There was no greater feeling in the world.

CHAPTER TWENTY-ONE

It was another wild Saturday night, partying with Calisto.

With Shadow gone over to New Orleans for some family business, I had decided to give Calisto a ring to see what she was up to. When Calisto answered the phone, she seemed genuinely excited to hear from me.

Within an hour of the call, I was out of my house and into the limo, speeding off to another nightclub. Lucky for me, Bria had decided to sit this one out.

It was a solid four hours of intense, alcohol-fuelled dancing between Calisto and I that scorched the dance floor, reducing everything around us to ash and leaving men salivating at the prospect of spending the night between our legs.

After tossing a couple of NFL linebackers—why did we seem to attract douchebag athletes?—Calisto's way, who devoured them like a carnivorous predator, it was my cue to leave the club.

Despite my protests, Calisto had called Abraham to personally chauffer me home, appalled by the fact that I had taken a cab last time.

A silver Mercedes Benz convertible—I was too drunk to

remember the model but it looked expensive—sat in front of the club doors, waiting for me, Abraham sitting in the driver's seat.

"God Abraham, I'm so sorry," I said. "I'm drunk."

"There's no need to apologize over having a few drinks," he said as he got out of the car and opened the passenger door for me.

"Did I get you out of bed?" I asked.

Abraham chuckled as he diverted my attention to his custom tailored grey suit. "I promise you, if I just woke up, I wouldn't be dressed in an expensive suit."

"What are you doing out at three in the morning?" I slurred as I entered into the car, sat back and closed my eyes.

"I was just finalizing some details on the Inferno's accounts…" he rambled.

I didn't catch the tail end of his reply. Whatever else he said was drowned in a sea of my alcohol-induced sleep.

In my drunken state I didn't recall stepping out of the car, entering into the condo, and going up the elevator, but somehow I wound up standing in front of my door, rummaging for my keys in my purse, which were gone.

Cursing, I decided to try pushing open the door anyway. Sure enough it was unlocked, which was strange.

I always made it a habit to lock all my doors, turn off all lights, and close all the windows before I left for anywhere. My father had engrained the importance of security and conserving energy since the day I started crawling.

Bleary-eyed, I entered into my condo and closed the door behind me. I would have to ask someone about making me another set of keys for my condo and possibly changing the locks.

Too tired and drunk to hang up my jacket, I dropped it in the foyer and went to the kitchen and poured myself a glass of water, draining it all in a single gulp.

After slamming the glass onto the table, I entered into the bedroom to rid myself of my sweaty dance clothes and into some comfortable yoga pants.

I stood in front of my full length mirror and scrunched my face. I looked like a wreck. Sweat and make up was caked on my face and I was exhausted.

And that was when I noticed something shift in the reflection in my mirror. My heart practically exploded in my chest as I spun around and saw a man, clothed all in black, wearing a balaclava over his face and a hoodie over his head.

I screamed.

His reflexes were fast as his hands lunged for my throat, springing with the speed of a coiled cobra. His fingers pushed into the base of my neck, choking me into silence while tears streamed down my face.

Who was he and why was he doing this?

I had never felt so helpless in my life.

The man shoved me onto the bed, where I curled up into a fetal position while gasping for air.

"You smell like soiled pussy," he said, his voice the texture of gravel. "Maybe I'll have myself a turn before I quarter and bury you."

I should have ran, but my entire body was paralyzed with fear.

Come on Aria, don't seize up, I thought to myself. If there was ever a time I needed a bit of courage, it was now.

"Never stop fighting," they always said in the safety police videos. I grabbed an empty glass off my nightstand table and hurled it at him.

I had piss-poor aim and a girly throw and my heart sank as the glass sailed harmlessly over his head, shattering against the wall. My attacker laughed at my feeble attempt to defend myself, his voice filled with a perverse delight.

"Pathetic," he said, lunging for me. I instinctively rolled off the bed, avoiding his talons by inches, and I bolted for the door. I felt something hard, striking me dead centre of my shoulder blades and I collapsed to the ground screaming.

"Run little girl, run," he said with amusement. "The chase is what I savor the most, even more than the penetration."

I was crying hysterically from both the pain of his attack and by the threat of his words. It wasn't until I climbed to my feet and caught my reflection in the bedroom mirror that I realized that I had a knife protruding from my left shoulder.

"I saw your piano girly girl," he said. "Can you sing as well? If I chew off your fingers, I bet you will—a pretty little song from a pretty little girl."

The sick fuck was enjoying every second of this.

I fled from my bedroom and into the kitchen, desperate to find myself a weapon.

"Don't stop fighting Aria," I whispered to myself. "Never stop fighting."

Pulling open the drawers, I grabbed the first weapon I saw. It was a Zwiggler butcher's knife that came with the condo.

I clung onto that enormous thing with complete desperation, both hands wrapped around the handle. My attacker strolled into the kitchen casually, as if he were at his own home.

"What's cooking my dear?" he asked, just before his eyes caught sight of the cleaver in my hand.

He wasn't intimidated. Instead, he laughed at me. I was as threatening as a bunny with fangs.

"Does the little girl want to dance?" he asked, pulling out his own massive knife from his boot. Its jagged bite looked deadly. I wanted to drop to my knees and scream out in fear, but I held myself together.

I had to fight.

My voice cracked as I screamed at him. "Fucker!" I shouted as I swung as hard as I could, but my attack was clumsy and uncontrolled and the man dodged it effortlessly. I felt a heavy blow to my stomach and I instantly dropped to my knees.

The butcher's knife fell out of my hands and onto the floor.

Had he stabbed me? My hands clung onto my abdomen, desperately prodding for an open wound. Luckily, I felt no blood. Perhaps I wasn't dead—not yet anyway.

"I hit you with my left hand as a warning," he said, pointing to his right hand which held the knife. "But the next time you attempt to be stupid again, it'll be with the other one."

I struggled to rise to my feet but the pain from my stomach along with the knife protruding from my back was crippling.

I was at his complete mercy.

I collapsed to the ground in a sad heap.

It just wasn't fair, I thought. Just when the future looked so bright, this masked asshole was going to steal it away from me. Tonight, I was going to get raped, murdered, and then butchered. Oh God, was this real?

His footsteps made no sound as he walked over to where I lay, hovering over me, like a black spectre of death. Out of the corner of my tear-stained eyes, I saw the knife in his hand.

"Are you going to still struggle girly? Or can I have some real fun now?"

"Fuck you," I cried out. "You damn asshole."

"My, my," he said. "Harsh words from such a pretty mouth. Your lips remind me of rose petals."

With a last ditch effort, I tried to climb to my feet again, but a vicious blow to my legs knocked me flat on my stomach.

"A girl should know when to quit," he said. "Let's see if a girl knows when she should die as well."

At least he wasn't going to rape me. I closed my eyes and waited for the sharp bite of the knife in his hands. It's funny, from all the things I've heard about death, I had the impression that my life would flash before my eyes.

I must have been the exception. The only thing I experienced was regret. I regretted not seeing Shadow again; just when we seemed to have things figured out between us. I'd never taste his lips, feel his warm touch, and caress his body ever again.

I also regretted not being able to fulfill the dreams that my father had set out for me. I was never going to be able to stand on that grand performance stage and tell the world just how important my dad was, and all the sacrifices he made for me.

And there was Justin too. I regretted not being able to make amends with him. He was my best friend and it was heartbreaking to know that I would leave this world with him despising me.

So many regrets, and no time left to fix them.

I opened my eyes and saw my attacker's shadow looming over me. His knife was raised high above his head, ready to deliver the death blow.

Maybe I'd be able to see my dad again.

"Get the hell away from her," a voice cried out, full of venom. I looked up and saw Abraham standing at the door way, my house keys in one hand and a gun in the other. I must have left them in the Benz and he had come up to return them.

"These are rather unfortunate circumstances," the assailant mused. "No one else was supposed to be here. It looks like you stumbled upon your death today as well."

"The only one dying tonight is you," Abraham said. If there was any fear in him, he concealed it well. "Do you know who she is?"

"Of course," the man in black said. "She is the lover of your stupid master."

"So you know that if you lay even a pinky on her, our entire organization will hunt you down like a mangy bitch and destroy you. You will suffer."

The man laughed, "Small threat. I will take my chances with the money promised instead."

"Who's money?" Abraham asked.

"It makes no matter. She will die," the man said, "And you sir, are at the wrong place at the wrong time."

I stared at Abraham, whose eyes were fiery like a dragon's breath. He was snarling as he gripped the gun tightly, his knuckles turning bone white.

"I'm not a man of mercy," Abraham said. "Especially to those that inflict harm on the ones I care about. The second you laid your hands on Ms. Valencia, you put this gun to your own head. Make no mistake you degenerate, you're going to die."

The man seemed amused by Abraham's threats. "Old man, do you know who I am and how many people I've killed with my bare hands?"

"I know who you are," Abraham said. "I could smell the stench of a Crow brother the second I walked through the door."

"Then why are you so eager to die? I'll tear apart your haggard face like a—" but before the Crow could finish his sentence, Abraham pulled the trigger. The explosive and harsh sound of gunfire echoed throughout my condo.

I covered my ears and screamed, which was pathetic in comparison to the Crow, who dodged the bullet like some super-human ninja.

His reflexes were unbelievable, moving with the strength and speed of a cheetah. He leapt across the room and connected his fist into Abraham's jaw.

I heard a sickening crack and watched Abraham drop to the ground clutching his mouth.

"No, stop!" I cried out. Fuck Aria, do something. Because of my weakness, my friend was going to die.

I heard the sounds of Abraham gasping for air like a wounded animal and it broke my heart. Meanwhile the asshole was hovering over him like a black phantom, laughing with perverse amusement.

"It must be hard to sound brave, now that you have a broken jaw," the Crow said. "I don't believe I like the sound of your yelping. It reminds me of a puppy I once had, who didn't know when to shut up. I killed him with a hammer and a butter knife. I can do the same for you."

Abraham struggled to his feet but a violent kick to his gut sent him crashing against a wall. The picture of a Parisian inspired vogue sketch I had hung crashed onto the ground, shattering the glass all around him.

The Crow walked over and inspected the wall that Abraham's body had struck.

"This is a well-built condominium," he said. "Usually when I toss my victims against walls, they break through the drywall. You must be hurting like a bitch."

While the Crow was ranting, he failed to notice Abraham grab a broken piece of glass from the ground. His grip was tight as it cut through his hands, droplets of blood trickling to the ground.

Abraham lunged at the Crow's stomach but the assassin had telegraphed the attack and deftly spun away, smashing his boot against Abraham's hand, grinding the broken glass into his flesh. Abraham howled with pain.

It was more than I could stand.

I struggled to my feet, enduring the sharp pulsing pains across my abdomen and shoulder blades.

Come on Aria, I thought. *Abraham needs my help. I've had cramps worse than this.*

I reached for the weapons within my reach. This guy was fast and smart, but with a bit of creativity, hopefully I could surprise him.

Meanwhile the Crow was taking great pleasure in tormenting Abraham, slapping him across the face with a back hand repeatedly. Every strike must have been excruciating considering Abraham's jaw was mangled.

"Fuh…fuh…fuh," I heard Abraham mutter through staggered breaths.

"You seem surprised," the Crow continued to rant. He was distracted making it the opportune time to strike.

He continued taunting Abraham. "When you face a Crow, there can be no result other than your complete and utter—"

I attacked him from behind. Even though I crept up on him silently, he was still aware of my presence through some unnatural sixth sense. His right hand gripped my wrist which was raised above my head, the butcher knife in hand, longing to shear the flesh of this bastard.

"Why Ms. Valencia, I am surprised at your continual efforts to struggle. Perhaps I should dispose of you now," he mused. "You are quite the pest."

"You talk too fucking much," I cried out. What the Crow didn't see was Abraham's gun in my left hand, concealed behind my back. With the weapon still held behind me, I turned ever-so-slightly so that the gun was pointing directly at his stomach and I pulled the trigger, the explosive sound of the gunshot echoing throughout my condo.

I stared deep into the Crow's eyes, wide with shock, and found satisfaction in knowing that an ordinary girl like me had bested him.

As he sank to the ground, I spat on him for good measure.

"Maybe if you finished the job instead of indulging in your ridiculously stupid soliloquies, I wouldn't have just fucked you in the stomach with a bullet," I said, aiming the gun at his head.

He tried to speak, but all that came out was a gurgle. I looked down at his wound and saw wetness pooling around the black fabric of his jumpsuit.

"I don't want to do this," I said, closing my eyes. But I had no choice. I had to save Abraham and myself. My hands were trembling and I hesitated for a moment. Was I ready to take another person's life? I suddenly felt a gentle hand rest upon my shoulder.

Abraham was standing behind me, his wounded hand buried underneath his suit jacket. Blood streamed down the corner of his mouth, and he looked at me with glistening eyes and shook his head.

"Du-du-dun't."

His hands reached for the gun, gently prying it away from me.

"H-h-hands fu-fu-fuh mus-si-sic." Abraham clutched the gun with his good hand and pointed it at the Crow's head. Instinctively I looked away.

My stomach wasn't made for this sort of thing.

Even though I was anticipating it, I still jumped at the sounds of the gun roaring. When I turned back around, the Crow was dead, and Abraham stood there like a man who had just been tortured.

I rushed over to him and wrapped his arm around my throbbing shoulder—knife still protruding from it—supporting the weight of his frail body as it threatened to crumple to the floor.

"Come on Abraham, you're alright," I said. "I'll get you to the hospital and they'll fix us."

Abraham nodded slowly as we made our way out of my condo and towards the elevator. I frantically smashed the button with my finger, cursing that the elevator wasn't here ten seconds ago.

"You're a brave and foolish old man," I said, keeping some type of conversation going. I was afraid that if he lost consciousness, he wouldn't wake up again. "You must have been quite the stud forty years ago."

I felt him slump further to the ground, but I used all my strength to hold him up. He looked at me with glazed eyes while his mouth was bloody, battered, and out of place. I had the urge to go back to the condo and put more bullets into the fucking dead bastard's skull.

Finally the elevator arrived and I half carried, half dragged Abraham into it.

"Do you want me to call anyone?" I asked. "Shadow maybe?"

Abraham shook his head. He tried to talk but I was quick to shush him.

"You don't need to say anything. I'll take care of you. I promise."

He looked at me affectionately, as if my words had brought him peace. He closed his eyes and tears streamed down their corners.

"Come on, no need to get sentimental on me," I said. "It's my turn to look after you from now on. Both Shadow and I will. Does that sound good?"

He nodded.

And then the elevator doors opened and there was an explosion of light and sound that assaulted my senses.

When I had regained myself, Abraham was lying dead on the floor, a bullet wound straight through his heart.

CHAPTER TWENTY-TWO

My father had died in a hospital bed in a tremendous amount of pain. I almost wished for his death to come sooner, just so he no longer suffered.

For the most part, I had held myself together, comforting him and talking to him, bringing up delightful stories from the past. In between bouts of pain, his eyes seemed to sparkle when I reminded him of pleasant memories from my childhood; like when he took me on a pony ride and I screamed throughout the entire thing or when he made me my Halloween costume—a princess—which made me look like a walking toilet roll.

I had stayed strong for him during his last moments on earth, never once shedding a tear. I needed him to know that as much as I loved him, I would be okay when he left me. It was only after he died that I lost my shit, screaming like a banshee until my throat was raw.

Death was never an easy thing to accept, but in the case of my father, at least he was at peace when he died.

The bullet that killed Abraham on the other hand was cruel and blindsided us completely. My stomach rushed to my throat and I stood there with my mouth open, stunned by the brutal slaying.

"Is my brother dead?" asked the man who had murdered

Abraham. I looked up with red eyes and stared at the killer, who was dressed in the same outfit as the Crow, but all in white.

I tried to speak but my voice had left me. I dropped to my knees and cradled Abraham's dead body in my hands.

"Answer me you dumb bitch, is my brother dead?" the White Crow asked as he pointed a gun straight at my head. I ignored him as I held Abraham's lifeless body. He deserved better than a bullet through his heart. Abraham had saved my life.

"Last time I ask, before I put one in your head. Is my brother dead?"

"Eat shit," I cursed, in between sobs. "Your brother deserves the death we gave him."

"Bullshit. How can an old man and a dumb bitch survive a fight with the Black Crow?"

"Because he was a cocksucker, that's why," I spat.

The look in the murderer's eyes was full of malice. There was no doubt that he was going to pull the trigger.

For the second time tonight, I was on my knees at the mercy of another man. I closed my eyes and waited once more for death, but it never came.

"Drop your weapon and put your hands in the air!"

I turned to see several police officers standing at the entrance of the condo, guns locked onto the killer.

"Another time bitch," he spat before dashing for the emergency exit. A volley of bullets flew at him, but he managed to dodge them as if they were snowballs thrown by children. He was faster than his brother.

A few cops pursued him while a couple stayed behind, examining the scene.

"We have at least four dead at the Metropolitan Condo," one of them radioed in. My gaze followed one of the officers, who examined the body of the hotel's concierge, still sitting in his swivel chair behind the desk, a single bullet hole through his head.

At the entrance two security guards were lying in a pool of their own blood, eyes wide and mouth agape.

"Miss, are you alright?" one of the cops asked me. I looked up at him, shook my head and unleashed a howl as I clung onto Abraham's body.

I closed my eyes and couldn't help but remember all the warm moments we shared together, the pleasant exchanges and conversations that touched my heart and made me happy to have a friend like him.

"You have a knife in your back. Let's get you to the hospital," the officer continued to drone in the background.

"I don't need anything from you!" I screamed. "Just find the asshole and kill him. Just kill him."

Everything that happened after was a blur—the trip to the hospital, the examination by the paramedics and doctors, and the statements the detectives took from me.

The one thing I did remember clearly was Shadow appearing in my private room at the hospital, several hours later, his fists clenched and a pensive look on his face. There was something about his presence that both comforted and terrified me.

"Shadow," I said, acknowledging his presence.

"Are you hurt?" he asked me.

"A few bruised ribs and thirty-two stitches in my shoulder to patch up the knife wound in my back," I said. "Hurts like a bitch but I'm not dead yet."

He stood up and examined my wounds for a moment and then kissed me on the forehead before sitting back down.

"I'm so sorry. I wish I could take the pain away. When I heard about the attack, I rushed back as fast as I could. I needed to know that you were okay. I need to know that you were safe."

"I'm safe with you around," I replied.

"Abraham…" Shadow began. "Did he suffer?"

I shook my head.

Shadow collapsed in the seat in front of my bed and leaned forward, resting his elbows on his knees as he exhaled.

After a moment of silence, he finally said, "That's good."

"If it wasn't for him, I would be dead," I said. "Abraham fought to protect me. He saved my life."

"The old man always did have fight in him," Shadow said with a forced smile. Despite the calmness in his voice, I could see that he was hurting deep inside.

Abraham was a guardian to Shadow. What kind of cruel world was it where a man suffered the loss of not one, but two fathers?

"I'm sorry Shadow," I began.

"Why are you sorry?" he replied with tenderness in his voice. "You weren't the one who killed him."

"I know he was close to you," I said, suddenly finding myself crying. "He was a good friend to me as well. He meant a lot to me."

"He did tell me that you had his daughter's smile," Shadow said. The sound of his voice cracking was unmistakable. I watched as he rose from his seat and stared out the window, his back turned to me. "The fucker who did this will pay. I've already put a hit out on the White Crow. With the vast network that the Midnight Society has, it's only a matter of time before he's caught."

"His brother tried to kill me," I said. "I shot him in the stomach and Abraham put the final bullet through his head. The Black Crow is dead."

Shadow turned to me, a look of surprise on his face.

There was a moment of silence as Shadow seemingly thought of something to say. Finally, he spoke. "Good," he said. "You did good."

"Why would anyone want to hurt me?" I asked.

"Because I'm the idiot who ended up choosing you," Shadow replied. "I was reckless and stupid. I should have known that if the Midnight Society was targeted, your life would be in danger without the backing of a recognized family name. I was selfish for selecting you and for that, I can't apologize enough."

"I see," I replied, staring at his silhouette by the window, the bright moonlight illuminating the room in a pale blue glow. "Do you feel anything between us Shadow? Do you have strong feelings for me?"

Shadow nodded. "Of course I do."

"Will you protect me?" I replied.

"You know I will."

I rose slowly from the hospital bed, stripping away the covers, and made my way towards him. My hands found his and they intertwined.

"I love you Shadow," I said. "I need to be with you. It's what's keeping me alive right now."

He nodded.

"I'm just so sorry about Abraham," I said, tearing up again.

"It's not your fault," Shadow said. "I'll find the White Crow and the person responsible for hiring them, and I will obliterate them."

"I'm tired," I said, suddenly feeling sleep overtake me.

"I'll take you home," Shadow said.

"They won't let me leave the hospital."

"They can and they will," Shadow said. "I'll make sure of it."

I felt Shadow lift me up into his arms, carrying me as if I were as light as a pillow.

"Can you take me back to your place?" I asked. "I don't feel like sleeping alone tonight."

He nodded, and like a fictional hero from a movie, he whisked me away from the hospital, stealing me from the clutches of the night's horrific events.

CHAPTER TWENTY-THREE

I always thought sex was more intense and gratifying when emotions were running high. With my ex-boyfriend, it was after we had our all-too-frequent fights. A lot of times, the issues we fought over were never resolved, and instead we'd both dive headfirst into mind numbering dirty talking sex.

Tonight, as Shadow lay me on the bed—his lips caressing every inch of my body—I was experiencing another type of raw emotion: Sadness.

While wrapped in his arms, I wanted to forget about the attempt on my life and the bullet that brutally killed Abraham.

In some ways, I thought Shadow needed a temporary escape as well, and he had chosen my body to provide it.

His lips found my hard nipples and I let out a sigh as I ran my hands through his soft, dark hair. Shadow's hands found the warmth of my sex which longed for his smooth touch.

After he pleasured me with his delicate fingers while suckling my breasts, he turned me over, his lips finding the nape of my neck and working its way down the length of my spine.

Instinctively I got on my knees, grabbed the headboard of his king-sized bed with both hands, and arched my back, readying myself to receive him.

His strong hands found the curves of my ass and I practically screamed with delight when his full length slipped inside of me. His hands moved up to my waist as he held me firmly, his raw power exuberating from his touch.

Shadow's thrusts were slow at first, sheathing his full length inside of me. I continued to groan and found myself sliding back and forth in a steady rhythm, countering his thrusts with a rhythm of my own.

Our physical union intensified as he began pumping faster—the feeling of euphoria so intense that I had to grip the headboard of the bed, slamming it repeatedly into the wall with every thrust of his.

"Fuck me Shadow," I moaned. I closed my eyes as his hard flesh satisfied me in every conceivable way.

I felt him tug gently on the back of my hair and that drove me wild. He was displaying his dominance and I allowed him to. I straightened my body out even more so he could fill every inch of me. I felt the tip of his manhood push against my G-spot and it wasn't long before a mind-bending orgasm seized my entire body— my muscles down below clenching tightly around his length.

I moaned with delight, begging for him not to stop.

Eventually he erupted and let out a loud groan as he unleashed his pleasure, filling me with hot cum.

Afterwards I rested my head on his massive chest and wrapped my arms around his body, listening to the sounds of his steady breathing.

The aches from my wounds were returning, but I didn't care. It was worth it to have Shadow once again.

"The stitches on my shoulder must look hideous," I said. "Probably makes me look like some Frankenstein woman."

"You're as sexy as ever," Shadow said. "Your scar is a reminder of how strong and dangerous you are. You killed a Crow."

I sighed and closed my eyes, recalling the events of my near-demise.

Death never did get its clutches on me, but Abraham on the other hand…

I looked up to see Shadow lost in thought. No doubt he was thinking about the old man as well.

"It's okay to cry in front of me," I said. "I was never one for this macho heart of stone bullshit. Men have emotions too."

Shadow shook his head. "I have no time for tears. I need to find out who hired the Crows and destroy him."

"Does the Midnight Society have enemies?" I asked.

Shadow practically snorted. "Every day the Midnight Society makes enemies," he said. "I've lost track the number of times in our organization's history that we went to war."

"Is that what's going to happen? War?"

Shadow nodded. "One of the council of seven is dead, murdered by a Crow. They also took a shot at you and nearly succeeded. If this doesn't spell out war, then the word's not in the dictionary."

"People are going to die aren't they?" I asked.

"Yes. Being a part of the Midnight Society, you get used to it," he said. "In our world, death is as common as the rising of the sun."

The funeral for Abraham was two days later. As people gathered around his solid oak coffin, watching it descend slowly into the earth, I couldn't help but feel that the weather was too nice for such an occasion. How could the clear blue sky smile down on us with a bright yellow sun, when Abraham was sealed in a casket, ready to decay in the earth for the rest of eternity? It just wasn't fair.

I sat by Shadow's side—first row dead center—as the ceremony took place. Words were spoken by several of the key members of the council. Takeshi gave a particularly beautiful speech, comparing the life cycle of man to that of a cherry blossom tree. Meanwhile, Shadow remained in his seat, his sunglasses making him seem distant and cold.

He was shutting down, both mentally and emotionally. Being the leader of our organization, he couldn't show any signs of weakness. I felt sorry for him.

A person should always be allowed to grieve for their loved one.

When Abraham was finally buried, the massive crowd made their way towards the funeral home—though it was more like a funeral mansion given the size of it.

I looked over at Shadow and squeezed him gently on the arm. His face was a mask of stone, hiding all his emotions underneath a grim exterior.

I wanted to say something to him but decided that silence was probably best at the moment.

He was lost in his own dark world, one that was haunted by the death of his parents, and now Abraham. It was a place I could never understand.

Takeshi strolled over to us and bowed his head.

"I know how much he meant to you," he said. "He was and always will be a man that has my respect."

"He was the last of the Constantines," Shadow said. "It's sad to know that the legacy and future of his house has now ended."

"A new house will have to rise and take his spot," Takeshi agreed. "Perhaps we should start this dialogue with the rest of the council sooner rather than later."

"I've already chosen my candidate," Shadow said.

"You made the decision without consultation from the rest of the council?"

"I didn't believe I needed council approval to make my decisions," Shadow said.

"You don't, but out of respect you need to take their considerations as well," Takeshi said.

"We have more important things to worry about, such as finding out the identity of the fucker who hired the Crows."

Takeshi turned his attention to me, amused. "Aria the Crow Killer," he said.

"What?" I asked, surprised. Out of all the nicknames I owned, Crow Killer was definitely at the top of the list of being bizarre.

"It's the name that's been circulating amongst our members over the past couple of days," Takeshi said, "Aria the Crow Killer."

"Can't say I'm a fan of it," I replied. "And why do I need a nickname? First I'm the Golden Virgin and now I'm the Crow Killer?"

"Trust me, the Crow Killer is a name you can take great pride in having," Takeshi said. "The Crow brothers are notorious assassins with the reputation of being both brutal and effective. Just to hire one Crow can cost an average man a whole year's salary, let alone both. Up until your encounter with the Black Crow, they have never failed to fulfill a contract, but somehow you managed to kill one of them. We are in complete awe of that accomplishment."

"I wasn't the one who killed the Black Crow," I said. "It was Abraham. He risked his life for me."

Much to my relief, Shadow interrupted our discussion of murderous assassins. It was something I wanted to forget.

"It looks like the council's waiting for us," he said.

At the top of the hill, where the funeral home was, stood Calisto, Lincoln, Donald Huff, and Brevin West.

Lucien was noticeably missing.

"Let's not keep them waiting," Takeshi said.

"Should I leave you guys alone?" I asked. I was tired and the last thing I wanted was more council scrutiny.

Shadow shook his head. "Our discussion today starts with you."

Fuck.

"We're at war," Shadow stated. "Aria was viciously attacked by the Crows two nights ago and it was only because of Abraham's intervention that she wasn't killed. Abraham…"

His voice staggered for a moment. The rest of us, seated in a large circle reminiscent of an AA meeting, listened intently.

"That old man always had fight in him," Brevin said, finally cutting through the silence. He cast his eyes over to me. "I'm still stunned that a girl, who dedicated her hands for the ivory keys, and an old white man, specializing in Chinese food, had enough grit in them to take down a Crow. I never thought it could happen."

"I can do more with my hands than just play the piano you know," I stated.

"My words weren't meant to offend," Brevin said. "I'm just stunned by what you two did. Up until now, I thought the Crows were practically inhuman."

"Am I the only one who notices the obvious?" Calisto asked. "Where the hell is Lucien?"

Takeshi cleared his throat and leaned back in his chair. "I guess now's the perfect time to discuss an investigation I was conducting after the Crows had attacked Aria," he began. "One of the main concerns is just how did the Black Crow enter into Aria's condo unit? The building itself is a fortress in terms of security."

"The bodies of several security guards and the concierge were discovered after the police did their sweep of the place," Donald said. "Pitting a Crow brother against a typical security guard is the same as tossing a wolf into a Mexican cockfight."

"Yes, but as far as entering into Aria's suite, the security system behind those doors is a vault. There are two methods of security to her entering. The first is her key to the door, and the second is the operator who unlocks the door for her after a visual confirmation."

"What visual confirmation?" I was surprised. I thought a key to get in was all I needed.

"You don't see it but there's a camera positioned right over your door," Shadow said. "When you insert your key into the lock, it sends a signal to an operator indicating your presence. The only way that door is opening is after the operator sees you and releases the remote locks on your door."

"What the fuck?" I was stunned. "So all this time I enter and leave my place, someone is watching me?"

"Yes," Shadow said.

Good lord. I tried to recall if I had ever done something visually embarrassing in front of my door such as fixing my bra or scratching an itch in my nether regions.

I hated the thought of being watched, and more vexing, being controlled.

"I don't appreciate having someone else dictate whether or not I can enter or leave my place and spying on me," I said. "I'm not the kind of girl that does well in front of cameras."

"They only monitor you entering," Shadow said. "It was only meant to keep enemies out of your place."

"So can I point out the obvious that your little security system didn't work and someone *still* managed to get inside?"

"Which is why we're all surprised," Takeshi said. "Our houses all use the same system by Skycom Security Inc. To have yours compromised puts the rest of us at risk as well."

"I assume you've investigated Skycom?" Shadow asked.

Takeshi nodded. "I've had my people find out who was operating the system that night. It's plausible an employee could have been bribed. With a bit of creative investigations into Skycom's log books, I discovered the name of the individual who was monitoring Aria's condo that night. Jason Weathers."

"Great, so we find Jason, lock him in a room and grill him about who paid him off," Brevin said.

Takeshi leaned forward in his seat. "My investigators already found him," he said, a grim expression on his face. "He hung himself last night."

"I'll get the police reports immediately," Donald sighed.

"The suicide has not been reported yet. My people left the scene untouched," Takeshi said. "But we can all come to the conclusion that Jason Weather's demise has been staged."

"So now what?" Calisto asked. "The mastermind has covered his tracks. Seeing as how we all have Skycom Security at our places, we've put ourselves in the jackpot."

"I've conducted my own investigation into Skycom's business. Just last year, their company was purchased by an overseas media communications firm," Takeshi continued.

Shadow smiled. "You solved the puzzle already, haven't you?"

Takeshi nodded grimly. "The communications firm that purchased Skycom is Blueleaf Inc, the same corporation that broadcasts and televises all of Kingdom United soccer games in the U.K."

"Lucien," Shadow spat. "That mother fucker."

"He's betrayed us," Takeshi confirmed. "Now the question is how do we approach this? Lucien knows the inner workings of the Midnight Society and all our weak points."

"We find him and we put his head on a spike," Brevin said, his voice filled with contempt.

"That's probably what Jesus would do," Lincoln leaned back in his chair and smirked, no doubt taking a jab at the fact that Brevin owned a Christian media empire.

"Now's not the time for jokes," Calisto said. "This is some serious shit that's happening here."

"I can't help myself," Lincoln said. "Consider it a defense mechanism for nervousness and anxiety. Some people have irritable bowels, I make wisecracks. Which do you prefer?"

Calisto ignored him and turned her attention to Shadow. "What should we do? It's been a long time since the Midnight Society faced an enemy that's one of our own."

I could see the gears were spinning inside Shadow's head as his eyes glanced over each member of the council. Finally he spoke.

"First thing we need to do is reinforce our defenses," he replied.

"Security to our homes and family is the first priority. We gut every single piece of Skycom equipment, down to the wire, and install a third party system. Calisto, I'll leave it to you to find us a reliable company to provide us with the physical security we need."

"I've already got one in mind," she replied.

Shadow nodded before turning his attention to Donald. "I need you to dig up any dirt you have on Lucien. Because he's a resident of the U.K., it'll be difficult to hit him on American soil, but find everything you can on all the key players in Lucien's organization. If they're American, do whatever you need to do to temporarily hold them in a cell. Any high ranking official in any big corporate business must have done something shady in the past. Discover what it is and use it to lock them away," Shadow instructed. "Meanwhile, pull all our resources over in the U.K. and see what they can do for us. By the end of the day tomorrow, I want Lucien's business empire razed to the ground."

"You got it chief," Donald said.

"Good." Shadow turned to Takeshi next. "Meanwhile, all of our own business assets may come under attack, if it hasn't already. I need you to secure our corporations and increase the cyber security around them. I'll leave the protection of our investments in your hands."

If Shadow was under any duress, it didn't show. He was doing exactly everything a leader needed to do. For him to doubt any of his own abilities to lead the Midnight Society was ludicrous.

Shadow was born to rule.

"That leaves the four remaining council members to hunt down Lucien," Shadow said, turning to Brevin and Lincoln.

"Four?" Brevin asked.

Shadow nodded.

"Sorry chief, but I think your arithmetic is a little off," Lincoln said. "Captain Christianity, you, and I add up to three."

"As of this moment, I'm nominating the house of Valencia to

take the house of Constantine's place on the Midnight Society's inner council."

His announcement surprised me and drew immediate backlash.

"Are you out of your fucking mind?" Brevin asked. "Look, you have a thing for cute musicians, I get it. You chose her as your partner, fine—whatever. But now you're telling me that she gets a spot on the council just for sleeping in your bed?"

"Sorry bro, but I have to agree with Brevin here," Calisto said. "As much as I adore Aria, she doesn't have the qualifications to have a seat on this council. In fact, she shouldn't even be at this discussion in the first place," she turned to me and frowned. "No offence sweetie."

"None taken," I said truthfully. I had no idea what the hell Shadow was doing. The last thing I wanted was to become a high ranking member of this dangerous social club. I just wanted to go to classes, play my piano, and then come home with Shadow and fall asleep in his arms.

"This isn't a democracy," Shadow said.

"You're seriously spitting on the family name of the Constantines," Brevin said. "He would be disappointed knowing that you replaced his seat with *her*." He emphasized the last word with disdain.

"I'm going to play devil's advocate here for a second, but didn't Abraham risk his life to save Aria?" Lincoln asked.

No one bothered to answer the rhetorical question.

"Clearly Abraham valued Aria's life over his own, so really, I don't think he'd be all too offended in having Aria sit in his seat," he continued. "In fact, I think the old man was extremely fond of Aria and would be glad to know that his seat went to someone he cherished in the twilight of his life."

"No one is questioning how loveable Aria is," Calisto said. "But come on, we're talking about a seat on the Midnight Society's council here. There's no power in her family name."

"Did you guys forget that I started off pedaling crystal to trailer trash and street walkers?" Lincoln noted. "But here I am now."

"You're an exception," Brevin said, "though more often than not, I think your inclusion into the council was a mistake."

"I appreciate you honesty," Lincoln sighed. "As always, it's refreshingly blunt."

"So girl," Brevin said, turning to me. "What makes you qualified to sit in that seat."

I was quick to respond. "I have no qualifications. Honestly, I don't want to be a member of the council. I'm just a lowly arts student who's struggling to maintain a 3.0 average that's required to stay in my program."

"What about your family name? What did your father do that was special?" Brevin continued his questioning.

I paused for a moment and thought about dad, and all the sacrifices he made for me. I knew what everyone here was thinking at the moment—they didn't deem his accomplishments worthy to grant me a seat as a member of the Midnight Society's pretentious inner circle, just because he didn't make the big bucks.

"My father made me," I stated. "He sacrificed money, power, and the chances of a prestigious life just so I could be sitting here today. You can look down on me all you want, but don't look down on the man who gave up his dream just so I could fulfill my own."

Brevin looked at me for a moment, and then nodded.

"She killed a Crow," Lincoln added. "If that doesn't deserve a seat on this council, I don't know what does. How many of us would have the smarts to survive an encounter with not one but both the Crow brothers?"

Silence.

Finally Shadow spoke. "I made my decision. The House of Valencia will take over Constantine's place. I have no doubt she'll be able to grow the legacy of her family name in time. She already has by ending the life of the Black Crow."

"Fucking crazy," Brevin shook his head. "All of you are fucking crazy."

"Now if we're done squabbling, we have a lot of work to do. None of us are resting until we've hunted down Lucien and nailed his nuts to the wall," Shadow said. "The Midnight Society does not forget nor forgive their enemies."

CHAPTER TWENTY-FOUR

I sat on the edge of the piano bench and allowed my fingers to dance across the keys while music flowed around me. At that moment in time, music was the only thing that made sense to me.

I closed my eyes and allowed my soul to shape the sounds, creating a haunting melody that melted away all the stress that had consumed me over the past few days. While I played I thought of Shadow—the sad and tortured man that he was—and crafted a song that was the epitome of him.

When I was finished and opened my eyes again, I saw Shadow standing at the foot of the piano, looking at me with affection.

"That was beautiful," he said. "Is that one of your own compositions?"

I nodded.

"What's it called?" he asked.

"Shadow's out of his fucking mind," I replied.

"Love the song, but the name can use some work."

I stood up from the piano bench and wrapped my arms around his chiseled body.

"What the hell were you thinking putting me on the Midnight Society's council seat? I thought you wanted to escape away from the entire thing, taking me with you."

"I do," Shadow said.

"Pulling me closer to the action isn't really distancing us from the Midnight Society."

"Do you trust me?" Shadow asked.

"I don't know."

"You should," Shadow said. "You let me go down on you after all."

"Hey, let's not mix business with pleasure here," I said. "Just because your mouth knows how to get a rise out of me doesn't mean I have to agree to everything coming out of it."

"I need you at the seat for two reasons," Shadow said. "The first is having you closer to me means I can protect you from another assassination attempt. Second, I'm not entirely convinced that Lucien was the only member that betrayed us."

"Why do you say that?"

"Despite Lucien hating my guts, he's never had the balls to organize a direct physical attack on me—or those I care about," Shadow said. "I've always thought of him as nothing more than a whiny bitch."

"Well it looks like he's becoming a dangerous bitch."

"Maybe," Shadow said. "But I also don't think he has the cunning to orchestrate such an attack. I've known him all my life. He's always been a spineless whelp. The only reason he's even on our council was because of his father's influence."

"So you think there's a second traitor?"

Shadow nodded. "With Abraham gone, I needed to fill his seat with someone I can trust."

"So you're using me once again," I sighed. "First you were using me as a trophy girlfriend, now you're using me as a trophy council member."

"I'm falling in love with you," he said.

I was taken aback by his words. Was he saying this just to shut me up so I didn't protest anymore?

"Say it again," I said, skeptical about the truth behind his words.

"I'm falling in love with you."

Damn it. If he was lying to my face, I couldn't tell.

He had me good.

"I'm falling in love with you too," I replied.

"Aside from you, Calisto, and Lincoln, there's no one else on the council I can trust."

"Well that's not bad, right?" I asked. "You have fifty percent of the council right there, not including Lucien who I'm assuming you've already kicked out of your little social club."

"Can you pass your university courses on a fifty percent average?" Shadow asked.

"Well…no."

"I can't run an organization on that either. Failure for me means death."

"I get your point," I said. "So what do I have to do as a member of the Scooby Gang? Investigate crazy killers and assassination plots?"

"You don't have to do anything," Shadow said. "Between Lincoln, my sister, and I, we can uncover the entire truth behind this ordeal. In the meantime, just stay safe."

"I want to help," I stated.

"Are you sure you want to get involved?"

"Hell yes," I replied. "You don't need to put kid gloves on me. After all, I am the Crow killer, aren't I?"

Shadow couldn't help but smile. "That you are Aria, that you are."

"First thing after classes tomorrow, I'll do whatever you need me to do," I said.

"You still plan on going to classes?"

"Damn straight."

I could see the look of concern on his face. "It might be

dangerous."

"I still have my own dreams to fulfill Shadow, and I'll be damned if I'm going to let one assassination attempt stop me from graduating this semester. I refuse to be a coward."

Shadow looked at me and sighed. "I'm not going to stop you," he said. "But can I at least send someone to protect you?"

"If I say no, you'll still probably have someone follow me anyway, right?"

"Yes," Shadow said, just before adding, "Have fun at school tomorrow."

"Can you at least keep the guy following me out of sight?"

Shadow nodded. "You won't even know he's there."

"Good. Then I'll allow it," I replied. "I won't lie, I'm a bit nervous."

"I promise you, I'll do everything in my power to protect you," Shadow said. "It comes with the territory of being with me."

He pulled me into his arms and held me while our lips converged. Our kiss was filled with an insatiable urge to satisfy one another. However this time it was my turn to please him.

"In that case, I'll do everything I can to satisfy you. It's one of the benefits of being my man." I whispered seductively. I licked my lips as I slowly undid the buckle of his belt.

If sexual gratification could ease Shadow's stress and take his mind away from his troubles for even just a little while, then I'd do whatever it took to please him.

"I'm going to suck you dry," I whispered.

He closed his eyes as I dropped to my knees and ran my hands over his incredibly hard chest and abs, his muscles tightening and flexing under my touch and I felt powerful yet completely vulnerable to him at the same time.

Shadow pulled his shirt over his head while I undid his belt and tore off his pants and boxers. I caught my breath as he took a step towards me.

"Aria, I need you. I need you now."

The conviction behind his words weakened me.

God, I will never get enough of this man.

I held his gaze as I took him in my hands. His full lips parted as I heard his breath hiss through his teeth.

The sound nearly undid me.

I ran my tongue along his hard length from the base to tip, swirling around the engorged head before I took him in my mouth. He let out a soft moan as his hands found the back of my head.

"Fuck, Aria," he growled. His hips jerked forward as I fucked him with my mouth and his movements became more uncontrolled with every stroke, his hands fisted in my hair. And then suddenly I was lifted off my knees as he carried me effortlessly to the couch, throwing me down. There was no time to adjust myself and before I knew it, he tore my clothes off and was on me, in me, filling me. My knees hit his shoulders as he slammed into me.

I came instantly, the sounds of our union drowned in a sea of our pleasured moans.

Eventually we laid on his couch, my head resting on his shoulder, our hands intertwined.

The warmth of his touch made me happy, but also scared me. This secret society he belonged to, the world he lived in, there was danger waiting around every corner—assassins, serial killers, kidnapping, and torture. On the peripherals of this blossoming love was the hand of Death, who was biding his time before snatching us into his cold embrace.

"Hey Shadow," I began. "Now that I'm a member of the council, can you finally tell me what the Midnight Society is really about?"

Shadow seemed to be drifting in between a state of awake and sleep. However, he still managed to reply to me.

"Not yet," he whispered. "Not yet."

CHAPTER TWENTY-FIVE

I had fallen way behind in my classes, which I soon discovered after the lecture started. My professor had already made it into the Baroque period of classical music history, which was two hundred pages further in our textbook than I had last read.

I unleashed a loud groan, which could have turned Chewbacca on, turning a few heads over in my direction.

As the professor began droning on about Bach and his fugues, I couldn't help but glance around the room to see if I could spot the tail that Shadow had put on me. It was rather awkward knowing that someone was watching my every move. What if I had to fix a wedgy, or something equally as embarrassing?

I glanced over Justin, who was watching me from afar. As soon as my gaze met his, he instinctively looked down, as if disgusted by my presence.

I didn't like the feeling of having things unresolved with Justin. For two lonely years, he was my only friend, and I was still sentimental to that.

Why did he have to go and do something stupid like fall in love with me?

My attention returned to the lecture as I concentrated on taking notes off the board.

There was only two weeks left in the semester and I was determined to see it through to the end. With all the drastic changes in my life over the past couple of weeks, the university was the only connection I had left to the past life that I once knew—the path that I had chosen for myself.

I sat alone in the campus cafeteria, staring at my plate of cold fries and chicken burger. After the amazing meals I had while being with Shadow, University food seriously tasted like ass.

As I pushed around a fry into a puddle of ketchup, Justin snuck up from behind and sat down in the seat across from me.

"Justin!" I was so delighted that I almost broke out into tears. "I missed you."

"Did you really?" he asked, skeptical.

"Of course you bonehead," I replied. "I hated the way we left things since I last saw you."

Justin nodded. "I've been a dick," he said, "And I'm sorry. You just have to understand that it's difficult for me to look at you right now."

I nodded, suddenly feeling a morose ache clenching at my heart. "I'm sorry as well," I replied.

"For what?" Justin asked. "For being true to how you feel?"

I had no response for him.

"I'll always love you Aria, that's never going to change," he said. "Buy maybe after some time it won't hurt so much anymore. You're the most amazing person I know—that's why I fell in love with you in the first place—and to have you completely out of my life would be the stupidest thing for me to ever do. But I just need a little time."

"And then we can be friends again?" I asked.

"I really hope so," Justin replied. "I just need to stop hurting every time I look at you. But I would like to imagine the possibility that I'll be able to get over you one day."

"You can smell my shit, if that'll help," I joked. "Whenever I need to get over someone, I just picture them taking a shit on the toilet and that knocks them off their pedestal. I'm offering you one better."

Justin flashed me an awkward look. "You're a strange girl."

"Yeah," I said. "I know."

"I appreciate the offer to inhale the fragrance of your poop, but I think this is one wound that can only be healed by time apart."

"But you'll promise when you're ready, you'll call me right?" I asked, "And then we can hang out together like old times?"

"Whenever I get over you, I'll call you," Justin agreed.

I leaned back in my chair and smiled. "I can live with that."

Justin looked at me with longing eyes, before rising from his seat. He was about to walk away but paused and turned around.

"You want me to smell your shit…really?" he asked incredulously.

"Hey, you should know by now that I always try to think outside the box."

"Forget the box. You're thinking outside of a different universe."

"Call me soon," I replied.

Justin closed his eyes and took a deep breath. "Goodbye Aria."

I watched him walk away from the table, his shoulders slumped and his heart broken while tears streamed down the side of my cheeks and onto my plate.

"Take you for a ride honey?" Calisto said as the silver S Class Mercedes convertible pulled up next to me. I had just finished my counterpoint theory lecture.

"Calisto," I said, surprised. "What are you doing here?"

"Shadow wanted to make sure you made it home safely," Calisto said. "Since you don't have a car, he's worried that you might encounter some unruly individuals on public transit; people shadier than the usual pocket jerking pervert."

"He really is the protective type, isn't he?" I sighed as I opened the door to the car and entered.

"He sure is," Calisto said. "You see that guy over there?"

My eyes followed the invisible line that her finger pointed to and zeroed in on a man serving sausages from a Bavarian-themed hotdog stand.

"The hot dog guy?"

"That guy is one of the Midnight Society's most trusted killers," Calisto said. "He can turn anything in his hands into a weapon, including those bratwurst sausages he's cooking up."

"Shadow is having me followed by the hot dog guy?"

"Well, not only the hot dog guy," Calisto said as her head tilted over to a couple of mean looking sons-of-bitches hanging out in front of an Asian-inspired bubble tea stand. Their eyes were fixated on the two of us.

"Those guys are Society guys as well?" I asked.

"Well they definitely don't look like bubble tea enthusiasts, do they?" Calisto laughed.

"Point taken," I said. "Man, I'm suddenly feeling like I'm on the Truman Show, where every move I make is being watched."

"It probably is," Calisto said.

"I hate it."

"Welcome to the lifestyles of the rich and dangerous," Calisto said. "Let's roll out before I'm tempted to grab a delicious looking fraternity boy and do some things to them that I'll most likely regret the next morning."

I nodded, as Calisto changed the gears on her standard convertible and we sped off from the University like a high end Thelma and Lousie.

I assumed that Calisto was going to take me back to the Tremaine estate, where Shadow was waiting for me.

On the radio, the rich and earthy tones of Regina Spektor were playing and I leaned back in my seat and decided to enjoy the ride. I still wasn't used to being chauffeured around all the time, but it was nice that I didn't have to endure a long subway ride back to the estate.

"My brother loves you, you know," Calisto said, her eyes fixated on the road. "It's been years since he opened up his heart to anyone."

I couldn't help but smile and felt my cheeks grow hot just thinking about him.

"He means a lot to me as well," I said. "Honestly, if it wasn't for you, I wouldn't have met him. I guess it's kind of funny how fate works."

"Sweetheart, I'm glad that my brother ended up choosing you over all those power hungry bitches—even if it was meant to be a 'fuck you' to the entire organization," Calisto said. "And I'm glad that he's taken a liking to you. There's something about you that's very sweet; very innocent."

"Something like a virgin?" I laughed.

"Yeah," she smiled. "If you haven't noticed by now, I tend to be a story teller when I'm schmoozing the scotch drinking, ass kissing fuckers. Someday, I'm tempted to tell them that sticking their thumb up their asshole is the key to eternal youth, just to see if they'll try it. I swear they're all mindless sheep that follow the trends."

"You dislike the society as much as Shadow?" I asked.

Calisto shrugged her shoulders, while making a left turn onto ninth avenue.

"There are things I like about it—like my massive wardrobe and the luxury of going anywhere in the world as I please—but there's a lot to it that I'm sick of as well."

"Such as?"

"The politics," Calisto replied without hesitation. "Aside from

Shadow, there's not a single person on that council that I feel like I can turn to whenever I need to talk to someone, get things off my chest."

"You can always talk to me," I offered. "I'm good for more than just a party."

Calisto smiled and nodded.

"I'd like that Aria," she said. "You know, I thought Shadow was being foolish when he named you to the council, but I'm starting to appreciate having someone on there that won't stab me in the back whenever there's a bounty on the table."

"What about Lincoln?" I asked, deciding to slip in another good word for him. I watched Calisto's expressions carefully.

"Shadow *does* put a lot of trust in him, but..." her voice trailed off.

"But what?"

"He was once a street rat," she replied. "And you know what they say about street rats."

"Not particularly."

"I won't go into the clichés, but the bottom line, Lincoln's roots involve lying, stealing, and cheating."

"How's that different from the rest of the Midnight Society? It seems like you guys do it under a veil of secrecy while street rats do their dirty business out in the open."

"A good point," Calisto said, "But with Lincoln, I just don't know. Don't get me wrong, he's a nice guy, he's been good to me, and he knows how to fuck my brains out, but I feel like he's hiding something too nasty for my liking."

"Shadow's the same way," I said.

"Yes...he is," she paused. "You do know about our tragic family history and the reason why Shadow's gone all dark knight on us, right?"

I nodded.

"I'm surprised you can accept something like that so easily."

"It's your past that shapes you, really," I said, "And a part of falling in love with Shadow is accepting all the skeletons in his closet."

The car pulled to a stop at a red light, and Calisto turned to me, sadness taking hold of her beautiful visage.

"Shadow hides a lot of the knowledge of my parents' murder from me," she said. "And sometimes, I don't know whether to love him or hate him for it."

"Why would you hate him for wanting to protect you from that horrible night?"

"Because I'm his sister, and they were my parents too," Calisto said. "Fuck, sometimes, when I'm sleeping at the estate, I wake up in the middle of the night and visit him in the study. He's often staring out the window like a zombie, and I know that in his mind, he's reliving those events. I have no idea what he saw that day, and if he'll ever share it with me."

"You've never tried to figure it out yourself?" I asked.

"I know the basics," Calisto said. "I know that my parents were murdered and their bodies were found in the study. As far as the gruesome details and the how and the why, I know nothing. Shadow kept that from me."

"With your resourcefulness, I'm sure you can dig out all the information pretty easily," I said.

The light turned green and Calisto put her foot on the pedal.

"Here's the thing as well," she said, taking a deep breath. "I'm also a giant pussy. Fuck, am I ever a pussy. I'm terrified about what I might discover."

"Well I don't blame you. Having your parents murdered is a pretty traumatic event," I said.

"I see what the details of my parent's death did to Shadow, and I'm scared it'll be too overwhelming for me to handle. But on the other hand, I want to be there for my brother, to support him in all of this. He's all alone on this crusade of his. Maybe if I was there to help him, I can ease his burden; distribute the hardships equally amongst the both of us, you know?"

I nodded.

"But I'm too much of a chicken shit to take that on," she replied as tears began rolling down the curves of her delicate cheeks. "So I wind up hating myself and I'm angry that Shadow shielded me from the truth."

"Your brother is being the man he thinks you need," I replied. "He's taking on all the suffering just so you can be happy and live your life."

"I never asked him too."

"If the tables were turned, would you do the same for him?" I asked.

Calisto nodded. "I'd take a bullet for him." She wiped her eyes with her finger tips and took a deep breath. "Abraham meant a lot to him; he meant a lot to both of us. I'm going to do everything I can to make sure that Lucien pays with his life."

The Benz turned into a ritzy looking plaza, stopping in front of the Velvet Beanery, a trendy café that sold overpriced coffee with the aftertaste of burnt beans.

"I need a caffeine fix," Calisto said, grabbing her hand held purse. "I'll be two seconds. Do you want anything, love?"

I shook my head. I had already three cups today in between lectures and I was afraid that another cup would rupture my tiny bladder. Calisto disappeared into the shop, leaving me alone in the car.

I glanced around, wondering whose eyes were on me at this very second.

The silence and open space made me feel exposed and vulnerable and the thought of being under surveillance was giving me a panic attack. I was swimming in open waters with sharks circling all around me.

"Come on Calisto, get your damn mocha java latte already and let's get out of here," I muttered to myself.

I glanced at the digital clock in the Benz. She was gone for five minutes.

Suddenly my phone whistled at me and I saw that I had received a new text message from Shadow.

'How were classes?' It read.

'Classes were good. I'm way behind. Just sitting in Calisto's car right now, waiting for her to come out of the coffee shop.'

'You're alone?'

'Yah.'

'My sister always had poor judgment. I can't believe she left you alone in the car just to get herself a coffee.'

'Well it's not like I'm a baby trapped in a hot car. I'm sure everything will be okay, especially with the number of eyes you have on me right now.'

'Still, I told Calisto to pick you up and drive straight back to the estate. No pit stops whatsoever.'

'You worry too much,' I texted back, though in truth I was quite worried myself. *'I'll see you soon.'*

'I love you,' he ended the conversation.

I glanced at the clock again and noticed that the exchange between Shadow and I had taken another seven minutes. Just how long did it take Calisto to get herself a cup of coffee?

I should have stayed in the car but I was growing impatient and decided to find out what was taking her so long.

As I pulled open the glass doors to the Velvet Beanery and glanced around the café, I noticed that Calisto was nowhere to be seen.

In fact, there was no one in the entire place, including the baristas that worked the coffee machines. A terrible feeling of dread took hold of me.

"Calisto, are you in here?" I cried out.

Dead silence.

Something was wrong. The right thing to have done was to run back to the car and call Shadow for help, but I wasn't known for always doing the right thing.

Instead, I strolled up to the counter cautiously and took a peek over it.

Lying on the ground in a pool of blood, her throat slit from ear to ear, was the barista, her empty eyes wide with shock.

It seemed like everywhere I went, I was surrounded by bodies.

I screamed.

CHAPTER TWENTY-SIX

I fled back to the car. My mind was filled with horrid thoughts and my hands were shaking as I tried to dial Shadow's number on my phone.

He picked up on the first ring.

"Aria?"

"Shadow," I cried. "She's fucking dead."

"My sister?" He sounded panicked.

Aria, you stupid girl, gather yourself together before this conversation went off the rails for both of us.

"No, not your sister," I said. "The woman working the counter inside the coffee shop is dead."

"Where is Calisto?" he asked, noticeably concerned.

I shook my head. "I don't know. She went into the café and never came out. I went in to look for her, and when I did, the place was empty...the woman working the counter was dead on the floor...dead...murdered...violently."

There was a brief pause.

"Where are you?"

"The Velvet Beanery on Ninth and Front," I practically shouted into the phone.

I needed to calm the fuck down so I could think with a level head.

"Are you in the car?"

"Yes. Calisto had the keys though."

"Stay inside and keep the windows rolled up and the doors locked," Shadow said. "I'll make sure someone comes and gets you right away."

"She took the convertible."

"Fucking hell…" There was a quick pause before Shadow spoke again. "I want you to reach down under the passenger seat."

I did as he instructed and my hands brushed against something cold and metallic.

"Do you have it?" Shadow asked.

It was attached to Velcro straps, which I undid blindly. The next thing I knew, I was holding a small firearm in my hands.

"I'm holding a gun," I stated.

"Good. If any stranger comes up to you, I want you to shoot them in the head."

"Seriously?" I asked.

"Yes."

"What if it's some old woman, asking me to help her open a door or something?"

"Aria, I'm not joking," Shadow said. "I need you to protect yourself."

"Alright, in the head," I agreed. "Fuck grandma."

"I can't even trust my own men anymore," Shadow said. "I'm an hour out of town--too long for you to wait for me. I'm going to send Lincoln. I'll have him over there as soon as possible."

There was a long pause before Shadow finally added, "Stay safe."

"I'll try," I replied.

The call ended, and I sat in the seat, my hand gripping the gun tightly. I was terrified and paranoid and having a weapon in my possession right now was the equivalency of giving a gun to a schizophrenic. I prayed that no one decided to get friendly because most likely, I was going to shoot them at 'hello.'

The next ten minutes were pure agony and I eyed every person walking past the car suspiciously.

Finally, when I saw Lincoln pull up next to my vehicle, I was flooded with relief. I had never been so happy to see someone in my life.

"Get in," Lincoln said, the tone in his voice a far departure from his usual cheery self. I leapt out of Calisto's Benz and entered into Lincoln's Porsche.

"Are you hurt?" he asked me, pulling out of the café and turning onto the main road.

I nodded. "Calisto's gone."

The look of concern on Lincoln's face was unmistakable. He cared deeply for Calisto.

"We need to find her," I said.

"I'm going to get you back to the estate," he said. "Your safety is first priority."

"She left the car and went into the café to get a coffee," I explained, despite him not asking the burning question, "And when she didn't come out, I went inside to check on her and she was gone. The barista was dead behind the counter, her throat slit."

I could see anger flash across Lincoln's face like a lightning bolt, and without any warning, he smashed his fist into the side of his car door.

"Damn it," he cursed. "Fucking Lucien."

"Do we know it's him?"

"Who else would it be?" Lincoln stated. "That fucker has had it in for the Tremaine's since day one. I swear, if he's hurt Calisto in any way, I'm going to rip his intestines out from his asshole."

The rest of the ride back to the estate was in complete silence.

I waited for Shadow at the Tremaine estate and when he arrived, he was relieved to see me, crushing my body with an embrace that was reserved for distant star-crossed lovers.

It was nice to feel loved again.

After making sure I was okay, we went to his study, along with Lincoln, where I told them in detail of every action taken from the moment Calisto picked me up at the university to the point where Lincoln had saved me from potentially shooting someone in the face due to jittery nerves.

By the time I was done, I was exhausted and both Shadow and Lincoln left me alone to rest on the leather couch, where I fell into a comatose sleep in a matter of minutes.

When I awoke again, Lincoln was staring out the large bay windows, sipping on a drink, while Shadow sat in front of his large cherry wood desk, his fists clenched.

From the expression on his face, I knew there was bad news.

"How long was I out for?" I asked.

"About two hours," Lincoln replied, staring into his glass.

"Is there any word on Calisto?"

Shadow shook his head. "No," he replied. "I had a few of my guys investigate the café. They found five other bodies in the kitchen, their throats all cut."

I swallowed hard.

"We'll find her Shadow. I promise," I tried to console him.

"Do you remember seeing anyone or anything that was out of place Aria?" Shadow asked, a hint of desperation in his tone.

I shook my head. "I was in the car the entire time. I couldn't see anything. I'm so sorry Shadow, I know this is my fault," I apologized.

"This isn't on you," he replied. "Calisto should have never gotten out of that car, though she's not entirely to blame either. I was the one who sent her to pick you up."

"The real bastard in all of this is Lucien," Lincoln added, "That tea drinking, scone-eating son-of-a-bitch."

"Have your guys found anything?" Shadow asked.

Lincoln shook his head. "Lucien's condo has been vacated," he said, "And when I say vacated, I mean everything inside is gone. Not even a single speck of dust."

"He's had this all planned from the beginning," Shadow said, rising from his seat. "I've always taken him too lightly."

"I had him figured for a fool as well," Lincoln said. "His yapping alone made him look as intimidating as a cocker spaniel."

Shadow turned to me. "Aria, I want you to stay here for a while," he said. "Lincoln and I are heading over to the condo Calisto owns on the waterfront. Maybe there's something there that can help us."

"I want to come with you guys," I said.

Shadow shook his head. "You've been targeted," he said. "Even allowing you to go to your classes was a bad decision on my part."

"I feel safer with you Shadow," I said. "I'm also not completely useless. I can help."

The two looked at me, dead silent.

"Well?" I asked.

"She is a Crow killer," Lincoln pointed out. "You have to give her credit for accomplishing that much, while others would have just soiled themselves before ending up six feet under."

Shadow seemed in awe of me.

"You're one of the most stubborn girls I've ever met," he finally said.

"Would you rather me be the weak, helpless, and submissive girl?" I asked.

He shook his head, and planted a gentle kiss on my forehead.

"Not a chance."

CHAPTER TWENTY-SEVEN

We pulled into the underground parking garage of Calisto's condo in Shadow's Aston Martin. There were five intimidating looking men standing by the entrance of the building, equipped with black body armor and heavy weapons. They reminded me of secret service agents, minus the black aviators and earpieces.

Before leaving his car, Shadow reached over me and opened up the glove box, removing a shiny, silver gun. He checked the clip and pushed it into the base of the gun, arming it for use.

"You think you'll need that?" I asked.

Shadow made no reply.

The intimidating guards acknowledged us as we approached them. "We secured the entire building," one of them said; a large brute with a shiny bald head.

"You guys did a search through Calisto's condo?" Shadow asked.

The man nodded. "Only a quick search to ensure that it was safe and secure. Everything else remains untouched, as you requested. Just a warning, my guys saw some pretty strange stuff inside."

"Strange?"

"Best you see for yourself."

Shadow nodded. "If you see anything out of the ordinary, run the Detroit police protocol on it."

"Right," the guard replied. "Shoot first and then hide the body."

As we entered into the elevator, I couldn't help but ask, "Was he serious about the entire shoot first thing?"

"During times of war, better safe than sorry," Lincoln replied.

When we arrived at the penthouse, there were two more guards waiting by the entrance to Calisto's condo. He pushed open the door for us, allowing us to enter.

To say things looked "strange" was an understatement.

I felt I had just stepped onto the set of a satanic cult movie.

Melted flesh-colored candles littered the room, burned right down to the stub. The wax bubbled and dried around the edges, forming grotesque blob shapes.

At the centre of the condo was the statue of a nude man, its body desecrated in dried blood and thorns. However the head was replaced with that of a pig's. Meanwhile, all along the square perimeter of the room were crude looking wooden carvings of animal heads mounted on poles, reminiscent of decapitated heads on a spike.

Whoever did this included most of old MacDonald's farmyard—dogs, cats, goats, rams, bulls, and roosters. Oddly enough, it was only the male counterparts of these animals.

"Now this is creepy," Lincoln said, his eyes fixed on the statue with the pig's head. "Lucien is one twisted fuck."

"What the hell is the purpose of all of this?" I asked.

"If there's a message to be had here, they've completely lost me," Lincoln said, walking over to the animal heads and inspecting them. "Grim little bastard, isn't he?"

"There is a message here," Shadow said.

Lincoln raised a brow. "Oh?"

"Animal Farm," he replied.

"Of course," Lincoln said, smacking his forehead with the palm of his hand. "Lucien is our little Napoleon."

"Huh?" I was confused. I had heard about the famous story before, but never read it despite having plenty of opportunities to do so. Instead I wasted my time indulging myself in scintillating romance novels and juicy erotic stories.

"Without going into the specifics, the farm animals overthrow the humans and take control of the farm. The pigs end up running the show, led by one porker named Napoleon," Lincoln explained. "This could be a strange allegory to Lucien's attempt to take control of the Midnight Society."

"It's a poor one if that's the case," Shadow said. "At the end of the story, the pigs are no different than the humans that they try to overthrow."

"Well, Lucien was never the brightest," Lincoln pointed out, "Though he did fool us all."

Shadow walked to each of the animal heads and examined them closely. It wasn't until he reached the dog that he stopped in his tracks.

"There's something in the dog's mouth," Shadow said as he reached down the statue's throat. When he pulled his hand out, he was holding a wooden box that fit into his palm.

"Jesus," Lincoln cursed. From the look on his face, he was just as concerned as Shadow was.

These two men loved Calisto—one by blood and the other by chance—and for anything to happen to Calisto would tear them both apart.

"Are you going to open it?" I asked. Shadow nodded, though I could tell he was hesitant to.

He pushed open the lid of the box and looked at the contents within. His face was immediately wrenched with anguish and he unleashed a scream that was fused with both anger and agony.

I watched as the wooden box containing a severed finger—a sparkling diamond band wrapped around it—fell to the floor.

I wanted to scream as well, but I held myself together. Shadow was in shock, and he needed me.

"Maybe it's not Calisto's," I said. "That could be anyone's finger."

"It's hers," Lincoln said, his face ghostly white.

"How do you know for sure?"

"Because I gave her that ring for her birthday," he replied.

Before we had a chance to mourn, shots erupted from outside.

Shit was really starting to hit the fan.

CHAPTER TWENTY-EIGHT

"Protect Aria," Shadow ordered.

Lincoln nodded, grabbing my wrist with one hand and drawing a gun from his belt with the other. "Stay down," he whispered. "Bullets always have a tendency of flying high."

I dropped to the ground, as instructed, and watched Shadow move towards the kitchen in a crouched position, his hand gripping his silver handgun tightly.

The main floor of Calisto's condo had an open concept, which provided horrible coverage for a take-no-prisoners shoot out.

Outside, a barrage of gunfire erupted in quick succession, followed by screams.

"Shit," Lincoln cursed. "They have automatics. From the sounds of it whoever's initiating this little attack is well armed."

Shadow positioned himself behind the island countertop facing the entranceway. He turned to us, and with his free hand, motioned for us to hide.

I watched him with wide eyes, fear seizing my entire body. I needed him to make it through this. I thought of Abraham and the bullet that tore through his heart and I bit my lip. I couldn't have the same thing happen to Shadow.

"He can't take on everyone by himself," I said. "You have to help him."

"You'd be surprised by what Shadow's capable of," Lincoln said as he led me up the winding staircase to the second floor. He guided me into the master bedroom.

"Quick, under the bed," Lincoln instructed.

"Can I even fit?"

Lincoln sighed and opened up a hidden panel on the side of the wooden bed post, revealing an electronic keypad. He punched in a sequence of numbers and suddenly, the entire king-sized bed folded upwards and the hardwood floors beneath parted, revealing a hidden stairway.

"It's a panic room," he said.

"How did you know about it?"

"Without getting into specifics, I've slept in this bed before. Now get inside and stay safe while I play Sundance Kid to Shadow's Butch Cassidy," he paused for a moment, thinking, and then added, "You'll notice the control center for the condo's security system inside. It's been activated with the passcode I punched in. It's complex, but if you know what you're doing, feel free to have some fun at the controls, otherwise don't touch anything. One slip of the finger and you may inadvertently kill us both."

I nodded and descended down the cold iron steps and into the secret room. The hatch automatically closed behind me.

I've only seen panic rooms in movies and on television before, but this one in particular was pretty impressive. It was *the* Cadallic of panic rooms, if there was such a thing.

At the center of the room was a massive eighty inch computer screen that was surrounded by several smaller monitors. The entire set up was reminiscent of a mainframe computer seen only in science fiction movies.

I took a seat in front of the system and switched on the monitor next to a thin microphone attached to the console. Just because I was safely hidden away in here didn't mean I had to be useless while Shadow and Lincoln were out there in a gun-blazing shootout. I was going to find a way to help them from inside with whatever security Calisto had installed in her condo.

One-by-one the screens came into focus, each displaying one of the rooms inside the condo. The large screen provided an overhead view of the entire place which was digitally superimposed onto an electronic blueprint of the space-aged security system.

The control panel itself was separated into sectors of the condo, each clearly labeled on the console along with the defense system available.

I never admitted this to anyone else, but back in high school I was a gaming geek, especially in those real-time war strategy games. My boyfriend at the time had dragged me into video game LAN parties and despite my protests at first, eventually found myself enjoying them. The control panel didn't seem all too different than a custom made gaming keyboard.

With all the functions tagged, it took me only minutes to figure out the system.

Once I had controls of the cameras, I zoomed in on both Shadow and Lincoln, who were hiding in different sections of the main floor—Lincoln behind the couch that faced the door and Shadow still hidden away behind the island kitchen counter top—both waiting for the attackers to enter.

I watched as the entrance's door pushed open and one-by-one men, dressed in black armor and ski masks, filed into the condo, fingers on the trigger of their automatic weapons.

For now, both Shadow and Lincoln seemed well concealed in their hiding spots. However they had underestimated the enemy's numbers.

I counted eight armored assholes that filed into the room and estimated that the most Shadow and Lincoln could take out on their own were two, maybe three before the rest turned their guns and annihilated them.

I had to do something.

I positioned the microphone in front of my mouth and spoke into it confidently.

"Hey assholes," I shouted. "You have until the count of three to drop your guns and get the fuck out of my space."

I watched as the assailants raised their heads, searching for the origins of my voice.

"One...two..." I began counting. However before I could get to three, Lincoln peaked out of his hiding space, lying on his side, and fired two shots that blew apart the knee caps of one of the attackers. Before the fucker dropped to the ground, a third bullet tore through his skull, ending his life abruptly.

With his position now given away, gunfire was immediately returned and tiny explosions erupted from the assassins' automatics, a hail of bullets tearing into the couch.

I thought Lincoln was finished.

Shadow popped up from behind the island countertop and took down another one of the bastards with a precise bullet to the head.

Six remaining, but Shadow and Lincoln were still outmatched. With their positions given away, it was only a matter of time before lady luck ran out on them.

"Hey fuckers, behind you," I shouted through the speaker system. Sure enough, by instinct, two attackers turned around which allowed Shadow to take one of them down with another shot through the throat. Two shots and two dead; Shadow had uncanny accuracy.

While the other assailants were distracted by the death of yet another one of their own, Lincoln took the opportunity and bolted from his hiding spot, rushing down the hallway and up the winding staircase.

The attackers regained their focus and began firing at him. I held my breath as I watched the bullets ricochet all around him, missing him by inches. It was an act of God that he was still standing.

"Christ," I heard him mutter through the control panel's speakers.

One of the assassins took charge, organizing his men that were still standing. "Hardball, stay with me. The rest of you go and find him."

Three men peeled off from the main group and made their way cautiously up the staircase, stalking Lincoln like savage predators. Meanwhile the other two who remained on the ground floor converged on the island where Shadow was hiding.

From their formation they were planning to take him from both sides. With only one gun, there was no way Shadow could take them both.

"Control panel, flash twenty-one," I heard Shadow shout, well aware of his situation. Was he talking to me?

"Aria, flash twenty-one, now!"

Yes he was. What the heck was flash twenty-one? I scanned the Control Panel and sure enough, discovered a button labeled F21. I pushed it and all of a sudden, the entire screen lit up in a blinding bright, white light.

"Fucking hell! I can't fucking see," one of the men cried out, dropping his gun to the floor, covering his face with his hands.

The other one had dropped to his knees in agony, rubbing his eyes. "I think I'm blind," he moaned.

Shadow emerged from behind the counter and pulled the trigger twice, putting an end to both of them with a single bullet each.

I had gone from an innocent aspiring concert pianist to an accessory to murder. While I was flooded with relief that Shadow and Lincoln continued to survive, my hands were trembling and I suddenly found it hard to breathe.

I was beginning to understand what being a member of the Midnight Society entailed: Shiny things, hot sex, and dead bodies.

Meanwhile, on the second floor, the three men split up,

searching for Lincoln. It was an incredibly stupid move.

One of the assassins entered into the guest bedroom, his footsteps as light as feathers. Little did he know that I was watching him and no amount of pussy footing was going to save this asshole. All I could think of was satisfying revenge for the people responsible for Abraham's death.

I explored the security options for the guest bedroom on the control panel and found something fitting for the situation. With the click of a few buttons, heavy metal doors sealed the room from the rest of the condo.

The bastard trapped inside sprung at the door and frantically pounded on it. It wasn't going to help him.

"Hey fucker, nobody—and I mean nobody—messes with my friends," I said as I pushed another button that began rapidly sucking all the oxygen out of the room. He continued hammering at the door before giving up and running to the window, which was also sealed. It took about two minutes before he completely stopped moving.

With a simple press of the button, I, Aria Valencia—who cried every time I watched the *Last Unicorn*—had just killed someone.

I didn't feel any remorse or guilt for what I did either. While watching him die, all I could think about was Abraham and his heart exploding in his chest. This son-of-a-bitch trying to kill us wasn't going to get any sympathy from me.

"Attention all remaining assholes, and by remaining, I mean the last one of you," I lied, watching as the two separated men stop dead in their tracks at my announcement. "I gave you the chance to walk away from this, but you didn't. Now you're dead."

I watched as Lincoln slowly snuck up behind one assassin, pointed the gun to his head, and executed him. Meanwhile Shadow blasted the last of them into oblivion.

It was over.

I leaned back in the leather chair, closed my eyes, and took a deep breath. My hands were now shaking and tears started rolling down my cheeks.

"Aria, it's over," Shadow called out from outside the panic room. "You can come out now."

I did as he said and flung myself into his arms, burying my head deep into his chest.

You killed a man Aria, the tiny voice in my head whispered to me. *You just killed someone.*

The reality of my actions tore through me like a wrecking ball.

"Is everyone alright?" Lincoln asked as he entered into the room.

"Aria's rattled," Shadow said. "I'm fine."

"Aria, you're brilliant. You saved both our lives," Lincoln said. "I know it's traumatic for you at the moment, but remember, you did what was necessary."

I lifted my head from Shadow's chest and wiped my eyes with the back of my hand.

"I'll never be a victim again," I said, and I meant it. Ever since my encounter with the Black Crow, my life had turned a dark corner.

"For a bunch of hired killers, these guys were very amateur," Shadow said, "Which is probably why we're still breathing."

"Agreed," Lincoln said. "They were very bush league. Lucien always was a cheapskate. It wouldn't surprise me if he used a Groupon deal to get these guys."

Lincoln knelt down in front of one of the bodies. "Let's see who they are."

One-by-one they peeled off the masks of the assassins, scanning their faces.

"You see what I'm seeing?" Lincoln asked.

Shadow nodded as he examined the neck of one of the bodies. "They're gangbangers," he stated. "From the tattoos on their necks, they belonged to the Talons."

"Why the hell would Lucien get a bunch of disorganized street thugs to come after us? It's quite the downgrade from the Crow

Brothers."

Shadow shrugged. "Lucien's an arrogant bastard. Maybe he thought sending eight morons were enough to take us down."

"Any ID on them?" Lincoln asked.

"Strip them down and let's find out."

While Shadow and Lincoln searched the bodies like scavengers, I made my way towards the guest bedroom where the man I killed laid face down on the ground. One of his hands was outstretched, reaching for the door.

I knelt beside him and rolled his head to the side.

I wanted to see the face of my victim—even though I knew it was a bad idea. Killing someone should never be this easy and I needed to see the dead man's face so I could live with it.

He was young, still in his teens and had a baby face that was pleasant to look at. He could have stolen the hearts of a few ladies had he been given the chance to live a decent life.

"I'm sorry." I felt pity for this kid.

If only he had known better. If only we had both known better.

"Aria," I heard Shadow's voice behind me. "You shouldn't look at him."

"He's just a kid," I said. "He's just another stupid kid who made a stupid decision in life. I killed him with a press of a button. How is that fair?"

I raised my hand and stared at it. My fingers, which I used many times to create music, had the same capacity to kill someone with a push of a button. It dawned on me that I didn't need to kill him; I could have trapped him inside this room and left him here. But instead, I allowed the anger of Abraham's death and Calisto's disappearance to take control. In the heat of the moment, I wanted him to die.

It was murder of the first degree.

"Aria, you did what you had to do. Who knows what would have happened if you didn't take him down? He could have surprised us. I could be dead," Shadow said.

I closed my eyes and reflected on his words. After a moment I nodded and rose to my feet.

Though there was truth to what Shadow said, the reality was this—the image of the boy, grasping for air on the video screen, will haunt me until the day I die. It was something I had to live with.

"Did you find anything on their bodies?" I asked.

Shadow shook his head. "Every one of them is clean. No wallets, no cellphones; nothing."

"On the contrary," Lincoln said as he entered into the room with a smart phone in his hand. "Look what I found hidden in between the ass cheeks of their ring leader."

"You dug through his underwear?" Shadow asked raising a brow.

"I'm very thorough," Lincoln replied as he held the phone out to him. "I did a quick search through the contacts and browsing history but found nothing. Want to see for yourself?"

There was a look of disgust on Shadow's face as he shook his head. "No thanks. You can hold onto it."

Suddenly the phone started vibrating.

"A call?" I asked.

Lincoln shook his head. "Text message looks like."

"From?" Shadow asked.

"Unknown," he replied as he scanned the message before turning to us. "But it looks like we just received a break in this little mystery of ours."

"What does it say?" I asked.

"Collect your payment at 465 Townly Street, unit 37, Passcode 9421," Lincoln said. "That address sounds familiar. What was over there again?"

"It's a storage facility," Shadow said, "One of the many side businesses that I own."

"No harm in checking it out then," Lincoln said. "Who knows, maybe Lucien might be stupid enough to show up himself with a burlap sack stuffed with unmarked bills."

"You actually believe that?" Shadow asked.

Lincoln walked over to where the box containing Calisto's severed finger laid on the ground. He picked it up as if it were a delicate flower. "At this point Shadow, all we can do is hope."

Shadow stared at the box and nodded.

"We'll find her guys," I said, sensing the grief that was shared between the two of them. "Calisto's a tough girl."

Lincoln took a deep breath. "Well come on then. Let's see what surprises wait for us at the storage facility."

Though he tried to remain calm, I could tell that Calisto's horrific kidnapping was tearing Lincoln apart. It was the worst part about falling in love with someone. At some point, they were destined to hurt you, whether they meant to or not—the dark side to every love story.

CHAPTER TWENTY-NINE

I was shocked to see the bodies of Shadow's men, along with a small army of hired killers, litter the outer hallways of Calisto's residence. It looked as if a war had been fought inside the condo building.

Shadow seemed distraught by the carnage. He had known some of these men personally.

It was Lincoln who consoled him, pointing out that for every one of Shadow's guards that fell, there were three killers who lay dead next to them. They had whittled away a death squad of at least thirty down to eight, giving up their lives to increase our chances of survival. In the end, they did their jobs and did them well.

We left the condo, and the massacre.

Shadow remained silent, his eyes focused on the road, navigating the Aston Martin through the city's highway, guided by the glow of the midnight lights.

"Her kidnapping makes no sense," Lincoln stated all of a sudden. "There's no ransom note, nor instructions for her safe return. Why give us her finger with no demands?"

"Lucien's sending us a message," Shadow said grimly. "He wants us to be afraid of him. He wants us to see him as a genuine threat."

Lincoln sat back in his seat and cursed. Tensions were high and we were all emotionally drained, which made for an uneasy car ride.

We finally pulled up to the steel gates of the storage facility. It had started to pour; heavy tears from the sky that reflected my own mood.

The security guard on duty recognized Shadow and opened the gate for us without a word.

"Why would Lucien choose a storage facility that you own as a meeting place?" I asked, puzzled.

"A lot of my personal businesses are kept secret from the rest of the society. I'm sure Lincoln has his own establishments kept off the records as well."

It took a moment for Lincoln to clue in on the conversation. He was too busy torturing himself by staring at Calisto's severed finger.

"Lincoln?" I tried reaching out to him, concerned for his sanity.

He looked up from the box and its horrific contents and pulled a Jekyll and Hyde, his morose demeanor morphing into a cheerful one. "If anyone ever wants a complimentary manicure and shellac that's out of this world, let me know," he said, putting the box away.

"Why keep all these businesses a secret?" I asked.

"Two reasons; the first being that people within the Midnight Society are nosy and love measuring their wealth against each other," Lincoln explained. "Consider it a 'my dick is bigger than yours syndrome.' It's childish, really. If people had the ability to be content with what they already have, wouldn't this world be such a happier place?"

"Tell that to the woman who just heard about the latest designer handbag from Burberry," I said.

"For us to keep a set of our own businesses off the record allows everyone to speculate each other's true worth. What's on paper will never be a true reflection of our net income. This removes the entire measuring our dicks…" Lincoln paused as he casted me a quick glance, "…or vaginas syndrome."

"I appreciate your effort to be politically correct in your analogy," I mused. "Though believe it or not, unlike men, girls don't tend to get jealous over the size of our vajayjays."

Lincoln ignored my comment and continued. "The second reason we hide our businesses is that some of us tend to deal in some shadier dealings and we need to launder the money coming through with secret side businesses."

"Shady dealings as in knock off sunglasses and black market electronics?" I speculated.

"Not exactly. It's better off you didn't know," Shadow said.

I turned to Shadow, surprised. "Tell me you're joking."

"Sorry," he said, "But I have no punch line for you."

"You're telling me my boyfriend is a criminal?"

"In his defense, we're all criminals," Lincoln said. "I have my illegal business dealings but I also own one of the most elite Montessori daycares in the country. I try to balance out the bad with the good; give myself a neutral karma rating."

"That doesn't make you good," I said. "A crack dealing Mary Poppins is still a criminal, no matter how many spoonfuls of sugar she shoves down a whiny kid's mouth."

"I'm not disagreeing with you Aria," Shadow said. "But as I said, it's better if you didn't know."

"Great, my lover is the Godfather," I sighed.

"Do you regret being with me?" Shadow asked.

I shook my head without hesitation. "I love you," I replied. "Although I can't say when I was a little girl, I had dreams of sleeping with Lex Luthor."

"I'm not bald," Shadow pointed out.

"You get the idea."

The Aston Martin pulled up to unit thirty-seven and the three of us filed out of the car and into the rain. I stood there and allowed every droplet of water to wash over my body.

I wanted to feel cleansed.

"Here goes," Shadow said, walking over to the storage unit. "Aria, stay back," he said, his gun in one hand while the other punched the access code into the security key pad.

A green light indicated that the entry was accepted and slowly, the heavy garage doors to the storage unit began to open.

The world froze all around us as we waited for the doors to open, and when they finally did, I was horrified by the nightmare that was waiting for us inside.

CHAPTER THIRTY

In the span of a few days, my life was flipped upside down.

I went from making passionate love with Shadow in the breathtaking kingdom of Cambodia to standing in the rain, staring at the corpse of a man, lying on a table.

"It's Lucien," Lincoln said, his eyes wide. "What the fuck is going on?"

At the centre of the room, a white light illuminated Lucien's pale body lying on a black marble table. Soft purple petals surrounded him, creating a sickly yet beautiful display, as if his corpse was the centerpiece of some twisted artistic expression. Resting at his feet was an envelope.

Meanwhile, the entire storage facility had been converted to a cold room with several heavy-duty air conditioners blasting frigid air throughout the unit, no doubt to preserve the body for when we found it.

What *really* drew my attention was the black tattoo of a goat's head, beautifully drawn onto his chest.

Was this referencing a scapegoat?

"How did he die?" I asked, shivering. I was freezing. The dampness of my clothes from the rain didn't help either as I felt the chill seep into my bones.

Shadow examined the body and shook his head. "There's no wound," he said, the vapors from his breath hanging in the air like smoke. He didn't seem bothered by the cold. "No ligatures or bruises either. My guess is either suffocation or poison."

Shadow walked over to the envelope, picked it up and pulled out the contents inside. It was a single white card.

"What is it?" Lincoln asked.

"It's an invitation," Shadow replied, showing us the card, "Dated for tonight."

"Come and play at Midnight," I read aloud. Following the message was a fiery logo that I didn't recognize. I was baffled. "Come play where? What's with all these cryptic messages?"

"They want us to come to the Inferno," Shadow said.

"A gambler's den inspired by Satan himself," Lincoln commented. He stared at Lucien's body for a moment, before turning away in disgust. "I can't say I ever liked the guy, but he didn't deserve this. We were chasing the wrong person all this time."

"Which leaves us with the question, who the hell is orchestrating all of this?" Shadow asked.

"Are you considering going to the Inferno?" I asked. "Not to dive right into a proverbial cliché, but I think it's a trap."

"What other choice do we have?" Shadow asked. "Calisto is still missing and in the hands of a complete psychopath. The only chance we have to get her is to play his game and win."

"Sink or swim it is then," Lincoln agreed. "Should we contact the rest of the Midnight Society and let them know what we're up to?"

"They're already messaging me," Shadow said as he drew his cellphone from his pocket. "All of them at once from the looks of it."

I saw the look of dread on his face as he scanned the messages on his phone. Something was wrong.

"Shadow, what is it?" I asked.

He turned the screen of his phone towards us so we could both see. It was the images of Brevin West, James Takeshi, and Donald Huff. They were all bound, and gagged—but still alive. The look of fear in all their eyes was unmistakable.

"For fuck's sake," Lincoln said, shaking his head. "The fucker has everyone else."

Shadow's phone buzzed again. The image this time showed Calisto--wearing an elegant white evening gown--tied to a stone table like a sacrificial victim. Standing over her was the tall figure of a man concealed by a black cloak, reminiscent of an executioner from medieval times. His face was hidden behind a white porcelain mask, red tears dripping down the sides of it symbolizing blood. I shivered upon first glance of this sadistic man.

There was an additional caption to go along with this image.

"Can you save her before I kill her, like I did your parents?"

Shadow's face changed from a look of concern to one of burning hatred. He stared at the image, his knuckles white from gripping the phone too tightly.

"Shadow, are you okay?" I asked.

He turned to me.

"I'm going to kill him. Tonight, I'll find whoever did this to my family and I'm going to crush his skull with my bare hands."

I suddenly felt my cellphone vibrate as well. I checked the message and was horrified to see an image of Justin, blindfolded, and tied to a pole. Beneath his feet was a pile of kinder.

Save him or watch him burn, was the text that followed, sent by an unknown caller.

"They have Justin," I became hysterical. "Oh god, they took Justin! He has nothing to do with any of this. Oh shit, shit, shit."

I was panicking and it took Shadow's strong embrace to calm me down.

"He has everyone," Shadow said. "I promise you Aria, we'll free them, and after we do, I'll find everyone responsible and I'll kill them all."

CHAPTER THIRTY-ONE

When we pulled up to the entrance of the Inferno hotel, the man waiting for us was well dressed—slim cut tuxedo, white gloves, and ink black shoes. His face however was crimson with paint, transforming his visage into something demonic.

He greeted us with a razorblade smile.

"Welcome to the Inferno," he said, gesturing towards the brightly lit entrance of the hotel. From outside, you couldn't tell the hotel was still under construction, aside from the upper floors of the high rise building, which were still a skeletal frame of support beams and concrete.

Shadow wasted no time attacking the man, slamming him against the outer brick wall. "Where are my sister and the others?" He pulled a gun from behind his back and jammed it under the demon-faced man's chin. "Answer me now or I'm painting the veranda of my hotel with your brain splatter."

"They're inside," the man replied calmly, ignoring the threat of the gun. "I assure you, they're all safe and unharmed."

"Unharmed?" Lincoln exploded, pulling out the box and

opening it, revealing Calisto's severed finger inside. "You call this fucking unharmed?"

"If they can still breathe on their own accord, then yes, I'd say they're in good shape," he replied.

"Who are you people?" Shadow spat, "And what do you want?"

"I'm nobody," he replied. "However, I do work for *somebody*. You'll find out who that is inside."

"Give me one reason I shouldn't shoot you in the face right now," Shadow threatened.

"Any harm that comes to me or any of the employees inside will result in the immediate termination of one of your friends, chosen at random."

Shadow released his grip on the man and let his gun drop to his side. "You're a smug piece of shit."

"Guilty as charged. Now, if you have your temper under control, the three of you may enter."

The explosive sound of gunfire startled me. The smug man grabbed his kneecap, which was now a bloody mess, and crumpled to the floor screaming.

"You asshole!" he cried as tears smeared the makeup on his face, "You fucking asshole!"

"What are you whining about?" Lincoln asked, the gun in his hand still smoking. "You can still breathe on your own accord. According to your definition, you're not harmed."

We entered into the hotel, leaving the wounded man screaming outside.

Inside, a petite woman with long flowing hair the color of plums greeted us. She was dressed in a provocative white-laced night gown. She was completely bare underneath.

"Welcome," she said with a seductive smile as she walked over to Shadow and placed her hands firmly against his chest. "You feel so warm."

"You rotten-crotched slut," I blurted out loud.

"Sticks and stones Ms. Valencia," she said, flashing me a wide grin. What was with these people? Was there some requirement to be a smug piece of crap in order to work here?

I sent telepathic signals to Lincoln to shoot her in the kneecaps as well, but alas, no such luck. Instead, I contemplated rearranging her face with the heel of my Jimmy Choos.

My teeth ground together with the force of tectonic plates shifting as I watched the little temptress reach up to her tip toes and plant a gentle kiss on Shadow's lips who—much to my relief—made no effort to return the favor.

"Don't kiss me again," Shadow said.

"Why?" the temptress asked. "Afraid to experience a real woman while your precious not-so-Golden Virgin is around?"

"No," Shadow replied. "I have no idea where your lips have been, but I assume nowhere clean."

Suddenly her slutty disposition melted away into a sour demeanor.

"Homo," she stated coldly.

"As an advocate of equality, I'm going to call you an ignorant wench," Lincoln said, pointing his gun at her. "I must also state that I'm equally opportune in blasting kneecaps as well. I'm sure you can still hear your co-worker screaming outside. Unless your employer offers an outstanding physical therapy benefits package, I advise you get to the point and take us to our friends."

I turned to Lincoln and grinned. "You read my mind."

"Follow me," she muttered as she began leading us down a long red velvet-inspired hallway.

After minutes of walking through a series of elegant corridors, I was curious of our destination. "Where is she leading us?" I asked.

"It looks to be the gambling suites," Shadow replied. "It's where all the private card games are held."

Eventually we stopped in front of double doors.

"Inside," the slut said.

Shadow gave her a suspicious glance.

"Standing here won't help your friends," she said.

"Sink or swim," Lincoln whispered, pushing open the doors.

It was a spine tingling scene, reminiscent of Shadow's party. Surrounding us were people wearing masks, similar to the ones I saw before. In fact, I even recognized some of the people in the crowd.

At the centre of the room were Donald Huff, Brevin West, and James Takeshi; still in their business suits, gagged, and tied to chairs. Luckily they were still alive.

They were situated around a circular table where at the centre were four silver-colored six-shooter pistols. Each one was well polished and glowed with a brilliant luster underneath the overhead lights. Behind them stood a woman in a black cocktail dress, wearing an owl's mask. She held a giant mallet, one that could be used to strike a large gong that was beside her.

"What the hell is this?" Shadow asked.

Silence from the crowd.

"Answer my question," Shadow demanded. "What's going on here? And where's Calisto?"

Out of the mass of onlookers emerged the man cloaked in black, the same individual that was seen hovering over Calisto in the image sent to Shadow's phone.

"If you want to save your friends, you'll have to gamble," the man said, his baritone voice sounding filtered through a voice scrambler.

Both Shadow and Lincoln drew their guns on him.

"Who are you?" Shadow asked.

"You may call me Sinister," the cloaked man replied.

"Did you kill my parents?"

Sinister unleashed a bone-rattling laugh. "You're still fixated on the past, are you?"

"You fucking slashed their throats," Shadow stated.

"Yes."

"Tell me why you did it," Shadow demanded, taking a step forward.

"Later Shadow, later. First let's see if you can save your friends."

"How about I shoot you in the neck instead," Shadow threatened, his gun still pointed towards Sinister.

"An eye-for-an-eye," Sinister said. Five men emerged from the crowd of onlookers, all in demon face paint, similar to the man who Lincoln had shot. "You may end my life with a bullet, but I promise you that once I die, none of you will be left standing either, including your precious love, the Golden Virgin."

Shadow reluctantly lowered his weapon, his face a mask of anger.

"Take their guns," Sinister ordered.

The masked demons obeyed and began scouring both Lincoln and Shadow for their weapons. When it was done and their guns were stripped away, Sinister turned to Shadow. "You always were easily intimidated. I guess her pussy must have some intoxicating power over you. For twenty years you tried to find me, and now that you have, you're willing to let the sweet nectar of revenge escape your lips without so much as a taste. Tell me, does the bitch's snatch taste that much better?"

"Fuck you," Shadow cursed.

"Who are you?" Lincoln asked. "You seem to know us."

Sinister didn't reply. Instead he turned his attention to the three captives at the table. "Let's try saving your friends now, shall we? Who will play?"

"You're insane," Shadow said.

Sinister turned to our direction and stared at us with dark eyes.

"You're one to talk Shadow. We're all a little insane in the end, don't you think?" he asked. "Now I'll ask again, who wants to play the game? It's the only way to save any of them."

"What if we say no?" Shadow spat.

Sinister sighed as he pulled out a gun from his cloak. Before any of us could protest, he pointed the gun at Donald Huff's chest and pulled the trigger.

It was hard to tell what came first, the explosive sound of gunfire or Donald's body going limp.

I was too stunned to make a sound, but James and Brevin weren't. Their eyes were wide open—screaming—as they moved frantically in their seats, horrified by the death of their friend.

"Oh Christ," Lincoln said as he dropped to his knees in disbelief.

"I've always been intolerant of indecisiveness," Sinister said. "A lack of patience is a flaw of mine. Now, I ask again, who's ready to gamble?"

"I'll do it," Lincoln said, rising to his feet.

"Have a seat," Sinister instructed. Two demon-faced men strolled up behind Lincoln and gripped his arms like a prisoner, forcing him to sit in the empty seat at the table where the pistols rested atop of it. One of the demon men removed a pistol, leaving three guns at the table for the three men.

I feared what came next.

Lincoln looked the other two in the eyes.

"We'll die with dignity," Lincoln said.

Brevin looked at him, tears streaming down his dark skinned cheeks. Eventually he nodded in agreement.

"The game is very simple," Sinister said. "I'm fascinated by high stake games of chance. I enjoy the mystique and magic behind the aspect of luck, which is why I've chosen for the three of you to play the romantic game of Russian roulette."

"Lincoln, don't!" Shadow cried out upon revelation of what Sinister had planned. "Don't do this. Let me play instead."

Lincoln turned to us and smiled sadly. "Forget it Shadow," he said. "Lady Luck never liked you much. Let me play with that bitch tonight."

"Don't play this game," Shadow stated. "You take Aria and walk on out of here. I'll play for all of us." It was clear to me how much Shadow valued his friend's life.

"They won't let us leave Shadow," Lincoln said, turning to Sinister. "He's here to watch us burn."

"If Lincoln wins the game, you'll let him go?" Shadow asked.

"Only if he wins the game," Sinister replied. "I swear on the souls of my mother and father, whoever survives shall leave this place a free man."

"Enough talk, let's play then," Lincoln said. He turned to both Brevin and James. "I'm sorry guys, but this is all I can offer you—a chance to live by killing me."

Both James and Brevin seemed to acknowledge Lincoln's words. Their lives were now in the hands of fate.

"There's a single bullet in each of the guns. The three of you will unlock the chamber, spin it, and lock it again," Sinister explained. "You will then point the gun to the person on your left and pull the trigger every time the gong is struck. Only when someone dies does this round end."

Knife in hand, one of the demon-faced men cut the straps that bound the hands of James and Brevin.

Anxiety filled my gut as I watched each of the three men reach for the pistols in front of them. I turned to Shadow to see if his nerves were as rattled as mine, but his face had become expressionless. His eyes however—those eyes of his had been touched by flames, watching the game unfold as if he were watching the world burn.

"Spin," Sinister ordered.

Lincoln opened up the chamber of the gun and stared at the single bullet inside the barrel.

"Spin," Sinister repeated.

The three did as they were told, rolling the palms of their hands across the cylinders of their guns, sending the single bullet twirling in a vortex of deadly chance.

"Load," Sinister instructed. I closed my eyes and heard the clicking of three guns and I took a deep breath. I was ashamed to say it, but I prayed that James and Brevin—two innocent men—would die. I wanted Lincoln to walk away from this.

"Aim."

My eyes remained closed. I already watched Donald die. I had no desire to see it happen to another person.

"Pull at the sound of each gong," Sinister ordered.

There was a moment of lingering silence. I heard the beating of my heart which echoed like war drums.

And then the sound of the gong cut through the silence and reverberated throughout the room.

Click.

The gong struck again.

Click.

It wasn't until after the third strike that the sound of gunfire erupted, followed by a loud groan.

I opened my eyes just in time to see Brevin slump over in his chair and fall to the floor. The tip of Lincoln's gun was smoking.

"I'm sorry Brevin," Lincoln was near hysterical. "I'm so sorry."

"I never liked Brevin," Sinister said. "Some say it's unethical to sell drugs, weapons, and sex, but honestly is selling false faith any more ethical?"

"Don't speak like you knew him," Shadow said. "Don't speak like you know any of us."

"Oh but I do," Sinister said. "Since the day I killed your mommy and daddy, I've watched you and your sister grow, waiting for the perfect day to introduce myself into your life. Tonight's games took almost over a decade of planning Shadow, and all for you. It's all for you."

There was a moment of tense silence before Shadow spoke.

"I'll bury you."

"Maybe you will, but wouldn't it be romantic if I dragged you down into the grave with me? We'd be locked in an embrace for all of eternity; dance partners in hell," Sinister laughed, "But enough with my dirty little fantasy. There's still one more round of this game to be played."

Sinister walked over to Lincoln and handed him another bullet. "One more to go," he said.

Lincoln loaded the bullet into his gun, his hateful stare never straying from Sinister. I could tell Lincoln wanted to use that single bullet on the bastard, but it'd only serve to get everyone killed.

He spun the chamber of the gun and snapped it shut, taking a deep breath after.

James did the same.

The second round of this perverse game had begun.

"Aim."

That was my cue to turn away.

This time there was only one chime of the gong as the deafening blast from the pistol immediately followed.

I watched as Lincoln dropped to his knees, tossing the gun aside. He buried his hands in his face and unleashed a horrific scream.

Meanwhile James's head hung over the back of his chair, his limbs dangling loosely by his side. Blood dripped down from the side of his temple and gathered into a red puddle on the ground.

Shadow made his way towards Lincoln, ignoring the demon faces, whom had their guns aimed directly at him.

"Lincoln," Shadow said, "We'll bury these fuckers. Every last one of them."

"Fuck, I killed them," I heard Lincoln sobbing.

Shadow pressed Lincoln's head into his shoulder.

"You didn't kill anybody," Shadow said. "Remember those words; you killed no one tonight."

Shadow glared in Sinister's direction, whose eyes danced with amusement beneath his shrouded visage.

I felt sorry for Lincoln. It was hard to imagine that he was the same man who bled confidence and boyish charm. He was now reduced to a husk of pity and self-loathing. Did Lincoln actually win in the end?

Shadow lifted his friend gently to his feet.

"Remember this man," Shadow said, his long finger directed at Sinister. "He's the one you hate. Together, we'll fuck him over."

Lincoln sat himself down in the chair, took a deep breath and closed his eyes.

"Congratulations Lincoln," Sinister said. "I honor my word. You may leave this place with the stains of their blood on your soul."

When Lincoln opened his eyes again, all the pity and self-loathing were gone. Instead there was pure animosity, as if his heart and soul had suddenly transformed into something dark and frightening.

"I'm not going anywhere until we all leave together," Lincoln stated, "You, me, Aria, her friend, and Calisto."

Shadow shook his head. "I'll finish this. Go while you still can."

Lincoln refused. "I'm not finished here."

Shadow gestured towards the dead council members. "I need you to make sure their families are okay."

Lincoln thought about it for a moment and finally agreed.

Shadow turned to Sinister. "As for Aria, let her leave with Lincoln."

"What? No!" I protested. "I want to stay. I *need* to stay."

"Let her go," Shadow repeated. "It's the Tremaine family you want in the end, is it not?"

"She is free to go on her own accord," Sinister said. "However should she leave the premise without playing the game, then her friend will burn."

"I'm staying," I cried. "I need to save him."

Shadow gripped me by the shoulders. "Aria, you may die. These fucking games are rigged."

"That's my decision then," I said. "If I let Justin die without even trying to save him, then the life I have is not one that I'll want."

"Does he mean that much to you?" Shadow asked.

I nodded.

Shadow's shoulders slumped and he gave in. "Then I won't stop you."

"Have a little faith Shadow," Sinister said. "I assure you that the next game, Ms. Valencia has the capabilities of winning with the skill set she has."

"What will you have her do?" Shadow asked, taking a step between the cloaked man and myself, acting as a human shield.

"Come with me," Sinister instructed, "And we'll see how well the Golden Virgin performs under a baptism of fire."

CHAPTER THIRTY-TWO

With guns pressed behind our backs, Shadow and I were led to the auditorium of the casino.

"I understand you dream of performing," Sinister said to me. "And it so happens that I adore classical music. I'd be honored if you'd play for me."

At the center of the stage, lit by a spotlight, was a majestic grand piano. However it was Justin tied to a pole and sharing the same stage as the piano, which drew my attention. He was unconscious.

"Let him go," Shadow ordered. "He's a commoner for Christ's sake. He has no involvement in anything we do."

"The day you chose the Golden Virgin to be your precious soul mate was the day you allowed commoners to be a part of the Midnight Society's affairs. You allowed them into the game," Sinister replied. "Everything you do Shadow sets precedence and we all know there's nothing more dangerous than precedence."

"Don't hurt him, please," I found myself begging. At that

moment, I didn't care about anything else in the world besides Justin's safety, whose only mistake in life was falling in love with me.

"Well my dear, that's up to you now, "Sinister said. "Are you ready to save your friend?"

"What do you want me to do?" I asked.

The man gestured towards the grand piano. "Play for me," he said.

"That's it?" I was skeptical. "I can do that. And then you'll let Justin go?"

"There's a catch though," he said. "I have a very fickle ear and absolutely detest mistakes. I can hear even the most minor ones. I demand an absolutely flawless technical performance."

"What will you have me play?" I asked.

"*Gaspard de la Nuit.*"

My heart sank at the cruel twist of fate.

"You can't be serious," I exclaimed, recalling all my failed attempts at trying to master the difficult song. What he was asking me to do was impossible.

"I thought you dreamed of being the world's best performer," Sinister said. "You can't be the best without taking on new challenges and facing pressure."

I turned to Shadow. "I'm not good enough."

"Aria, you can do this," Shadow said to me, his voice void of any doubt. "You're one of the most gifted pianists I've ever heard."

"It's impossible," I shook my head. "I make at least ten mistakes on every play-through of the song. It's far from perfect."

"Is the Golden Virgin giving up already?" Sinister mused.

"No," I said without hesitation.

"If the pressure is too much, then concede. I'll take pleasure in listening to the melodic sounds of your friend's screaming while he burns."

Out of the corner of my eye, I noticed Justin stirring. His eyes slowly fluttered open and he fixed his gaze on me.

I ran to him.

"I'm so sorry Justin," I said as I wrapped my arms around his shoulders and held him. The warmth of his tears trickled down my shoulders and I couldn't help but cry with him. "I promise you I'll get you out of this."

I held him at arm's length and looked into Justin's eyes. "I'll save you just like all the times you saved me during those first years of school. I promise."

He closed his eyes and nodded, placing his life within my fingertips.

"If we're done with the melodrama, let us begin," Sinister said, taking a front row seat. The doors to the auditorium opened and the masked guests began to file in, filling the empty seats. Sinister patted the seat next to him, motioning for Shadow to join him.

"Go fuck yourself," Shadow replied.

"Fine, stand there then," Sinister said, nodding to one of the demon-faced guards.

The thug jammed his gun into Shadow's spine and left it there, making it seemingly uncomfortable for him.

"Come on then," Sinister said. "Time's wasting. We still have the bitch Calisto to deal with after this."

I was incredibly nervous as I strolled over to the piano and seated myself at the bench in front.

I rested my fingertips atop of the keys and tried to remember *Gaspar de la Nuit* and its complex melody. Like a computer, I began downloading the sequence of notes from my brain onto my fingertips.

"Any day now," Sinister was growing impatient. It was never good to leave a psychopath waiting and so I began.

The sounds from the piano immediately flooded the auditorium as my fingers danced across the smooth ivory surface of the instrument. Never had I taken greater care in playing a piece, my mind focused solely on the music. I prayed that the muscle memory in my fingers didn't fail me as they rapidly scaled up and down the piano, filling the room with the beautiful song.

As I continued to play, I channeled all my emotions into it, injecting life and personality into the piece. I was determined to make this performance a masterpiece—one that had the equivalent value of another human life.

I had lost track of time as to how long I played for, but when I reached the finale of *Gaspar de la Nuit*, I was exhausted.

But I did it. I had no idea how, but I did it.

I had played *Gaspard de la Nuit* flawlessly.

The silence that followed the last note of the song was unnerving. What did Sinister think? Was it good enough for his standards to allow Justin to live?

From listening to the song so many times before, I knew technically that it was flawless.

Sinister slowly rose to his feet and began applauding.

Was that a sign of his approval? I held my breath as I waited for him to speak.

"Brilliant," he said. "It was absolutely brilliant. That performance does solidify you as one of the world's best."

I was relieved.

"You'll let Justin go then?" I asked.

"Good heavens, no. I'm afraid he'll have to burn." Sinister's reply tore me apart.

"You bastard!" I shouted. "I did what you asked. I played Gaspard de la Nuit perfectly."

"Actually, there was one minor error in your piece," Sinister pointed out.

"There was none," Shadow said. "I listened to that song thousands of times. It was perfect."

Sinister shook his head. "Uh-uh," he refuted like a ten-year old.

I was in complete disbelief. I thought everything was perfect. What did I do wrong?

As if the sadistic bastard had read my mind, he looked at me with a sick delight in his eyes as he revealed my 'error.'

"The forty-fifth bar in the song, second stanza, it should have been played as mezzo forte instead of forte," he stated. "Aside from that, the performance was flawless, really."

I wanted to die. The mistake was a petty one, open to interpretation. It was the equivalent of saying tomato one way instead of the other.

"Don't do this," I pleaded. "Let him go. He's innocent."

Sinister laughed. "Now that's a lie my dear. None of us are innocent. It's true that he's an outsider and unfortunate collateral damage to this game we play, but don't mistake him for being innocent. He knows about the Midnight Society, and that in itself is a sin."

Oh God, this was my fault. I should have never told Justin about the party and the Midnight Society. At the time, I had thought to myself, what's the harm of telling just one person?

Now I knew.

If I had only kept my mouth shut; and now, Justin was going to die because of me.

"Take me instead," Shadow said suddenly. "Let them both go and burn me instead and end this feud."

Sinister was surprised by the suggestion. "Well look at you," he jested. "Shadow's trying to be a sacrificial Messiah all of a sudden. You're willing to give up your life so your whore girlfriend can end up screwing a sad, pathetic commoner in the end?"

"Just let them go," Shadow repeated. "We have history between us Sinister. I know it's my life you want. Let Aria, Justin, and Calisto walk out of here safe and unharmed and you can have me instead. Finish what you started with my father and mother."

Sinister thought about it for a moment and then shook his head. "I would have considered it but Calisto doesn't get off so easily. She's the guiltiest of them all." He then turned to one of his henchmen and barked out an order. "Burn him."

I dropped to my knees and watched in horror as the demon-faced henchmen doused my best friend in gasoline. The way Justin was writhing and screaming was agonizing to watch. I wanted to save him but all I could do was drop to my knees and beg Justin to forgive me for getting him killed.

From afar I heard Shadow shouting, but his words faded into the background. All I heard was the splashing of gasoline and Justin's muffled screams.

"I'm sorry, oh God, I'm so sorry."

Sinister laughed at me. "You must be mistaken girl. God's not here right now. There is me however and my cigarette lighter." The pad of his thumb flicked the metallic lighter, sparking a flame.

I tried to lunge for the lighter but I was too slow and it found its way to Justin's pyre. Both the kindle on the ground and Justin erupted into a blanket of flames.

My screams were hysterical and echoed throughout the auditorium while my insides turned into liquid. The sickness in my stomach started off as nausea but by the time it reached the back of my throat, it tasted like poison.

"Turn away Aria, turn away," I heard Shadow calling from behind me. "Don't look at Justin."

I didn't. My eyes were focused on Sinister instead and I stared at the man with such a hatred that could make even the Devil quiver.

Eventually Justin's screams stopped. He was gone.

"When you are ready, you'll be taken to see Calisto," Sinister said, taking his leave. The crowd in the auditorium began to disperse as well. I wished for every person who took pleasure in watching Justin die to suffer.

I wanted to kill them all.

I felt Shadow's warm touch as he lifted me off the ground and held me.

"I'm so sorry," I heard him whisper.

I should have been crying but I had no more tears left in me. I was all cried out.

So instead of sadness, I felt hate.

"I know how you feel now Shadow," I whispered. "I know why revenge is so important to you."

Shadow shook his head. "Don't end up like me. I am flawed and I am miserable. Let me obsess about revenge for the two of us."

"We'll get him, won't we?" I asked.

"I'll kill him," Shadow replied. "I promise you."

The heavy footsteps of Sinister's guards surrounded us. "Come on, let's go," one of them said.

"Go to hell," I cursed.

"No thanks," he replied as he jammed his gun into the back of Shadow's head. "Now if we're done slinging meaningless insults, I believe there's a whore you both wanted to see."

As we left the stage, my eyes gravitated towards Justin's body. I could only wonder what explanation would be given to his family about his horrific death. He always spoke fondly of his parents and his sister, but because of me they'll never see him again.

The doors to the auditorium closed behind us and with it I was leaving behind my dreams of performing. After enduring that nightmare, how could I ever think about touching a piano again?

Today, my desire to play music died along with my best friend.

CHAPTER THIRTY-THREE

"Four," Shadow muttered underneath his breath before shaking his head. "Fuck."

For a moment his eyes flashed to the direction of one of the demon-faced guards in front of us. It took me only a second to realize what he was getting at.

Shadow was contemplating taking out the four guards, escorting us, on his own and without a gun.

It was suicide.

But then again, so was walking into whatever game they had in store for us next. After watching Justin burn, I realized there was very little hope for us to get out of this alive. Sinister was cruel and a liar and at this point, there was no reason not to think that Lincoln was dead as well.

I wanted to scream.

"I know what you're thinking," one of the guards said to Shadow. "You're thinking about taking us out."

I froze in my tracks. How did he know?

"The odds are against you," he continued, "But then again, I've always been one to play the odds. The question for you Shadow is, are you a risk taker like myself?"

"Hey, we're not paid to talk," another one of the demon-faced thugs said, turning his attention to the yapper.

"I'm just trying to create some dialogue, unlike you, you anti-social conversation Nazi."

"What the fuck is the problem here?" another one of the masked men asked. "Can we please all just shut up, get them to the helipad already so we can finish the job? I want to get paid and go home."

"Why can't we be friends?" the talkative one asked.

"Just shut the fuck up," the first guard said, his patience worn thin. "Please, just shut the fuck up."

"You shut up," the yapper said. In a moment of complete surrealism, I watched as the chatty guard raised his gun and blew apart the thug next to him with a round of bullets to the chest.

I dropped to the ground, hands over my head, and watched as Shadow tackled another guard to the ground, trying to wrestle the gun out of his hands.

"Lincoln, there's one more," Shadow cried out as he continued to struggle with the guard beneath him.

Lincoln?

The yappy guard immediately turned to the last demon-faced man standing and pulled the trigger, spraying the walls with red matter.

Lincoln wiped the makeup off his face with the back of his sleeve and nodded at me.

Meanwhile Shadow managed to tear the gun out of his adversary's hands after delivering a crushing fist into the man's throat. It took only one bullet to end the fight for good.

"I thought I ordered you to leave here," Shadow said, wiping the sweat off his brow.

"You honestly thought I'd listen to you?"

"Nope."

"And did you expect anything less from me?" Lincoln asked, looking at the bodies of Sinister's men on the ground.

"Of course not," Shadow replied, patting Lincoln on the back. "Come on, let's go save my sister."

It had stopped raining but the night air harbored a chill. Calisto stood at the center of the helicopter landing pad, hands bound behind her back. She must have been freezing in the white evening gown, her shoulders and legs bare.

The large torches that aligned the circumference of the helipad didn't seem to provide much warmth for her, though it did succeed in creating a creepy atmosphere.

Calisto tried to shout something at us, but the gag covering the lower half of her face muffled her. Instead, all I could hear was a desperate scream.

Shadow's first instinct was to run to her, but after no more than three steps, Sinister stood behind Calisto and pressed a knife against her bare neck.

"One more step and I end her life," he said.

"Move a fucking muscle and I put a hole in your head," Lincoln threatened, his gun aimed at the bastard. "If I see so much as a drop of blood spill from Calisto, you're finished."

"I give you credit for being such a sneaky bastard," Sinister said, "But you lose points for being an impatient little shit. In fact, I'm disappointed in all of you. You'd think to examine your surroundings before rushing head first into an obvious trap."

"Put down your gun," a voice echoed from above us.

A high powered rifle was pointed in our direction, held by the fucker who had murdered Abraham.

The sight of the White Crow made my blood boil. I could still feel Abraham's lifeless body in my arms, a phantom memory that will haunt me forever.

"Fucking coward," Lincoln shouted. "Come down here and fight like you have balls."

The White Crow laughed as he directed the red dot from his rifle onto the centre of Lincoln's forehead.

"Crows like to be perched up high," the assassin replied. "I'm sure the guys down on the ground would be happy to accommodate your request."

From out of the shadows, two more demon-faced men emerged, guns in hand. I could see the look of anger and disappointment on Shadow's face. He gave Lincoln a glance that said, *we fucked up*.

"The fault isn't yours," Sinister said. "It's human nature to allow emotions to overcome logic and reasoning. That is why you fail and I succeed."

"What are you then?" Shadow asked, "An emotionless psychopath?"

"I gave up on relationships long ago," Sinister said. "It was the only way to get ahead in life, the true way to obtain power. Once you start caring for someone, you allow yourself a weakness." He grabbed a handful of Calisto's hair and pulled her head back, exposing the pale flesh of her neck and pressed the edge of the knife against her throat. "This stupid bitch over here is one of yours Shadow."

"Don't even think about it," Shadow warned.

"Oh hush now," Sinister said. "Don't you see? I'm trying to free you of one of your weaknesses. You were destined to do great things Shadow, but you allowed your human frailty to control you. You had the genius of Julius Caesar and the ambition of Napolean, yet you sadly wasted most of your time trying to avenge the death of your parents; countless hours wasted searching for me."

"Who are you?" Shadow asked.

"All shall be revealed soon enough," Sinister said, "But the game comes first."

"No, I'm done with your games."

"Then you're done with your sister's life." Sinister pushed the blade deeper into Calisto's neck until her skin broke and red began trickling down her throat.

"You'll kill her anyway," Shadow said. "All your games are rigged."

"That's not true," Sinister replied. "Lincoln was freed after winning my game."

"I don't feel free," Lincoln said, gesturing to the two guards who had their guns fixated on us.

"You can only blame yourself. Instead of walking through the open door, you decided to kill my men and play dress up, which I had already anticipated." The blade of the knife moved half an inch across Calisto's throat and she let out a muffled scream underneath the gag.

"Are you ready to play yet?" Sinister asked.

Neither Shadow nor Lincoln responded.

"Good," he said. One of the guards walked over to us brandishing a large bowie knife. He dropped it at Shadow's feet.

"The game is fairly simple," Sinister continued. "I will count to three and you will either stab your girlfriend in the heart or I'll kill your sister."

Shadow stared at the knife on the ground.

"I don't have to repeat the rules now, do I?" Sinister asked.

"You can't expect me to do that," Shadow said.

"Sure I can. It's a simple choice. Choose who will live—Calisto or the Golden Virgin. You have until the count of three."

Shadow ignored the knife on the ground. "No," he cried out. "I will not make this choice."

"Three seconds," the cloaked man said. "Pick up the knife and choose a life. There is no negotiation."

Shadow's weary eyes turned to me and I saw the helpless expression on his face. I knew what decision he needed to make, and I couldn't blame him. Calisto was family after all—his twin. There was a bond that they shared that was far deeper than our love which had *just* blossomed.

"One," Sinister shouted from the helipad.

I turned to Lincoln, who was frozen in place. "Shadow…" he began while staring at Calisto longingly.

"I love you" I said to Shadow just before closing my eyes.

I thought of my dad holding me tightly as a child when I was most scared. He always made me feel safe.

"Two," I heard Sinister shout from the distance.

I let out a deep breath and waited for Shadow's knife to enter me. I couldn't help but think about the kid I had murdered in Calisto's apartment. Not only did I feel remorse for what I done but fear also. If there was a hell, I had punched myself a one way ticket and the kid was probably waiting for me down there along with the Black Crow.

I would never see my dad again nor Justin who I needed to apologize to.

Suddenly I heard both Shadow and Lincoln scream.

I opened my eyes in time to see the knife protruding from Calisto's heart, a trickle of blood painting a thin red line down Calisto's white gown.

"Fuck it," Sinister said. "You took too long. I made the decision for you."

I looked at Shadow, who was gripping the bowie knife in his hands, pointing it in my direction.

"You fucker!" Lincoln cried.

"You disappoint me Shadow," Sinister said. "I thought this was an easy choice. Instead you had to think about saving the whore while your own blood's life was in jeopardy. Hasn't anyone ever taught you that family comes first? In the end, it was *you* who stabbed her in the heart."

There was a blank, catatonic look on Shadow's face as the knife fell from his hands and onto the ground. I ran to Shadow and held him.

"I'm so sorry," I whispered as I held him tightly.

"You surprise me Aria," Sinister said. "I thought you'd be pissed that given one more second, Shadow was going to kill you."

"None of us know that," I shouted. "You never gave him a choice."

"Of course I did," Sinister said. "He just took too long to make it."

"You promised him three seconds," Lincoln shouted.

"He shouldn't have *needed* three seconds. Hell if it were me, I would have stabbed the Golden Virgin in a heartbeat. No one in this world is worth the life of my own blood."

I looked at Shadow who was visibly shaking. I wanted to say something to him, but there was no combination of words in existence that could make this right. Instead I held onto him.

From the distance, the sounds of a helicopter approaching signaled the end of Sinister's games. He was going to escape cleanly with the blood of the Midnight Society on his hands. In one single night, he had destroyed the organization.

"The game is done," Sinister said. "I'm tired. Let's call it an evening."

His words cued the demon-faced guards to pull the trigger on the guns that were pointed at us.

I blinked hard, anticipating a round of bullets to rip us all to shreds. However there was no barrage of gunfire—only an empty click.

"What the hell?" one of the guards cursed.

"Do it the old fashioned way you lazy shits," Sinister cried out. "And entertain me. You goons are unworthy of any more of my bullets."

Lincoln was quick to react and lunged for the knife that Shadow had dropped to the ground.

Shadow, still in shock over Calisto's death, remained unmoved.

"You have to help Lincoln—" I began shouting, but was

suddenly blindsided by a muscular arm wrapping itself around my neck, choking the life out of me.

"My employer promised me your head," the White Crow whispered into my ear, his breath emitting a foul stench of tobacco and vodka. "I hope my brother has a front row seat in hell as he watches me tear you apart."

Tears stung my eyes as I watched Shadow spring to his feet, reaching out for me. I extended my arm to him as well and for a brief second, our fingertips touched, but the contact was short lived.

I abruptly felt myself plummeting over the edge of the building, the White Crow's arms still wrapped around my body.

Did this man hate me that much that he was willing to dive headfirst into the mouth of hell just so he could drag me down there with him?

I closed my eyes—and without screaming—waited for darkness to come.

CHAPTER THIRTY-FOUR

I hit the ground quicker than I had expected, and it hurt like a bitch. I was winded and struggled to gasp for air.

Air—I could still breathe, which meant I wasn't dead.

Yet.

I opened my eyes and saw the large rifle pointed at my face. I was still groggy from the fall but I managed to piece together what had happened.

The White Crow had grabbed me and jumped off the edge, landing one level below. I had crashed onto the balcony of the unfinished penthouse suites.

"Now that I have you alone, I believe we can have a chat," the White Crow grinned, "About how you killed my brother and how I'm going to put you down like the miserable bitch you are."

I stared at the White Crow with a venomous gaze.

"You murdered Abraham," I seethed. "You killed him in front of me."

"That old shit needed to go," the White Crow replied. "Be happy it was quick. He deserved to suffer much more than he did."

He walked over to me and licked his lips with his long slug-like tongue. "You however…"

I found myself taking a few steps back. The rifle was focused on me like a homing beacon. It was only a matter time before he pulled the trigger.

I was deer thrown into the den of a lion.

This brought me to now. I was a lonely girl with the shattered dreams of being a musician.

Two people that I cared for were dead because of me—one of them six feet under and the other a pile of ash and bone. It only made sense that I was next to die.

It seemed foolish to think that only three weeks ago, my biggest worry in life was scrounging enough money to have a hot meal. Now, my fears included assassins, serial killers, hit squads, and the devil that waited for me in the afterlife.

The White Crow was still waiting for my decision—die by a bullet or take the plunge fifty-stories down. Both were equally unappealing.

"Make a decision girl," the White Crow said. "Be happy I'm giving you a choice."

"You expect me to thank you for that?" I asked; bitterness stitched into my words.

"I don't have time for this," the White Crow said. "If you don't make a decision on how you're going to die, then I'll make one for you. I'm starting to lean towards senseless and uncontrolled bludgeoning."

While the White Crow continued his threats, I saw Shadow sneaking up behind him concealed in a blanket of darkness.

I allowed my eyes to divert away from the White Crow and looked over his left shoulder while I let out a sigh of relief.

The White Crow grinned.

"I see what you're getting at," he said, "Sadly you need a better poker face."

He spun to his left and fired off a quick shot, but was surprised to see that no one was there.

"Wrong side asshole," Shadow said as he blindsided the White Crow from the opposite direction and drilled him in the shoulder with a two-by-four, causing the assassin to drop his weapon.

The White Crow growled like a wounded bear, taking a step back while clutching his arm.

"Ugh, what the fuck," he cursed. "That hurt like hell."

"Nothing compared to this," Shadow said as he lunged at the White Crow, hands still gripping the large piece of wood.

Despite being wounded, the White Crow's reflexes were bursts of lightening. He was much faster than his brother, dodging Shadow's attack and retaliating with a boot to his gut. Shadow dropped to his knees, writhing in pain.

"You fucking coward," the White Crow spat. "This is what fighting me fairly actually feels like." He followed up with another kick to Shadow's ribs. I heard a sickening crunch.

I couldn't stand here like a useless damsel in distress and watch Shadow get pummeled. I scoured the ground for the closest weapon and discovered a full bucket of primer lying mere inches away. The White Crow continued his assault on Shadow, who struggled to get to this feet but was struck back down to his knees with the White Crow's heavy fists.

"This is what you deserve for trying to be a snake," The White Crow continued taunting. "I can do this all fucking-"

Before he could finish his sentence, I took the opportunity to attack him with the bucket, swinging it awkwardly with two hands, and managed to catch him across the side of his head.

"Argh," he screamed, clutching his head. "Seriously, what the fuck is wrong with you people? Stop fighting like cowards."

I came at him again but had the wind knocked out of me when he countered with an elbow to the soft spot of my stomach. The pain felt like an electric shock, originating from where he had hit me, all the way to my fingertips as I struggled to suck in air.

The White Crow picked up the paint bucket with one hand, raised it over his head, threatening to bring it down on my skull.

Shadow snuck up from behind, a hammer in one hand, and grabbed the White Crow's wrist—still clinging onto the bucket—with the other. He pulled the bastard's arm as far back as he could and delivered a punishing blow to the assassin's elbow with the hammer.

The White Crow howled in pain as Shadow crushed the bones in his arm.

"You murdered my friend," Shadow said as he continued his assault, driving the hammer into the White Crow's kneecap, smashing it to oblivion.

The killer's howls intensified as he took a few staggered steps back. Shadow continued the attack, making contact with every swing. The White Crow shielded his head with his arms while backing away in retreat. The two were drawing closer to the edge.

"Shadow, watch out," I cried out. My warnings were ignored. Shadow was too focused on obliterating the White Crow to pay any attention to me.

One of Shadow's blows landed on the White Crow's head and I thought for sure that was the deathblow.

Astonishingly, the White Crow failed to stay down and instead—with a surge of superhuman adrenaline—charged into Shadow like an angry bull. Shadow tried to get out of the way but wasn't quick enough as the White Crow barreled into him, sending them both flying over the edge.

"Shadow!" I screamed, rushing towards the spot where they had both fallen over. I couldn't stand the thought of him dying on me. I needed Shadow in my life. He was all I had left in this world and I loved him.

He was clinging onto a flimsy piece of scaffolding gutting out of the side of the building. The White Crow was gone, reduced to a smear on the concrete. I hoped he was with his brother, dancing with the devil in hell.

From the creaking of the scaffolding, it wouldn't be long before it all went tumbling down.

I lay flat on my belly, just at the edge, and reached out to Shadow. He extended one hand upwards but we were still inches apart.

I willed my body to stretch further, hoping to defy all physical odds written by the universe. The tips of my fingers touched his and for a moment, I thought I could do it. I thought I could save Shadow's life.

One of the bolts securing the scaffolding to the side of the building came undone under the stress of Shadow's weight. I was devastated as Shadow sank a few inches further away from me.

He drew his hand back.

"What are you doing?" I cried. "Don't give up."

He shook his head and smiled at me sadly.

"I'd never hurt you Aria," Shadow said. "Never in a million years."

He was referring to the moment when he had the knife in his hands and I thought I was a goner. Had Sinister waited for the full three seconds, would I still be alive?

A loud creek came from the scaffolding. Any second, it was ready to give.

"Shadow, please," I said, reaching out to him again.

"Just tell me you love me," he said. "That's all I need from you." His face was red from strain, his voice hoarse.

"I love you," I said without hesitation.

I saw peace on Shadow's face as he closed his eyes, accepting that this was the end. If he was going to die, I wanted to join him.

"I love you too Shadow," came a third voice. The sight of Lincoln lying down next to me, reaching out for Shadow made my heart sing. "Now come on, hold my hand damn it."

A smile crept across Shadow's face as he nodded and extended his hand upwards. I was relieved to see that he was able to grab Lincoln's hand, and just in time too. A split-second after Shadow released his grip on the loose scaffolding, it came crashing down, plummeting to the ground below.

"And to think, I used to get teased for my gorilla-long arms," Lincoln said. He clenched his teeth and using both hands, pulled Shadow up and back onto solid ground.

Shadow collapsed onto his back and sucked in a heavy breath of air.

"Remind me to fire the construction crew for installing such shitty scaffolding," he said. "No more cash deals, ever again."

I dove on top of Shadow and pelted him with a hundred butterfly kisses.

"Maybe you two should wait until the hotel is finished and then get a room," Lincoln said, wiping sweat off his brow. The right side of his face was swollen and his lip was fat and bloodied.

"You look like shit," Shadow said.

"My abilities to stay beautiful seemed to have deteriorated with each subsequent attempt on my life," Lincoln replied.

Above, the sounds of the helicopter blades were growing louder. The chopper was fast approaching.

"The helicopter," I said, pointing out the obvious.

"Well ahead of you," Lincoln acknowledged as they both rose to their feet and bolted for the stairwell that led back to the helipad.

"Sinister's mine," Shadow said.

"Leave a piece for me," Lincoln added. "I want the softest and fleshiest piece."

By the time we reached the helipad, the chopper was already on the ground and Sinister was entering into it.

"No you don't," Shadow said as he began sprinting for the chopper, leaping over the unconscious bodies of the two guards that Lincoln had dispatched.

Shadow was fast, but when it came down to man versus machine, the latter always won. By the time Shadow reached the helicopter, it was already fifteen feet up in the air.

"This isn't over," Shadow cried out to him.

"Of course not," Sinister shouted over the noise of the spinning blades. "This has been too much fun. I'm glad you survived all of this Shadow, I really am. You may not believe me, but I still do love you...brother."

And then the chopper was gone. Sinister's final words reverberated in my ears.

Brother?

Shadow stood on the helipad, his eyes staring into the distance at the chopper which had become a speck in the sky.

"It's not her," Lincoln said, his voice pulling Shadow's attention from the city skyline back down to us. "Thank God, it's not her."

"What?" Shadow asked.

"It's not Calisto," Lincoln repeated, cradling the dead woman in his arms, knife still buried in her heart.

I had a look for myself. He was right. From afar it was easy to be fooled.

With a new hairdo and a gag over her mouth, it was easy to transform Bria into a Calisto look-alike.

The poor girl didn't deserve to die like this, despite her antagonizing me. Bria wasn't a bad person, just confused and misunderstood; and now she was gone.

Lincoln laid her body back on the ground and then stood up. In his hands was an electronic tablet.

"I found this next to the body," Lincoln said.

Shadow's eyes narrowed when he saw the tablet. He took it from Lincoln's hands, tapped on the screen and saw that it was loaded with a video.

The screen image was of Sinister, sitting on what looked to be a throne.

Before even watching the video, I already knew that Sinister's message was not going to be good.

Shadow held the tablet out for everyone to see and hit the play button. I held my breath and listened to the bastard's words, which I knew would change us all forever.

CHAPTER THIRTY-FIVE

Despite the shitty quality of the tablet's speakers, the true voice of Sinister was unmistakable. With the voice scrambler removed, we ended up listening to Calisto's delicate falsetto instead of the deep baritone drone of Sinister.

"I wish I could say I know what you're thinking at this very moment Shadow," she said in the pre-recorded video, "But the truth is, I don't. But God, I wish I was there to see the look on your stupid face."

Calisto removed the mask and revealed herself to us. She had a smug look on her face.

The three of us congregated on the helipad, huddled over the screen, absolutely dumbfounded. I turned to Shadow and saw the hurt on his face.

I reflected on my own emotions and discovered only hate for Calisto. She had murdered Justin and for that, I wanted her to die.

"The first question that must come to mind is regarding the death of mommy and daddy," she continued. "Yes, I take full credit for that one, though I know it's probably hard to believe. How could a ten year-old girl have the mental capability to commit murder that has baffled police—and my stupid brother—for over thirteen years? The answer is simple.

"I'm smarter than all of you. I always have been. But seeing as how mom and dad invested all their time on you, Shadow, I was always on the outside looking in—like a forgotten puppy left out in the cold on Christmas Eve, staring through the windows while everyone else feasted on their fat Christmas turkey.

"*I* was the one deserving of their attention. *I* was the one that was always smarter, and *I* was the one that listened to everything that our parents told us. *I* should have been groomed to be the next leader of the Midnight Society but because I was born with no balls between my legs, I was regulated to the sidelines like a second-rate hack.

"No matter what I did, it always failed to impress mom and dad. While you were drawing stupid stick figures on snot-stained pieces of paper, I was composing ballads on my violin. But did mom or dad care?

"No, of course not; they ogled over your imbecile drawings and told me to hush my playing so you could concentrate on studying the works of Leonardo Da Vinci and Pablo Picasso. Do you know how I felt being second to you Shadow? Do you know how it felt being second to someone who was mentally inferior?

"It's pretty amazing how much hate a ten year old can develop. Let that be a lesson for all parents—don't neglect your kids because you'll never know when they'll murder you for being an asshole parent."

"This brings us to the night that has altered the shape of your life forever, Shadow. You were asleep, if I recall. Dad was in the study, deep into his after dinner drink. I remember him passing out in his favorite arm chair; his head tilted back, neck exposed while Liszt's Hungarian Rhapsody played. It was easy to sit in his lap and stab him in the jugular with the box cutter.

"Oh the blood, you should have seen the blood. It was brilliant.

It was magnificent. What really made my day however was watching his eyes loll over to me in complete and utter disbelief. I stabbed him again, and the gurgling sound deep in his throat was the true music in the room, overshadowing Franz Liszt.

When dad was dead, I decided to saw his neck open with the box cutter. I didn't know why at the time, but it felt like the right thing to do.

"Daddy's death deserved to be gruesome. It deserved to be horrific in every sense. After all, he was an asshole. After I was finished with dad, it didn't take long for mom to enter the study to investigate what my crying was all about. She screamed like a banshee when she saw dad lying in a pool of blood. She completely ignored me—as she always did—and ran to dad, cradling him in his arms.

"I surprised her with the blade from behind, giving her the same treatment I had given dad.

"When the deed was done, I hid the box cutter along with my blood-stained clothes in the large stuffed bear our grandma had given me on my fifth birthday. I hated that bear, by the way. It always reminded me that while you got the shiny new bike, I got that furry oversized piece of shit—though it did come in handy in disposing the evidence.

I cleaned myself up along with any evidence that I had been in that study that night, and then I went to bed and slept peacefully for the first time in a long while.

"The next morning, you found their bodies. I thought it was ironic, yet sweet how you were trying to protect me from seeing the crime scene, despite the image already engraved in my photographic memory. I created the masterpiece after all."

"My God," Lincoln whispered out loud.

Shadow said nothing and continued watching the monitor.

Calisto sighed. "After killing our parents, I thought it was the end of my blood lust. I had tried my hand at murder once and once was enough for me. Soon it became a fond memory, one I occasionally would replay in my mind and smile. I'm sure you know what I'm talking about, all those times you caught me in a daydream smiling and I told you that I was thinking about some cute guy I had met off the streets. Well that was a lie Shadow. In reality, I was thinking of mom and dad's blood-soaked corpses.

"So while I moved on from that night, you were possessed by the incident. I have to admit, I didn't think it would haunt you as much as it did, but at the time I was young and I didn't understand the concept of emotions as much as I should have, and I underestimated just how much like our father you truly were. Whereas father obsessed over Julia's death, you obsessed over father's demise. It was very poetic.

"To this day, I sometimes find it hard to understand the emotions of others. I guess that makes me a sociopath doesn't it?" she paused. "So this is the part where my confession gets a little sappy. Believe it or not, I care about you Shadow, and I never wanted to hurt you—physically that is. While mom and dad treated me like I was some bastard worth forgetting, you treated me like family. The only reason I discovered love was because of you. Yes—though you may not believe me after all that has happened—I love you Shadow. You are my twin after all and we share a bond that only other twins can understand.

"I'm still smarter than you, apply myself much better than you— but I'll never hate you because of your stupidity or naivety. You're probably wondering why I decided to do all of these things to you if I loved you so much.

"It's because I wanted to recreate you; give you a new life. Let's face it, the murder of our parents turned you into an empty shell— and I seriously felt guilty about it. I couldn't just sit here idly and watch you waste your life away, trying to bring their killer—me—to justice.

"A few years ago I read how the Incata, an aboriginal tribe living in the remote rainforests of South America, believed that the sins an individual committed over their lifetime possessed your spirit and your body, transforming a person into a walking monster. The only way to be cleansed was to be stripped of everything you owned and take a pilgrimage deep into the center of the rainforest where a certain purple plant grew. This plant acted as both a powerful hallucinogen and a strong poison with its beauty being its defense mechanism.

"The sinners were to pick this plant and bring it back to their village as the first part of their absolution. Many of them ended up dying in the jungle from starvation, dehydration, or killed by the wildlife inside. Only a few returned back to the village, where the final step of the cleansing involved ingesting the plant and dying for a brief period of time. During the transition between life and death, the village elders resurrected the sinners by some voodoo magic, which suspiciously looked like CPR to me. If a person survived, only then were they were deemed fully cleansed and alive again.

"Shadow, this is what I have done for you. In order for you to be born again, I needed to strip everything away from you, which I have done. The leadership of the Midnight Society has been destroyed and all its past members now belong to me. It wasn't difficult convincing them that under your leadership, the Midnight Society was going to crumble. After all, you broke a sacred tradition and allowed a common whore—Ms. Aria Valencia into our organization.

"I anticipated you choosing her far in advance. How? Well for the past year, I've been fucking with your mind. Before you went to sleep at night, I drugged you and with a little help of some subliminal cognitive hypnotherapy, I was able to mold the ideal woman in your mind—every single detail including her height, her weight, her characteristics, her interests. I even went down to the finest details such as her speech and her mannerisms. For the past year, I've been constructing your dream girl, and that girl was Ms. Aria Valencia. She was someone I chose at random while enjoying a free piano concert at the University one evening. I admit, I will miss her lovely music.

"Oh yes brother, your love for Aria was programmed into your little walnut brain. Naturally when I brought Aria Valencia to your birthday party and had her play the piano for you, you immediately gravitated towards her. The desire for the Golden Virgin was too strong to resist. So when it came time to choose your life partner, you defied all logic and reason and you chose Aria. It was an artificial true love at first sight, and it pissed the hell out of everyone.

"If there's one thing the mindless sheep in the Midnight Society respect, it's tradition. They're afraid of anything new and revolutionary. Your decision to have a commoner join the ranks of our prestigious organization was a massive slap in the face. Everyone was already unimpressed by your utter disregard for the responsibilities of being the Midnight Society's leader, spending every waking second trying to solve the mystery of mom and dad's gruesome murder.

"But don't worry Shadow, with the way things turned out, you're no longer burdened with the responsibility of leading a powerful secret society. I am.

"I know, you're probably thinking that I must be the greatest sister in the world for taking on this heavy burden of leading all these idiots and assholes, but don't worry. I'll do it for your benefit. As of this moment the Midnight Society ceases to exist, and instead is replaced by the Order of the Revenant—named after that beautiful flower I was talking about.

"Presently the first step of your cleansing should be complete. Everything you own has been stripped away from you. The estate and all your money now belong to me. Your best friend Lincoln— who mistakes my vagina for a heart—should be dead; though I'm sure he'll surprise me and find a way to survive. It's the nature of a cockroach.

"By now, you would have also killed your new love, Aria, and chose to save your loving sister from having her throat slit by...your loving sister. It's irony at its finest isn't it?

"You have nothing left Shadow, nothing. You are now ready to go out into the harsh nature of the jungle alone, to be hunted by the predators. Every single cop in the country will be coming after your ass. After all, you just killed a prominent senator, along with a wealthy Japanese businessman and a devoted black Christian as well—well the prints on the gun from my rigged game said you did. Oh yes Shadow, the game was rigged. There was no way for you to lose, especially since pistols given to Brevin and James were tampered with.

"Welcome to the beginning of your rebirth Shadow. I anticipate you'll be searching for the Revenants, and more specifically, me. I can't wait to see you again brother, however don't be sad if I have to kill you, because only then can you truly be reborn."

I watched in confusion as tears began to stream down Calisto's face. She truly was a psychopath.

"Goodbye Shadow, with all my love."

The video ended and we stood on the helipad in complete silence, bathed by the morning sun. I could only imagine what was going through Shadow's head, and what bleak emotions he was feeling.

As for me, my heart was breaking into a thousand pieces at the revelation that Shadow's love for me was engineered by Calisto for her twisted little game.

We were not meant to be; the video made that abundantly clear. My life had been manipulated by Calisto for her personal game and if it weren't for her brainwashing of Shadow, he would have never given me a second glance.

"So what now?" Lincoln asked, his voice cracking.

The tablet fell from Shadow's hands and smashed onto the ground. He turned to me and was about to say something. Whatever it was, I didn't want to hear it.

Sometimes you could read a person's face and just know that the news wasn't going to be good.

"Aria, I don't-" he began, but I shook my head and cut him off.

"Whatever you want to say, don't say it," I said. "If it will break my heart, please just don't say it."

Shadow paused for a moment, and then nodded. That nod felt like a bullet tearing through me. I wanted him to tell me that he would never break my heart, that the love we shared was real and had nothing to do with Calisto's sick, twisted games.

But he didn't. He nodded.

"I'm lost Shadow," Lincoln said. "For the first time in a long time, I have no idea what to do."

Shadow turned to him. "I'll tell you what we're going to do Lincoln. We're going to rebuild the Midnight Society," he said with a fiery resolution. "And then I'm going to find my sister and kill her."

Lincoln closed his eyes for a brief moment, and when they opened again, he wore the same determination on his face as Shadow had.

I had nothing to offer, feeling like I had no place here with them—no place in Shadow's heart anymore. I turned and began to walk away but it was Lincoln—not Shadow, that called my name.

"It's safer staying here with us," he said.

I looked at Shadow, but he didn't look at me. His thoughts were elsewhere.

Memories of the past three weeks flashed like snapshots. Twenty-one short days and the life I knew had been obliterated. I hated Calisto more than the cancer that stole my father away from me.

Shadow wanted to find his sister and kill her, but he'd have to get in line.

END.

A WORD FROM LOGAN PATRICKS

Thank you.

A writer without readers is like a sad clown holding a broken umbrella in the rain during a thunderstorm. The fact that you made it to this page means that you're a reader--not just a one-click book addict (nothing wrong it you are).

Semblance was a tough one to write because I wrote much of this book on the train ride to work and I struggled to keep nosy readers from staring at my screen while writing the words "nipples" and "erection."

If at any point in this book you swooned, blushed, gasped, cringed, cried, locked yourself in the bathroom to read more, and stayed up to the wee hours of the morning finding out how Semblance would end, I did my job as a writer. I graciously ask for you to:

a) Leave me a wonderful review on Amazon so I get motivated to get book two of the Midnight Society out faster. (Seriously positive reviews are like power ups for me).

b) Sign up for my EXCLUSIVE GUEST LIST @ www.loganpatricks.com and be the first to hear about new releases and get exclusive sneak previews as well receive some cool swag!

c) Tell your friends about Semblance so you can speculate what happens in book 2 of the Midnight Society series together. (Reading shouldn't be a lonely hobby. Save that for writing).

d) Say hi to me on my blog: www.loganpatricks.com, or on twitter @LoganPatricks so I can share with you all the details about the Midnight Society series while I write it, as well as providing you self-depreciating stories about my bizarro life.

ABOUT THE AUTHOR

Logan discovered both love and heartbreak at the tender age of seven, when the pretty little blue-eyed girl next door stole his kit-kat bar and shared it with the bad boy from across the street. Devastated, Logan found solace by escaping into the imaginary worlds he forged with his words, creating kingdoms where chivalrous knight always got the princess.

Twenty three years later, Logan spends his days in a suit and tie, working for the government on matters of network security. However his thoughts never strayed too far from the incendiary nature of love -- the passionate fire that's both scintillating and dangerous. Obsessed with exploring the steamy and mysterious side of human nature, Logan continues to create worlds filled with thrills, mystery, and of course, sex.

PENUMBRA

THE MIDNIGHT SOCIETY BOOK TWO

COMING SPRING 2014

LOGAN PATRICKS